**TEACHER'S BOOK**

# Exploring Texts
# Extended Reading B

*Richard Brown*

**General Editors**

*Richard Brown
and Kate Ruttle*

**Consultant Editor**

*Jean Glasberg*

**CAMBRIDGE**
UNIVERSITY PRESS

PUBLISHED BY THE PRESS SYNDICATE OF THE UNIVERSITY OF CAMBRIDGE
The Pitt Building, Trumpington Street, Cambridge CB2 1RP

CAMBRIDGE UNIVERSITY PRESS
The Edinburgh Building, Cambridge CB2 2RU, United Kingdom
40 West 20th Street, New York, NY 10011–4211, USA
10 Stamford Road, Oakleigh, Melbourne 3166, Australia

Exploring Texts: Extended Reading B
Text © Richard Brown 1999
Illustrations © Cambridge University Press 1999

First published 1999

Printed in the United Kingdom at the University Press, Cambridge

*A catalogue record for this book is available from the British Library*

ISBN 0 521 63413 X

**Notice to teachers**

# Contents

## Part One: Introduction

# Part Two: A choice of literacy activities

# Part Three: Resources for further work

# 1 PART ONE: Introduction

# An overview of *Cambridge Reading*

*Cambridge Reading* is an innovative series of books and support materials for the teaching of reading throughout the primary years. The books, by both new and established children's authors and illustrators, offer children breadth of choice and a wealth of different writing and illustration styles.

The scheme guides the child from short picture books for sharing, through several developmental phases in reading to skilled and independent reading of many kinds of text. For children at the first four phases of the scheme (i.e. Preparing to Read, Beginning to Read, Becoming a Reader and Towards Independence), this is achieved through:

- a balance of text types and genres which include fiction, non-fiction and poetry;

- a structure which facilitates progress and continuity in the teaching and learning of reading;

- a careful control of language;

- a range of support materials aimed at developing reading skills, including comprehension and personal response;

- an integrated phonics and sight vocabulary programme.

At the last two developmental phases of the scheme (i.e. Independent Reading and Extended Reading), reading is further developed and extended through:

- a range of extended narratives in different genres;

- poetry anthologies;

- picture books and graphic novels;

- anthologies of short stories;

- teacher's and pupil's support material in a series of teacher's books to cover text, sentence and word level work around each of the children's books.

## A clear and flexible structure

*Cambridge Reading* is structured into six **phases** which reflect the developmental phases in children's reading: Preparing to Read, Beginning to Read, Becoming a Reader, Towards Independence, Independent Reading and Extended Reading.

- **Preparing to Read and Beginning to Read**: these phases lay the foundations for future progress in learning to read. They develop concepts of print, the beginnings of a sight vocabulary, phonological awareness and early phonic knowledge, letter formation, approximate reading of known stories and rhymes, some accurate reading based upon recall, and an understanding of the link between text and pictures.

- **Becoming a Reader**: this builds upon the first two phases. It develops children's ability to read most of a familiar short, illustrated text aloud; the use of a larger sight vocabulary concentrating on high-frequency words; the use of a variety of cues to predict unknown words; the beginnings of self-correction, recall and discussion of some main points of the text; and some responses through drawing and writing.

- **Towards Independence**: in this phase, children are becoming increasingly independent. They are able to read much of a 32-page picture book with a relatively wide vocabulary on their own, giving a variety of responses to it.

- **Independent Reading:** in this phase, children are ready to explore more challenging texts, including non-fiction; their stamina and concentration are developing to cope with sustained reading over several sessions; they are developing a range of reading strategies to deal with a widening variety of texts; and they are becoming more willing and knowledgeable about choosing books for themselves.

The six phases are divided into **stages** to provide manageable and easily identifiable steps in the children's learning. As teachers record children's development through these stages, they can feel confident that the children are making suitable progress.

There are two stages each for Independent Reading and Extended Reading: stage A and stage B. Stage B is more demanding than stage A. The progression is thus:

- Independent Reading A

- Independent Reading B

- Extended Reading A

- Extended Reading B.

For a list of the titles in each stage, see page 156.

- In the second and third phases, Beginning to Read and Becoming a Reader, the books are organised into genre strands to give the children an introduction to different styles of writing. The books in the final two phases are organised into forms: short narratives, picture/cartoon books, poetry and extended narratives. The range of books provided gives the children a wide experience of different text types and narrative genres.

- Each of the children's books is accompanied by a wealth of teaching ideas, lesson plans and pupil's material. In the first three phases, these were designed to support children's acquisition of reading skills in terms of reading for meaning, personal response and phonic development; the focus was very much on learning to read.

- In the final two phases, the focus moves to higher-order reading skills. These include:
  - an introduction to a wider range of quality children's authors and their books;
  - skills in reading aloud in different contexts;
  - comprehension at different levels and for different purposes;
  - knowledge about language, its vocabulary, forms, structures and styles.

- The four *Exploring Texts* teacher's books (one for each stage of the last two phases) focus mainly upon the higher-order reading skills outlined above. In addition, there are companion teacher's books which develop other language aspects of the children's books (see p. 156).

# The *Cambridge Reading* approach for the Independent and Extended Reading phases

During the first three phases, success in learning to read will often be influenced – and in some cases determined – by a range of factors. They include:

- the child's motivation to read;
- the quality of the book being read and its appeal to the child;
- the child's understanding of how different kinds of texts work;
- the social context within which reading takes place;
- the child's prior knowledge of the text;
- the child's engagement with literacy activities related to the text;
- the child's understanding of language patterns and how texts cohere;
- the extent of the child's sight vocabulary.

These factors are described in more detail in the first three teacher's books in the scheme. They will continue to influence reading at the later stages of development but in a slightly different way. The following is an outline of the operation of these factors at the Independent and Extended Reading phases.

## The quality of the book and the child's motivation to read

Perhaps the key factor in reading success is the child's motivation to read, for without it progress will be delayed. Children need books by authors they have already encountered as well as by new authors. They need narrative genres which reflect their growing personal preferences for certain kinds of stories. They need poems and stories which grab their attention at the beginning and keep them riveted throughout with characters they can respond to and readily imagine, and language that is accessible. They need books which reflect both their reading stamina and the time available to read them. The provision of children's books in these two phases has been organised with these factors very much in mind. Not every book will appeal to every child, but the wide choice should cover most tastes, and hopefully extend them too.

## Understanding how different kinds of texts work

In the first four phases of *Cambridge Reading*, children were formally introduced to genre strands and text types which included contemporary, traditional and fantasy stories, autobiographical accounts, poetry and rhyme as well as non-fiction. This will have helped to prepare them for the range of narrative and poetic forms they will experience in the last two phases, particularly with regard to fictional narratives. These will widen the children's experience by the addition of historical fiction, comic reworkings of traditional stories, graphic novels and supernatural tales. The poetry featured at these phases includes poems written for more than one voice, chosen for oral performance.

Discussion and work around the text should help to bring out the essential features of each narrative genre and text type.

### The social context within which reading takes place

In the first four phases it is important that the child sees reading as a social activity in which they are given all the support they need while they are learning to read. At the Independent and Extended Reading phases, reading develops both at the individual and at the social level. Children increasingly enjoy choosing their own books and reading them by themselves at school and at home as a leisure activity. However, this is not sufficient for the full development of reading skills. Alongside their individual reading, children need reading activities within the class which will help them to read aloud to others, discuss and explore texts with their peers and the teacher, and receive teaching and guidance from the teacher on how texts work and how to get the best from them. The social context for reading at school needs to be supportive. It should provide for positive interactions and foster a creative, exploratory and personal approach to literature, in order for real learning to take place.

### Prior knowledge of the text

It was noted in the first phases of **Cambridge Reading** that children will have greater success in reading a text if they have some prior knowledge of its content. In many instances, this meant the teacher reading the text to the children first. At the later phases, it means discussing the expectations raised by the cover and blurb, and by any introductory passages. It might mean knowing the traditional version of a story that has been adapted or the historical background to a period novel. It might also mean having an awareness of a theme explored by a novel or anthology, such as protecting the environment or bullying. The 'Before reading' suggestions at the beginning of the teaching notes for each book will give some ideas on this.

### Engagement with literacy activities related to the text

If the activities chosen to follow up the reading of a book or chapter do not appeal to the child, they are unlikely to be successful; they may even have a negative effect on the child's experience of the book. It is important that the activities and the way they are carried out should be interesting and challenging but kept within the child's capabilities. The activities should be relevant both to the text and to the child, and should be seen to have benefits in terms of understanding, knowledge and appreciation.

The follow-up activities in *Exploring Texts* have been drawn up with these criteria in mind. They develop literacy principally at the text level and are usually carried out through a mix of class, pair and group work to facilitate discussion and to give the necessary social and teaching support. Apart from the more formal comprehension questions for discussion and writing which accompany most of the narratives, most of the activities are examples of *active* learning. The child is led to discover and develop aspects of literacy through interesting language activities rather than, for instance, being told about them in a didactic way by a text-book or by copying from the board. Even the comprehension questions can be used actively in group discussion and paired writing.

### Understanding language patterns

This aspect of literacy is principally covered by *Passports to Literacy: Sentences* and *Passports to Literacy: Words*. Some aspects of language, however, are so fundamental to the text that they should be explored as part of the wider search for meaning. Where this seems to be the case, *Exploring Texts* has activities which look closely at language use. Examples might include aspects of poetry (e.g. form, simile, metaphor), speech acts (particularly those set out in speech bubbles), and the use of vocabulary (e.g. synonyms, definitions, colloquialisms, dialects). Activities which require gap-filling (cloze) or the sequencing of texts also draw on children's knowledge of how passages cohere and what links them grammatically, and a few examples of this kind of activity are provided.

### Sight vocabulary

The reading level of the books at each of the four stages in the Independent and Extended Reading phases increases step by step to reflect the children's growing sight vocabulary and to help develop it further. In the first four phases, these steps had to be relatively small. Now that the children have acquired a sight vocabulary, thus achieving a real measure of independence in reading, the stages in difficulty reflect broader steps in reading development. The reading level of the pupil's follow-up material is consistent with that of the books. Support at the vocabulary level, then, is less overt but still has an important part to play, particularly at the Independent Reading phase.

# Choosing the appropriate phase/stage

## Independent Reading: the preceding phase

Children's reading develops at different rates. There may be many children in the class with whom you are intending to use the Extended Reading *Exploring Texts* books who are still operating at the earlier phase, Independent Reading. (Indeed there may be a few who are still at the Towards Independence phase.) These children may not be ready for reading the books independently or for many of the follow-up activities. You need to look closely at the description of the Independent Reading phase set out on pages 6–7 *of Exploring Texts 1* and *2* in relation to each child in your class to whom you think this may apply. If neither of these books is to hand, use the abbreviated profile given below.

### Independent Reading

**Reading aloud**

The child:

- reads aloud with increasing skill, fluency and confidence;
- is tackling a variety of unknown texts of different lengths;
- reads aloud appropriately in group and class contexts.

**Comprehension**

The child is learning to:

- monitor the sense of what they are reading, self-correcting appropriately;
- use knowledge of the text's subject matter to make predictions and test understanding;
- respond imaginatively to characters and situations;
- find, recall and summarise items at a literal level of understanding;
- construct meaning at the inferential and evaluative levels of understanding;
- recall a narrative or procedural text in the right order;
- skim to get the gist of a text and scan for specific information.

**Knowledge about language**

The child is learning to:

- appreciate the differences between fiction, poetry and information texts;
- identify different narrative genres.

**Attitudes to reading**

Hopefully, the child is learning that reading:

- is intrinsically worthwhile, for enjoyment and information;
- is the key to learning;
- is valued by the school, at home and by peers.

## Differentiated use of *Exploring Texts*

This can be achieved in three ways:

**Mainly class reading and group response**

- By having groups work on differentiated activities based on the same book, which you have read to the class. Most books will have at least one activity which is less demanding than the others.
- By adapting the activity chosen for the whole class to bring it within the learning range of those working at an earlier phase. Learning support assistants obviously have a role here.

**Mainly group reading and response**

- By using texts and activities from different stages of **Cambridge Reading** within the class or through setting within a year group. In practical terms, this will probably mean that groups are reading the children's book on their own, in pairs or in a group reading context, with variable support from you, before they tackle the follow-up activity. You or another skilled adult may, however, read the book to the group or participate in a shared reading.

This approach means that you will need access to more than one stage of the books and to more than one stage of *Exploring Texts*.

# The Extended Reading phase

Children at the Extended Reading phase will have had a wide and positive experience of a range of genres, text types and literary forms, from picture books to hundred-page novels, from nursery rhymes to thematic anthologies of poems, from simple information books to children's encyclopedias. They will be developing preferences for different genres and authors, and will be reading increasingly widely for different purposes. Their independence in reading – now well established – will be characterised by their ability to choose books appropriately, to read at length to themselves in a variety of contexts, and to discuss the content of the books they read with growing perspicacity. They will be keenly aware of what their peers are reading, and will often be reading successive books within a popular publisher's series or by authors highly rated by their peer group. TV and other media tie-ins will also be increasingly influential in this phase. The literature available for children at this phase is extensive. It is often challenging in terms of concepts, content and language; and it is sometimes controversial, too, in its exploration of contemporary modern life. There is a wide variety of literature to intrigue and entertain at whatever level each individual child requires.

Support for the reader at this phase is most useful when it opens children's eyes to new reading experiences (e.g. new authors, different genres and contemporary themes), and when it capitalises on enthusiasms and personal preferences. Much of the teaching will be focused on raising awareness of significant children's authors, and on exploring the language, purpose and meaning of texts at higher levels. At home, support is most effective when it is positive, practical and uncompetitive, for example when the child is given space and time to read, when books are valued as presents and reading is seen as a valuable and pleasurable activity.

Surveys show that girls read more than boys at this phase, and possibly also at a more sophisticated level. Whatever the reasons for this, it poses a challenge to the teacher which must be met before reluctance to read becomes habitual.

## Reading development at the Extended Reading phase: a profile

What reading skills and behaviours are developing at this phase? They may, for convenience, be listed under four headings:

- the skills of reading aloud;
- comprehension;
- knowledge about language;
- attitudes to reading.

Adding detail to each of these headings will give a profile of the reader at the Extended Reading phase. Profiles such as the one given here are neither definitive nor exhaustive. Teachers may wish to amend this profile to reflect their own understanding of the extended reader.

### Reading aloud

The child:

- reads aloud with fluency and confidence;
- has developed the use of pace, pause and expression;
- tackles a variety of texts of different lengths with confidence;
- reads aloud and behaves appropriately in group reading contexts;
- is willing to read aloud to larger groups such as the class;
- reads poetry with appropriate expression, making good use of cues such as rhyme, rhythm and line-breaks;
- can dramatise some short texts for performance.

### Comprehension

The child demonstrates through a variety of texts at an instructional level the ability to:

- use a variety of cues to predict the meaning of unfamiliar words;
- monitor the sense of what they are reading, at paragraph as well as at sentence level, self-correcting appropriately;
- use knowledge of the text's subject matter to predict and test understanding;
- make good predictions based on textual clues;
- form sensory images based on textual information;
- respond imaginatively to characters and situations;
- find, recall and summarise items at a literal level of understanding; sequence recall of a narrative or a procedural text, including all relevant details;

- evaluate viewpoints within a text;
- locate and deploy evidence to support a point of view;
- give the gist of a passage;
- skim to get the gist of a text and scan for specific textual items;
- integrate information from more than one text;
- generalise and extend their own knowledge in response to a text;
- identify and evaluate bias in texts (e.g. stereotypical characters, characters' opinions, author's apparent stance);
- identify or speculate on the author's purpose, giving clear reasons;
- choose books appropriately, closely matching text to task or purpose.

## Knowledge about language

The child can:

- discuss the main differences between fiction, poetry and information texts;
- discuss the differences between and the purposes of more ephemeral forms (e.g. newspapers, magazines, leaflets, posters, publicity brochures);
- identify different narrative genres (e.g. contemporary, fantasy, historical, science-fiction) and discuss their distinctive features;
- identify and make good use of content guides in fiction (e.g. cover, blurb, key quotations, plot summaries);
- identify and make good use of structural guides in non-fiction (e.g. contents, index, glossary, headings and sub-headings, captions and labels, fact-boxes, charts);
- discuss the structural features of text grammar (e.g. chapter, paragraph, sentence);
- identify and make appropriate use of punctuation (e.g. capital letters, full stops, commas for lists and clause boundaries, speech marks, question and exclamation marks, dashes);
- make good use of typographical clues (e.g. italics and capitals for emphasis);
- identify and discuss features of poetry (e.g. verse, rhyme, rhythm, line-breaks, free verse, refrain, sound patterns, simile, metaphor, imagery, traditional forms);

- talk with confidence about the structure of narratives using terms such as 'beginning', 'middle', 'end', 'trigger', 'conflict', 'clues', 'surprise', 'exciting episodes', 'climax', 'resolution';
- use terms such as 'character', 'setting', 'mood', 'plot', 'sub-plot' when talking about a story;
- recognise and name different text types within non-fiction texts (e.g. description, explanation, instruction, reports, personal accounts, letters, diaries).

## Attitudes to reading

The child should feel that reading:

- is enjoyable;
- is the key to learning;
- widely for different purposes is the norm;
- in a group and silent reading are a highly valued part of the curriculum;
- is an activity endorsed by the peer group;
- is valued at home;
- is an area for continual exploration – that it is good to be on a personal reading quest (e.g. for an author's work, or to explore a genre or subject);
- is intrinsically worthwhile, giving its own rewards.

The child should feel:

- confident in tackling unknown texts;
- that it is appropriate to seek support when reading more difficult texts;
- that they are a 'good reader'.

### A note on monitoring and assessment

The profile of the reader at the Extended Reading phase has been set out in checklist format in *Exploring Texts: Extended Reading A* (See Reading Record 1, p. 16). You can use this checklist to monitor children's reading behaviour and to record evidence as it emerges and/or becomes more secure.

# Children's responses to literature

The relationship between a story (or a poem) and the child reader is unique. The child responds to the text through imagination, feeling and understanding in a personal and individual way; that is the nature of reading literature. The author seeks to shape the reader's response as much as possible but recognises that each reader will have their own unique response to the text.

The *skills* used in reading aloud, commenting on a text or demonstrating comprehension in different ways, and at many levels, may be practised and developed. However, it should be recognised at the outset that what moves back and forth between text and child has a unique quality, a personal dimension, which teaching needs to nurture and respect.

Teachers can help to strengthen the relationship between child and text by, for example:

- setting up activities which help children to make links between the text and their own lives;
- helping them to appreciate the way language has been used;
- making them more aware of the way the text has been constructed;
- helping them to reflect on the points of view expressed in the text;
- helping them to become more aware of the layers of meaning a text may contain;
- making children more aware of what they as readers bring to the text.

Good teaching, quality texts, interactive and relevant activities: these are the necessary conditions for developing literate readers.

By observing children talking about texts, particularly in class and group reading contexts, it is possible to describe the kinds of broad response to literature which teachers should seek to develop. For convenience, these responses may be listed under the following headings:

- personal growth;
- imaginative response;
- appreciation of language;
- understanding of textual structures;
- critical awareness;
- communication skills.

These six broad areas of response provide a framework within which to plan schemes of work for literature-based English. The activities and teaching contexts set out in part 2 have been planned with this framework in mind.

## Personal growth

Literature can play a significant part in children's personal growth because it deals with characters – their experiences, motives, aspirations, dilemmas and problems. All the stories have characters, providing opportunities for discussion and reflection about how people behave and the different ways in which they relate to one another. Issues which affect relationships are the stuff of fiction: friendship, family crises, bullying, personal beliefs and values, aspirations. Activities which help children identify and explore these relationships and issues (e.g. group discussion, character profiles, sociograms, thought-tracking, hot-seating and drama) help them to make the link between the characters' experiences and their own. They make connections between what they are reading and what is happening – or could happen – to them. One of the teacher's duties is to help make these connections clear and meaningful to the children.

What may emerge from this is a greater understanding of the self, of relationships and of the larger themes which govern them: life, death, love, hostility, safety, danger, destruction, preservation and so on.

## Imaginative response

The bridge between child and text is created by the imagination. Its strength depends partly on the author's skill in conveying images, partly on the child's prior knowledge of the text's subject, and partly on the degree to which a child can visualise a written text.

At a simple level, an imaginative response can be mainly pictorial – that is, the child 'sees' the story unfolding in their mind or 'sees' the picture being described. This is a fundamental aspect of responding to texts. Not everyone has it, however; there are readers who do not visualise but access the text through other cues, for example through the other senses and through the shape and sound of the words themselves.

At a more advanced level, good stories and poems exercise and develop the imagination. This is done in a number of ways, for example:

- by providing original models of how imagination can be shaped into texts;
- by leaving 'narrative gaps' in the story for the reader to fill in;
- by presenting individual, even idiosyncratic, views of the world;
- by providing original treatments of common or universal themes.

Teachers can help children to develop imaginative response through, for example:

- asking children to imagine what is happening 'off-stage';
- asking children to make informed predictions;
- asking for or suggesting alternative plot-lines;
- asking for descriptions of people and places;
- through 'genre switch' (i.e. asking for re-creations of the text in other forms).

## Appreciation of language

Every author has their own style; it is as unique as a fingerprint. Some authors have styles that are so idiosyncratic that they are instantly recognisable; others strive to achieve a style so transparent that you hardly notice the words on the page. The majority of texts lie somewhere in between. The author's particular use of language provides an opportunity to examine how words are used to create effects that help to make the story work successfully.

At a simple level, children can begin to develop an appreciation of how language is being used by, for example:

- discussing the effect of story openings;
- seeing how syntax and sentence length determine the pace of a passage;
- discussing the choice of vocabulary;
- looking at the proportion of dialogue to narrative;
- comparing the tone and register of two very different stories;
- comparing versions of the same traditional story.

At a more advanced level, language appreciation can be developed by, for example:

- considering alternative vocabulary and discussing the effects of substitution;
- pronouncing and defining dialect words;
- noting how language has changed over time;
- looking at syntax as a feature of style;
- discussing the appropriateness of colloquialisms;
- learning to use appropriate terminology when discussing parts of texts (e.g. the terms 'metaphor' and 'simile' when writing about a poem).

The most important point is that children should develop their understanding of the use of language in context.

## Understanding textual structures

Texts are structured at many different levels. The wider the range of literature which children experience, and the more opportunities they have to explore and reflect upon their reading, the greater will be their understanding of how authors put texts together and of the rules and conventions which shape the texts.

Moving down from the broadest level, children can be brought to understand the various levels of structure:

- the main differences between text types (story, poem, play, diary, letter, report, information text);
- the notion of sub-genre – for example, the many different forms of poetry, or the many different text types in information books;
- different narrative genres and their main features – for example, contemporary, fantasy, historical, traditional, autobiographical – and the way that these can combine or sub-divide further;
- how purpose and audience can shape the way a text is written;
- how stories, plays and poems are structured and laid out on the page;
- the way paragraphs are structured sentence by sentence to achieve pace, coherence, musicality or even ambiguity;
- the terminology for different parts of the structure, for example:
  - word, phrase, sentence, paragraph;
  - verb, noun, adjective, adverb;
  - beginning, development, climax, resolution;
  - rhyme, rhythm, metre, metaphor.

As children respond to literature, their attention can be drawn to the way it is structured and they can be encouraged to note such structures for themselves.

## Critical awareness

At the same time as developing responses and exploring language and structure, children should also be developing a critical awareness of the quality of texts and an appropriate vocabulary to express it. They should begin to evaluate how well an author has written the text by looking critically at, for example:

- the creation of character;
- the originality (and plausibility) of plot;
- the use of foreshadowing and textual clues to create anticipation and suspense;

- the appropriateness of the dialogue;
- the way dramatic conflict is built up, sustained and resolved;
- the pace, rhythm and tone of the text;
- the appropriateness of the vocabulary;
- the different points of view expressed within the text and by the text.

At primary school level much of this will be done by:
- the teacher modelling responses;
- discussion and writing around questions such as 'What makes this a good story?', 'Why do we like this character?', 'How does the author keep you guessing?', 'Why does this story disappoint us?', 'Is this a good metaphor?';
- a close study of extracts;
- book reviews and book talk times.

The intention is to give children the confidence and vocabulary to say what they think are the strengths and weaknesses of particular texts, and in the process to help them develop preferences for particular authors, genres and perhaps text types. Such critical awareness should also help develop the quality of the children's own writing by giving them the critical tools with which to evaluate it.

### Communication skills

The various kinds of response to literature set out above imply opportunities for interesting and, at times, challenging acts of communication, for example:
- reading aloud to an audience;
- dramatisations;
- discussions;
- writing;
- performing;
- listening critically.

These responses imply a range of contexts and interactions:
- child to child;
- child to group;
- child to class;
- child to teacher;
- child at home.

They develop speaking and listening skills through such activities as:
- story telling;
- acting character parts;
- participating appropriately in a group;
- summarising, explaining or developing a point;
- summarising a discussion;
- collaborating on problem-solving tasks.

# *Exploring Texts* in the English curriculum

The previous section sets out in broad terms the value of developing children's responses to literary texts and gives some examples of classroom action. The practical challenge for teachers has always been to create frequent and progressive opportunities for these key responses to occur in the classroom. *Exploring Texts* provides teaching suggestions and pupil's material for each book in the Independent and Extended Reading phases of **Cambridge Reading** to enable teachers to plan individual lessons and units of work which will, over time, give children many different opportunities to respond to literature in the ways suggested.

The English curriculum covers a variety of areas but *Exploring Texts* is mainly concerned with **composition** and **comprehension**. Other teacher's books in **Cambridge Reading** are dedicated to teaching other areas of the curriculum, such as punctuation and spelling.

## Comprehension

Comprehension is an umbrella term used to describe different kinds of understanding of the text. It includes:
- the literal (what the text states unequivocally);
- the inferential (what the reader can plausibly infer from the text);
- the evaluative (the value judgements the reader makes about the content of the text);
- the critical (what the reader thinks of the way it has been written);
- the personal (how the content links with the reader's experience and concerns);
- the aesthetic (the way the text appeals to the reader's senses);
- the philosophical (what the reader makes of the ideas and themes in the text).

Comprehension is not a fixed quality; it is a search for meaning and a construction of that meaning, not just through reading but, crucially, through activities and discussion around texts. *Exploring Texts* provides more traditional comprehension questions, mainly aimed at literal and inferential understandings, for most of the narrative texts in both phases. (There are no comprehension questions on the poetry collections.) The text-based activities provide many more opportunities for the wider development of comprehension.

## Composition

Composition refers to text-making. *Exploring Texts* has many ideas for the development of story writing, poetry writing, dramatic writing and writing in other forms, often based on models given directly in the books. Reading and writing are thus closely linked, both drawing from and supporting each other.

## Activities and learning objectives

The index on pages 18–23 lists the activities suggested for each book together with their learning objectives. These give a clear overview of the opportunities *Exploring Texts* provides for the teaching of the English curriculum. In addition, the teaching notes for most books suggest discussion points for before, during and after reading. It will be clear from this that *Exploring Texts* can play a major part in resourcing and delivering the teaching of English in the primary school.

# Reading contexts

*Cambridge Reading* books will take their place within the contexts for reading normally provided for seven- to eleven-year-olds. These include:

- individual reading in class;
- individual and shared reading at home;
- teacher reading aloud to the class;
- teacher (or another adult) sharing the text with a group;
- children sharing the text without an adult present.

### Individual reading in class

Individual *Cambridge Reading* titles may be integrated into class and school library collections. Some of them will take their place beside other books by the same author published elsewhere. For children who need guidance on what to read next, teachers can make use of the background notes on each book to inform the children about the book and to whet their appetites. Book reviews could be written for some of the books.

*Cambridge Reading* books may also be kept separately in class, together with the relevant comprehension questions. From time to time, children may be given a *Cambridge Reading* book for more in-depth individual reading and response.

### Individual and shared reading at home

As children establish their independence in reading and widen their reading experience, they will increasingly prefer to read on their own. Parents and other family members who wish to continue to play a part in their child's reading should recognise that the nature of their involvement may have to change. For example, the child may no longer wish to read aloud but may want to continue to have books read to them. Or a book may be read separately and then discussed. Each family will have to work out the approach which best supports their child's reading progress and helps sustain their confidence and enthusiasm for good books. Schools can give guidance to help family members to achieve this, both formally through leaflets and informally through discussion.

The comprehension questions for the prose titles may be used for homework. One or two of the questions (perhaps photocopied onto card) could accompany the book home for the child to respond to in writing.

There are two practical points to consider before making *Cambridge Reading* books available for home reading. If some of the titles are going to be used for class or group reading, it is best to keep these in reserve and not include them in class or school collections. On the other hand, once the children have enjoyed them in either of these contexts, it is a good idea to release the books – or additional copies of them – for borrowing. For example, releasing a set of a title you have just read to the class will give a number of children the opportunity to re-experience the story through their own reading.

### Teacher reading aloud to the class

*Cambridge Reading* can help to answer the question 'Which books shall I read to my class this year?' The collection includes:

- different forms (i.e. short narratives, picture/cartoon books, poetry and extended narratives);
- different genres both within books (anthologies) and within stages;
- books by significant children's authors;
- books which have cross-curricular links.

Short texts can be read aloud in one session, while longer texts will, of course, require serial reading. Teachers should try to ensure at least two good reading aloud sessions per week so that the gap between episodes is not too long. Some teachers like to record their reading aloud so that children who want to hear it again can do so, and any that missed it can catch up.

It is always best to read the book beforehand to judge its suitability for your class. This becomes essential if you are intending to make use of some of the accompanying activities.

All the prose books come with ideas and material for individual lessons and units of work for English. There are also comprehension questions on most of them. By using the books in designated core English or 'literacy hour' time, it may be possible to make more time for reading aloud.

### Teacher (or another adult) sharing the text with a group

Regular group reading sessions can have many advantages. They include:

- allowing children to share reading and discussion of a text;
- providing a supportive context in which to develop reading aloud skills;
- creating a context for developing speaking and listening skills;
- providing opportunities for developing collaborative and problem-solving skills;
- ensuring that children work closely with their teacher over a sustained period;
- giving the teacher opportunities for informal assessment of each child's reading development.

The teacher's role is to guide response, clarify meaning, help the children to define words in context, point out particular language features, and help the children reflect on the content of the text.

Sets of *Cambridge Reading* books, together with the teaching suggestions and activities in part 2, will resource a substantial part of the children's group reading needs.

### Children sharing the text without an adult present

As you work intensively with one group, you may have several other groups reading together without an adult present. In these self-managing groups, discussion and response will be undirected and teaching opportunities will be lost. This, however, is balanced by the likelihood that the children's discussion about the text will be more spontaneous, exploratory and wide ranging. The children will seek support from each other rather than the teacher.

### Selecting texts for group reading sessions

It is important to make sure that the text chosen for a group reading session is pitched at the right reading and interest level. Selection will also be affected by:

- the book's links to other areas of the curriculum;
- the focus of the book (e.g. contemporary fiction by a significant author, or poems on a theme);
- the group's likely concentration span;
- the learning needs of the group;
- the nature of the follow-up activities;
- the curriculum time available;
- possible links with the book currently being read to the class.

Texts for taught groups can be more challenging than texts for self-managing groups. There is a wide range of difficulty within each phase. Some books (e.g. *Spindle River*) may be best used towards the end of a term or year, while others (e.g. *Sandstorm*) will provide a good introduction to this kind of study.

# Reading strategies

## Before reading

### Class and group reading

Orientate the children towards the text by:

- discussing the cover and illustrations;

- asking questions which focus on the theme or content;

- giving useful background information to create prior knowledge;

- making links with other texts, perhaps by the same author or on similar themes;

- whetting the children's appetite, for example by discussing the blurb and highlighted quotes, or by asking questions about the pictures.

### Group reading

1. Many of the stories have lots of dialogue. Where this is the case, draw up a list of the characters and assign children to character parts. Some doubling up of minor parts may be necessary. If you have a mixed-ability group, reserve the easiest parts for the less fluent readers.

2. Less confident readers may benefit from being allowed to scan the text ahead to see where their character speaks.

3. The main part will be the narrator – that is, the author's voice or, if the story is a first-person narrative, the main character's voice. Children can take turns to read this aloud, intercutting it with the dialogue.

4. Let the children decide how much they wish to read aloud before passing on to the next reader. You might want to give less experienced readers some indication of an appropriate length.

5. Join in the reading yourself so that you are part of the experience. Children will learn a lot from the way you read the text: your use of pace, pauses, expression, intonation and so on.

6. Make sure that background classroom noise does not interfere with the reading and discussion. The rest of the class should be engaged in tasks which do not require your immediate support. Make it clear that while you are working with the group you are not to be interrupted.

## During reading

1. When a child has difficulty with syntax (the shape of the sentence) or with pronunciation, give support through example or encourage others in the group to do so, thus modelling appropriate behaviour.

2. Explain words which are unfamiliar, encouraging the group to say what they think the words might mean within the context. List these words and write a definition for each one. Display them or keep them in the group's record folder for future reference. Alternatively, you could write them in a class dictionary.

3. As the story unfolds, comment on and question the text, ask for predictions and clarify meaning, thereby modelling responses. This will encourage the children to do the same in independent groups. These interruptions should, however, be brief and to the point in order not to disrupt the flow of the narrative.

4. If you are using a poem, read it through first without interruption. Poems can then be read several more times, with children taking parts and with different purposes in mind.

5. The author may have left some 'narrative gaps' (i.e. where events happen 'off-stage') in the story to allow the reader's imagination to work and in the interests of pace and economy. It may be appropriate to pause between two scenes separated by a narrative gap and invite descriptions of what might have happened. In other cases it might be better to return to such points after the reading is over, when the group can discuss them with hindsight.

6. Reading aloud in a group is not a performance. Nevertheless, some attention should be paid to good delivery, taking the needs of the group into account (e.g. appropriate volume, pace and expression). These give clues to the text's meaning and indicate whether it has been understood.

## After reading: developing understanding of the text through literacy activities and comprehension questions

1. All *Cambridge Reading* books have text-related activities. These can be found in part 2. There are two kinds: literacy activities and comprehension questions.

   What you choose to do as a follow-up to the group or class reading session will be determined by:
   - the time available;
   - the needs of the group;
   - the nature of the task;
   - the task's links with broader schemes of work in English;
   - any follow-up work on the text already completed.

2. The skills and experiences covered by the literacy activities are listed in the index on pages 18–23. As explained on pages 10 and 11, these cover the main areas of **comprehension** and **composition**.

3. Most of the prose titles have comprehension questions which may be photocopied and made into individual question cards for discussion and written work. They can be used for homework and for formal assessment of a child's understanding of a text (see p. 17).

4. You may wish to devise your own literacy activities in addition to those supplied or as a substitute for them. Part 3 contains further general ideas on developing language study which should help you do this.

5. It is a good idea to build up records of the class's or group's experience of texts and follow-up activities. This will help to inform planning.

# Recording and assessing reading development

All teachers of children who are developing their reading skills recognise the importance of keeping records of a child's progress. These records range from a teacher's individual notes to internal records, reports, national test results and the children's own informal records. The record formats which follow should be seen in this wider context.

Keeping records of progress in reading has many advantages. It will help you to be sure:
- that children are learning at a satisfactory rate;
- that you identify children who are not making the progress expected;
- that your teaching is effective;
- that you are offering the range of opportunities required to develop wider reading skills;
- that you are carrying out school policy;
- that you are using appropriate resources;
- that other interested parties can be kept informed of the child's progress.

Records and assessment for reading tend to fall into three categories:
- summative (e.g. a summary of what a child has experienced and achieved over a period of time, noting reading behaviour which is emerging, being consolidated or is secure, and noting what is influencing reading development);
- quantitative (e.g. a list of books a child has shared, read and responded to, often categorised into levels of difficulty);
- formative (e.g. a record of how a child responds to a particular text).

For examples of quantitative and summative record-keeping formats see Reading Records 1–4 in *Exploring Texts: Extended Reading A* (pp. 16–22). If you want a formative record too, use existing miscue analysis or running record procedures or use Reading Record 2 in the teacher's book for the Towards Independence phase of *Cambridge Reading* (pp. 64–65).

# 2 PART TWO: A choice of literacy activities

# How to use this book

This section sets out all the information you will need to get the best out of each book in this phase of *Cambridge Reading*. The teaching notes on each book usually include:

- bibliographic details;
- a synopsis of the story or a description of the contents;
- suggested discussion points for use before, during and, sometimes, after reading;
- a table showing the focus of and learning objectives for each activity;
- concise, detailed teaching notes for each activity;
- comprehension questions (prose titles only);
- activity sheets where appropriate.

There are two kinds of follow-up activity: **teacher-led activities** and **comprehension questions**.

## Teacher-led activities

For each book there are a number of suggested activities from which to choose. These activities are designed to help children understand the main elements of narrative and poetry, for example character, plot, structure, viewpoint, setting, mood, theme and genre. They develop comprehension *actively* at several levels of meaning and extend children's knowledge about language. They are designed to be used flexibly as a follow-up to a class or group reading of the text. It is often best for the children to work on the activities in pairs but some may also be done individually.

Extended narratives will require serial reading if you are reading them aloud to the class. Therefore, for these books, most of the activities are intended for use *during* rather than after the reading of the text.

**Nearly all the activities are self-contained and can be completed within an hour.** Where an activity might take longer, it is suggested that it be split into separate sessions.

Each activity follows the same basic teaching model.

- **Introduction**. This usually lasts no more than fifteen minutes and sets up the activity.
- **Development**. This focuses on the children's work in pairs and groups.
- **Review**. This rounds off the session and focuses on what has been learnt, or what can be learnt, from the activity.
- **Extension**. Sometimes, further work may be appropriate to the activity or for some of the children. This section gives some suggestions.

## Selecting the activities

Your choice of activities will be influenced by:

- the needs of the children;
- the intellectual demands of the task in relation to the ability of the group;
- the skills developed by the activity (see 'Index of activities', pp. 18–23);
- whether it is a whole-class or a group activity;
- whether it is going to be the only follow-up or you are planning to do more than one;
- the time you have available;
- the degree of teacher input required;
- the relationship of the activity to medium- and long-term plans for English;
- the availability of multiple copies of the text.

## Teacher-led class work, or group work?

The following symbols are used in the teacher's notes to indicate whether the activity can be carried out with most of the class or whether it needs to be confined to smaller groups. Both contexts are dependent on the number of copies of the books you have available.

### C | The child needs to read the text (in a group)

- These activities are more appropriate to group rather than whole-class work.
- If you have only six copies of the children's book being used, up to twelve children can do the activity, working in pairs.
- Some of these activities will require you to be teaching and guiding the group for a good deal of the time.
- In this context, reading skills are developed through reading the text, not just hearing it.

### T | Teacher reads text to class or group

- The children may need to check the book occasionally, but they do not need to have a copy of it in front of them in order to do the activity.
- This allows most of the class to do the activity at the same time, usually working individually or in pairs.
- In this context, reading skills are developed indirectly through listening, recall and response.

**The activity may be done either way**

- Some adaptation of the teaching notes may be required if the activity assumes that the child can see the book.
- An alternative approach would be to have up to ten children working independently with the book (sharing copies in pairs), while you work directly with the rest of the class using the remaining copy.

**No symbol**

If there is no symbol, reference back to the book after reading is either not required or is incidental. The activity will be based on recall of the text or will be of a compositional nature (e.g. writing a poem).

## Comprehension questions

In addition to the teacher-led activities, most of the prose titles have a set of comprehension questions. With the longer narratives, the questions cover only one section of the text. Some are straightforward, literal comprehension questions while others require children to infer the answer or to give an opinion of their own. They can be used in a variety of ways:

- as one of the follow-up activities;
- to check children's understanding of a book read individually or in pairs;
- as prompts for group or class discussion;
- as questions for written responses;
- for homework, where you and/or the child selects a few of the questions to answer;
- to give children practice in responding to more formal comprehension tests carried out for assessment purposes.

The comprehension questions may also occasionally be used as the preferred follow-up activity, but it should be remembered that comprehension questions cover only a narrow range of comprehension skills. (See the section on comprehension in the profile of the extended reader on pp. 6–7 for a wider range of comprehension skills.) The comprehension questions would not therefore be sufficient as a response to these texts, particularly if they are used simply for individual written answers.

## An author's classroom account

In a departure from the standard format, *Exploring Texts: Extended Reading* A and B contain sections written by Frances Usher, author of *That Rebellious*

*Towne* and *The Hermit Shell*. Frances, a trained teacher, took her two books into two different classes and worked with the children for many sessions alongside their own teachers. She reports on how the children responded to the stories and to the activities she devised, describing briefly each activity and reflecting on how it went. These sections give unique and inspirational insights into the interaction between author, text and class; and should help the teacher to construct a scheme of work around each of the novels.

## Skimming and scanning

Many of the activities in part 2 require children to use the skills of skimming, to get the gist of a passage, and scanning to find specific quotations, information or reference points. Children who have not yet developed these skills will need to understand the very different approaches required for each. You will need to demonstrate how to skim and scan, and you will need to give the children some simple exercises for each to start them off. Big books and multiple copies of the same book in small groups are useful for introducing the different approaches to these two skills.

For skimming, leaf through the pages of the book slowly, asking the children to say what impression they get of what is happening or what the text is about, for example by saying the first thing that comes into their heads about it. You can then pause and ask the children what signals they picked up to give them this impression. Home in on headings, sub-headings, pictures and brief captions. Also, if appropriate, run your finger quickly down the text, pausing at key words (i.e. words which help to sum up what the passage is about). Emphasise that when skimming you seldom read more than a few words at a time. Your eye and mind are more concerned with getting a general idea about the content of the passage.

Scanning is the act of searching for something specific. It often requires close reading to find clues to meaning, quotations, references and descriptions. Demonstrate some simple specific searches, first by using skimming to locate the relevant passage, then scanning for the precise information you require. Follow this up by asking the children to search for some items themselves. Keep the search within a limited field at first (e.g. a page or two) and at a simple, literal level of comprehension. As the children progress, widen the search and introduce comprehension at the inferential level.

The many activities in part 2 which require skimming and scanning will give the children plenty of practice in these key skills.

# Index of activities

| Title | Activities | Learning objectives |
|---|---|---|
| **By the Pricking of My Thumbs**<br><br>Editors: Helen Cook and Morag Styles<br><br>Poetry<br><br>pages 25–28 | (Ideas for activities for most of the poems in the collection.) | exploring the meaning of poems through discussion; developing the skills of reading aloud; understanding the meaning of a word by looking at the context; exploring the use of non–standard English; examining the way poetry is patterned; developing poetry-writing skills |
| **Heroes and Villains**<br><br>Editor: Tony Bradman<br><br>Short narrative<br><br>pages 29–58 | | |
| **Christmas in the Other House**<br><br>Judith O'Neill | 1. Summarising characters' thoughts in relation to key events. | identifying key events; empathising with characters; using skills of inference and deduction to look at key events from multiple viewpoints |
| | 2. Writing a profile of Aunt Ina. | examining characterisation; using skills of inference and deduction |
| **Heroes and Villains**<br><br>Paul Stewart | 1. Examining characterisation; compiling fact files. | collaborating in a group; examining characterisation; scanning; representing information in a fact file |
| | 2. Hot-seating the main characters. | using information; practising oral skills; empathising with characters |
| | 3. Writing a case-study report (*for able writers only*). | projecting beyond the story; report writing; examining characterisation |
| **Invisible**<br><br>Richard Brown | 1. Discussion and writing about the main characters' relationships. | using inference and deduction; scanning; text recall; developing vocabulary |
| | 2. Assembling evidence for character development. | examining the idea of character development; developing empathy with the main character |
| | 3. Looking at the story's structure; assembling evidence. | examining the basic problem/solution structure of the story; gathering textual evidence |
| **Making Rain and Other Magic**<br><br>Monica Furlong | 1. Sequencing and retelling the story; thought-tracking. | text recall and sequencing; oral retelling of the story; empathising with a character |
| | 2. Finding and classifying information; note-taking within a framework. | scanning; classifying information; note-taking; considering major influences on the main character's life |
| **Tags**<br><br>Ben Bo | 1. Class debate on the ethics of graffiti. | defining and classifying aspects of graffiti; developing opinions in speech and writing; participating in a class debate |

| Title | Activities | Learning objectives |
|---|---|---|
| **The Visitor**<br>Keith Ruttle | 1. Reading and understanding the complex language of the prologue. | using a dictionary effectively |
| | 2. Drawing information from the text to create a fact file. | scanning; using inference and deduction |
| | 3. Interviewing; story recall in pairs using prompts. | text recall; interviewing; developing skills of inference, deduction and reasoning |
| **Whitney Snow**<br>Richard Brown | 1. Using a writing framework to examine characters' actions and their consequences. | examining characters' actions and making moral judgements; writing persuasively, drawing on textual evidence |
| | 2. Looking at the use of metaphor and cliché. | considering the meaning of common metaphorical phrases; providing definitions of their meaning in context |
| | 3. Vocabulary extension; dictionary work. | widening vocabulary; discussing the meaning of unfamiliar words in context; using a dictionary; writing definitions |
| **In the Court of the Jade Emperor**<br>Rosalind Kerven<br>Short narrative<br>pages 59–73 | 1. Retelling the story; chanting a verse; compiling a list of Monkey's transformations. | exploring the character of Monkey; oral retelling in a group; speaking and learning a new verse; using imagination to draw up a list |
| | 2. Sequencing; retelling; thought-tracking. | recalling the sequence of the story; retelling orally and in writing; using inference |
| | 3. Recall; retelling. | recalling the story orally; retelling in writing |
| | 4. Identifying within the story recurring elements of traditional tales. | analysing the story into elements common to traditional tales; seeing how many of these elements apply to another traditional story; retelling orally or in writing |
| | 5. Retelling the story; describing the settings. | retelling the story using a pictorial map; describing in writing the story's settings |
| | 6. Identifying colloquial language; quiz. | examining colloquial language in a first-person account; scanning; giving opinions |
| | 7. Story telling in a circle; improvised drama. | text recall; developing story-telling skills; working collaboratively to dramatise a short scene |
| **Letters to Henrietta**<br>Nell Marshall<br>Picture/Cartoon<br>pages 74–80 | 1. Writing a letter in the character of Henrietta or one of her brothers. | scanning; using inference and empathy; writing a letter creatively and in character |
| | 2. Collecting and scribing family stories. | drafting questions for an interview; selecting relevant material; identifying elements of spoken and written language and transforming one into the other |

| Title | Activities | Learning objectives |
|---|---|---|
| | 3. Listing the advantages and disadvantages of various types of schooling. | scanning; using empathy and imagination; writing persuasively |
| | 4. Writing a description of life in the trenches. | skimming and scanning; using inference and empathy; extending vocabulary; writing imaginatively |
| | 5. Comparing definitions from various dictionaries; writing definitions. | using dictionaries; extending vocabulary |
| **Sandstorm**<br>Judy Cumberbatch<br>Extended narrative<br>pages 81–92 | 1. Discussion to clarify what happens at the beginning of the story. | evaluating different interpretations of events; discussing the genre |
| | 2. Thought-tracking the main character. | developing understanding of the main character; empathy |
| | 3. Illustrating a descriptive passage. | extracting relevant information from a short text; transforming written information into graphic information |
| | 4. Writing a letter from a character in the story. | developing understanding of the relationship between two principal characters; writing in a personal style, using the conventions of letter writing; filling in a narrative gap using inference and deduction |
| | 5. Identifying textual clues about the school and Abla Selma, the teacher. | visualising Rashida's school; building up a picture of a principal character; understanding how authors create impressions of places and people |
| | 6. Exploring characters' points of view. | exploring each character's view of two key events, using inference and empathy; scanning; using textual evidence to support a point of view |
| | 7. Setting out arguments for and against a course of action. | considering alternative plot-lines; marshalling arguments for and against possible actions |
| | 8. Group or class discussion. | developing oral skills (discussion) |
| | 9. Group or class discussion. | developing oral skills (discussion) |
| | 10. Writing the end of the story. | practising discussion, looking at the links between characters in the past and the present; planning and writing a piece of narrative |
| | 11. Discussion. | developing oral skills (discussion) |
| **Sorcery and Gold**<br>Rosalind Kerven<br>Extended narrative<br>pages 93–109 | 1. Completing cue-question charts for some of the main characters. | exploring characterisation; using inference; note-taking |

| Title | Activities | Learning objectives |
|---|---|---|
| | 2. Exploring a key relationship; looking at textual clues. | developing understanding of two key characters and their attitudes to one another; scanning; practising oral skills (discussion and reading aloud); summarising |
| | 3. Class discussion about the Sorcerer; drawing. | practising oral skills (discussion); scanning; transforming written information into a visual form |
| | 4. Summarising interactions between characters. | considering the extent to which information is given through dialogue; considering characters' motives; summarising |
| | 5. Discussion. | developing understanding through group discussion; skimming and scanning |
| | 6. Summarising what the characters think about one another. | looking at characters from different points of view, using inference and deduction; summarising; using textual evidence to support a point of view |
| | 7. Cloze procedure; looking at descriptive language; drawing. | using contextual clues to find missing vocabulary; examining descriptive language; transforming written language into a visual form |
| | 8. Completing a chart of Ingrid's fears. | considering the main character's fears at crucial points in the narrative; using inference and deduction |
| | 9. Recall; prediction. | text recall; practising oral skills (discussion) |
| | 10. Sequencing; group recall; role-playing. | recalling events through sequencing and retelling; using inference and deduction to consider events from different viewpoints; inferring and discussing characters' feelings |
| | 11. Recalling the whole story. | recalling the plot; considering the importance of places and objects in a story; writing summaries based on recall |
| **Spindle River**<br><br>Judith O'Neill<br><br>Extended narrative<br><br>pages 110–126 | 1. Looking for period clues; creating fact files; drawing the setting; compiling a glossary. | scanning; note-taking; using textual evidence to support a point of view |
| | 2. Discussion; writing from one character's point of view. | examining characterisation; practising oral skills (discussion); using empathy; writing creatively |
| | 3. Completing a chart to compare nineteenth-century and modern views of the Sinclairs' new living arrangements. | scanning; using empathy |

| Title | Activities | Learning objectives |
|---|---|---|
| | 4. Drawing and captioning a sequence of diagrams to illustrate work in the mills. | scanning; translating written information into a graphic sequence; writing explanatory captions; collating information from several texts |
| | 5. Devising and commenting on a 'silent monitor'. | exploring a philosophical idea through discussion and experiment; arguing for or against a point of view; speaking and writing discursively |
| | 6. Discussion; role-play. | becoming familiar with a central experience of the Industrial Revolution; using empathy in role-play; arguing for or against a position |
| | 7. Compiling a timetable of Jockie's day as a servant. | scanning; using inference and deduction; using reasons to support an argument |
| | 8. Improvised drama. | adapting text from prose to unscripted drama; using gesture, intonation and expression to rehearse and prepare a performance |
| | 9. Discussion. | practising oral skills (discussion); text recall; using empathy; making predictions |
| | 10. Writing a short novel based on an outline (*for able and motivated writers only*). | developing story-writing skills; writing historical fiction; working to an outline; writing in stages over a long period |
| | 11. Shared reading of the chapter; discussion of historical references. | understanding historical and political ideas; understanding how such ideas can be reflected in a novel; practising oral skills (reading aloud and discussion) |
| | 12. Writing the end of the chapter. | drawing on knowledge of the story to predict the next event; writing in the style of the author |
| | 13. Group discussion. | practising oral skills (discussion); using inference and deduction; giving coherently argued answers |
| | 14. Writing song lyrics based on a model. | writing song lyrics; using a rhyming verse form; appreciating the meaning of the song in relation to the story |
| | 15. Hot-seating; interviewing; writing a newspaper report. | using empathy, inference and deduction; scanning; writing in a particular style |
| | 16. Role-playing in group discussion to determine Dan's fate. | using inference, empathy and deduction; arguing a point of view; listening to and taking account of differing points of view; reaching a group consensus |
| | 17. Discussion and prediction. | practising oral skills (discussion); making predictions |

| Title | Activities | Learning objectives |
|---|---|---|
| **The Hermit Shell**<br>Frances Usher<br>Extended narrative<br>pages 127–134 | 1. Discussion. | |
| | 2. Research. | |
| | 3. Discussion and personal writing. | |
| | 4. Oral and written prediction. | |
| | 5. Writing diaries. | |
| | 6. Writing letters. | |
| | 7. Agony aunts or uncles. | |
| | 8. Hot-seating. | |
| | 9. Drama. | |
| | 10. Artwork. | |
| | 11. Sequencing; making a time-line. | |
| | 12. Alternative plot-lines. | |
| | 13. Imagining the future. | |
| **Twinkle, Twinkle Planet Blue**<br>Editor: Morag Styles<br>Poetry<br>pages 135–141 | 1. Group reading and discussion. | exploring and considering a variety of styles in poetry; practising oral skills (discussion and reading aloud) |
| | 2. Classifying the poems in terms of their form and their approach to the 'green' theme. | developing a vocabulary with which to discuss poetry; understanding that one poem can contain many ideas |
| | 3. Looking at the language of poems which use non-standard English. | understanding that there are many dialects of English and that poetry can be written in any dialect; appreciating the sound-values of non-standard dialects |
| | 4. Using some of the poems as models for the children's own poems. | writing creatively, using a model; recognising and understanding the elements of several poetic forms |
| | 5. Annotating more challenging poems. | practising annotation; developing understanding of difficult concepts and language |
| **Whisked Away**<br>Richard Brown<br>Poetry<br>pages 142–145 | (Ideas for writing activities for most of the poems in the collection. Ideas and advice about performing the poems can be found at the back of the book itself.) | |

# By the Pricking of My Thumbs

**Selected by**  *Helen Cook and Morag Styles*
**Illustrator**  *Chris Coady*
**Poetry**  *An anthology of poems about the supernatural, originally published as part of the Cambridge Poetry Box*

## Description

A collection of modern and traditional poems on the theme of magic and the supernatural: omens, spells, witches, ghosts, strange shadows, fears of the night and the unknown.

## Introducing the book

- Give the children some clues about the theme of the book – for example, discuss the cover and title, read the blurb, read some of the poem titles. Ask the children what sort of poems they think the book contains. What led them to this conclusion?
- Read the first two poems (p. 5) and then brainstorm what might be meant by 'creeping things that run in hedge bottoms' and 'night's black agents'.

- Check through the poems in the book to see if any of them are about creatures that appear in the children's brainstormed list.
- One child who was introduced to the book in this way described it as 'goosebump poetry'!

## A choice of literacy activities

Activities are suggested for nearly all the poems in the collection. They cover the following learning objectives:

- to explore the meaning of poems through discussion;
- to develop the skills of reading poetry aloud;
- to develop the skill of understanding the meaning of a word by looking at it in context;
- to explore the use of non-standard English in poetry;
- to develop knowledge and understanding of the way poetry is patterned;
- to develop poetry-writing skills.

### 'Charm' (p. 6) Choral reading; looking at rhyme patterns

- All the children can join in with a reading of this poem. (Put it up on an OHP or copy it out on the board or flipchart.)
- Ask the children what sort of world the rhyme describes and why the editors chose to put it near the beginning of the collection.
- Ask the children what rhymes they can find in the poem. Do they spot the internal rhymes – mole/hole, bay/play, red/fled? What is the effect of the internal rhymes? And of the final rhyme which rounds off the poem?

### 'Omens' (p. 7) Vocabulary extension; writing individual and class poems

- Before reading the poem, explain what an omen is – a symbolic event which seems to show what is to come, often something unwelcome. Omens are 'signs', often things which break the natural pattern of experience, and this is the theme of the poem.
- Explain what 'Traditional, Gaelic' means – the poem's indeterminate age, its lack of an identifiable author, its geographical origins, and the fact that it was originally written in another language.
- Read the poem. Explain words like 'stock-dove', 'copse', 'flag-stone', 'rump' and 'snipe'. Alternatively, ask the children to look them up in the dictionary.
- Discuss which of the omens are natural occurrences and which appear to be unnatural. Is the poet being too superstitious?
- Brainstorm with the children omens in nature, seen and heard, natural and unnatural. Sort the best ideas into a free verse class poem.
- The children could write their own omen poem. Here is an example written by a Y6/P7 pupil:

  I heard an owl spooking about a wood.
  I heard a galloping horse with no one on its back.
  I heard a cow mooing wildly.
  I heard a woodpecker pecking very loudly
  and breaking its beak,
  and I foresaw that bad luck was coming.

### 'Applemoon' (pp. 8–9) Imaging; considering the effects of alliteration; exploring portmanteau words; illustrating a word picture

- Before reading the poem, talk to the children about the experience of waking in the night and of looking out of the window onto a moonlit scene, or even of going outside. Have the children ever done this? What did they feel, hear and see that was strange? Read the poem 'What Was It?' on page 12 to enrich this discussion; its theme is that even familiar things can seem strange at night.
- Once you've read the poem, check that the children understand the basic plot. Then read it again, asking the children to think about the 'word pictures' being painted. What is the strongest image in their minds after hearing the poem a second time?
- Look at the patterning of the language. Start with the use of alliteration – for example, 'midnight'/ 'moon-flood. Mazy moon...' Read the poem again, pausing after the use of alliteration and inviting the children to repeat it. What effect does the use of alliteration have in this poem?
- Next, look at the use of portmanteau words: 'startle-sound', 'moon-flood', 'sea-stones', 'mouse-went', 'quick-ran', 'sleepy-warm'. Ask the children how these words would normally be expressed – for example, 'a startling sound', 'a flood of moonlight'. What advantage does the use of portmanteau words give to the poet?
- Focus on the imagery. Ask the children to choose a 'word picture' from the poem and to illustrate it, perhaps no bigger than postcard-size.

### 'Where Would You Be?' (p. 10) Looking at the patterning of the poem

- Ask who in the class would take up the implied invitation in this poem to join the poet 'Out in the Night' and who would stay 'Safe in a chair'?
- Re-read the poem slowly, asking the children to put up their hand each time they hear an example of nature disturbed by powerful forces – for example, the howling wind, the twisting trees, the lost moon, the roaring waves.
- Ask the children about the patterning of the poem. (Make sure they know the appropriate vocabulary for this kind of discussion – 'stanza', 'rhyme scheme', and so on.) Do the children notice:

  – that the five-line stanzas are extended by two lines in the third stanza;
  – the question-and-answer form;
  – the rhyme scheme (a-b-c-c-b)?

  What is the effect of each of these patterns?

### 'The Hansel and Gretel House' (p. 11) Story telling; looking at omens; deducing the poem's 'message'

- This poem won't make much sense unless the

children know the story of Hansel and Gretel. It can be retold in a story-telling circle.

- Can the children connect the use of omens in the third verse to the poem 'Omens', which they have already read?
- Ask the children to say what they think the 'message' of the poem is. (The second verse gives the clearest clue.)

### 'What Was It?' (p. 12) and 'House Fear' (p. 13) Discussion and writing

- These two poems provide a good stimulus for discussion and writing – including poetry writing – on fear of the dark.

### 'The Phantom Lollipop Lady' (pp. 14–15) Writing a poem based on a model

- Ask the children whether they think this poem is a ghost story (it is) and what sort of ghost story it is (a sad one rather than a frightening one?). Point out that the story focuses on one person who loved her job so much that she could not give it up, even in death.
- Look briefly at the form – four-line, unrhymed stanzas. Time passing is signalled at the beginning of four of the stanzas ('When', 'One day', 'After a month', 'Now'), giving the poem the feeling of a story.
- Ask the children to write a poem using the same form about someone else who loved their job too much to give it up when they died, for example a teacher, a doctor, the custodian of a museum or castle, a shopkeeper. You can brainstorm a list with the children for them to choose from.

### 'The Frozen Man' (pp. 16–17) Brainstorming; story telling; debating in speech and/or writing

- Re-read the poem down to 'ring/and ring'. Ask the children to say what the frozen man sees and hears.
- Brainstorm a spider-chart for 'Out at the edge of town' to include images, feelings and sounds not explicitly mentioned in the poem but appropriate to it. Then do a contrasting spider-chart for 'at the heart of town'.
- Ask the children to invent (perhaps in writing) a set of circumstances to explain why the man is wandering, frozen, at the edge of town.
- Then ask the children to argue for or against the advice (or order) to let the man in when he knocks on the door. Again, this could be done in writing if you prefer.

### 'Duppy Dan' (p. 18) Looking at the use of dialect; commenting on the patterning of the poem

- Make sure all the children can see the poem. (If you do not have a class set of the book, copy the poem out on an OHP, the board or a flipchart.)
- Ask the children to identify dialect words and phrases in the poem, and to underline them. Ask what would be lost in terms of style, sound and rhythm if the poem had been written in Standard English.
- Ask the children to comment on the patterning in the poem; that is, the repeated 'Duppy Dan', the two-line stanzas, the a-b-a-b rhyme scheme. What effect does this patterning have?

### 'A Spell to Destroy Life' (p. 20) Writing a spell based on a model

- This is a rather chilling spell. To counteract its bleak effect, you could invite the children to write 'A Spell to Revive Life', to be chanted over someone who is sick. The form of the poem can be taken from 'A Spell to Destroy Life'; that is, it can start with 'Listen!' and follow the wording of most of the lines, with appropriate changes – for example, instead of 'I bury your soul under earth', the line might be 'I breathe the life of the earth on your soul'. To do this activity, the children will need to have a copy of the poem.

### 'La Belle Dame Sans Merci' (pp. 22–23) Introducing a 'difficult' poem and exploring its meaning

- This has been described as the greatest of Keats's ballads, not least because however many times one returns to it, and thinks about it, it remains ultimately mysterious. Love and death entwine: the knight moves in a wintry landscape that seems to reflect his own despair; the lady is beautiful and alluring, a dreamlike phantom that has enslaved him. The bleak landscape is shot through with images from the world of fantasy: a faery's child and a faery's song, an elfin grot, ghostly knights and princes. It has the air of an old legend.
- For Y6/P7 children, introducing the poem will be sufficient. Hopefully there will be many opportunities for them to come back to it and ponder its meaning when they are more mature. Begin by explaining that it was written in the early nineteenth century and uses the vocabulary of the time, some of which may be unfamiliar to modern readers.

- Most children will find it easier to follow the poem if they have a copy of it in front of them.
- Explain briefly what the poem is about, read it through, discuss what is happening and then re-read it.
- Focus on some of the archaic words and phrases – the children can volunteer these themselves if you wish – and discuss their meaning
- Alternatively, give pairs or groups of three one verse of the poem to discuss and to report back on its meaning to the class. (Make sure you cover the whole poem.)

### 'The Cunjah Man' (pp. 24–25) Choral reading; looking at the use of dialect; writing a spell based on a model

- Having read the poem through once, ask four fluent, confident readers to read one of the four verses again, with the whole class joining in with the two-line refrain. (You may have to write the refrain up on the board.)
- The 'Cunjah Man' is the equivalent of the 'Bogey Man'. What variations on these two do the children know about?
- Re-read the poem, asking the children to indicate whenever they hear a dialect phrase. What would the Standard English equivalent be?
- The children could write a spell to ward off the threat from the Cunjah Man.

### 'Why?' (p. 26) Writing a poem in reponse to another poem

- The children could write a poem in which Susanna gives her reply to the poet. Ask the children:

  - What did Susanna see?
  - What did she think and feel about the guy?
  - Why does she fear that he was alive?

### 'Wolf-Cub Meets the World' (pp. 28–29) Exploring the meaning of the poem through question and answer; writing additional verses

- This poem should be read aloud in two voices. Point out the question-and-answer form of the poem.
- Ask the children to re-read the poem with these three questions in mind:

  - What does the wind do?
  - What does the sun do?
  - What does the river do?

- Some children might like to write a further question and answer in two verses to add to the poem.

### 'Overheard on a Saltmarsh' (p. 31) Paired reading and performance; story writing

- Before reading this poem, explain what nymphs and goblins are. (A nymph is a semi-divine water-spirit in the form of a girl; a goblin is a small, grotesque, supernatural creature, usually male.) Establish the setting of the poem – a reedy, moonlit and deserted seashore or marsh, probably at night.
- The poem is in two voices. Choose a confident reader to take the part of either the nymph or the goblin, and make sure they know which lines are theirs.
- Discuss with the children:

  - the two protagonists (Who are they? What are they doing there? Where might they live?);
  - why the goblin wants the beads so much;
  - the beads themselves (Where do they come from? Are they magical?).

- If you have enough copies of the poem, get pairs of children to perform it with appropriate expression.
- The poem could be used as a prompt for story writing. You could suggest a title like 'How the Nymph Stole the Glass Beads from the Moon and the Consequences'.

# Heroes and Villains

**Editor**   *Tony Bradman*
**Illustrator**   *Tony Kerins*
**Short narrative**   *A collection of contemporary short stories*

The short stories in this collection cover a range of genres including fantasy, war, comedy and science fiction. Most of the stories will take 45 minutes to an hour to be read aloud – longer if you allow pauses for discussion.

The activities for this book will be found under the titles of the individual stories, which appear in alphabetical order.

## A choice of literacy activities

# Christmas in the Other House

**Author** *Judith O'Neill*

**Short narrative** *A family story set in the recent past*

## Synopsis

Alec looks back to when he was twelve or thirteen and recalls a strange Christmas and the events that led up to it. He and his mother lived near his grandparents in a village by the sea. He loved being at his grandparents' house and often spent the night there. Until, that is, his widowed great-aunt Ina moved in, bringing her precious furniture with her. Although it is never stated, Aunt Ina's aim is to move in permanently and to change the ways of the house – not just the furniture – to suit herself. She does this by stealth: first taking over the cooking; then, in the months leading up to Christmas, moving out much of Grandma's beloved old family furniture and replacing it with her own. Aunt Ina's belongings had been stored in the 'other house', an old building at the bottom of the garden. On Christmas Eve, while Aunt Ina is at church, Grandma finally rebels and has her old table and chairs brought back in from the other house, while Aunt Ina's are returned to it. Aunt Ina sees this as the final challenge. The next day she insists that the Christmas lunch she has cooked should be eaten in the other house on *her* table. The other adults refuse, but Alec, drawn by the delicious smell and sight of the food, almost succumbs. However, at the last minute he realises where his loyalties lie. Accepting defeat, Aunt Ina moves out into a house of her own.

## Discussion points

### Before reading

- Explain that this story is told in the first person by someone looking back some sixty years at an important event in his boyhood. If this were a true story, it would be described as a 'memoir' – a personal account of the past – but since it is fiction, it only borrows from the form.

### During reading

- It is worth pausing briefly after the first paragraph to sort out who's who and how they are all related.

### After reading

- Help the children to recall and retell the main events of the story by splitting it into the following four 'movements':
  - **July:** Aunt Ina's letter arrives; she moves in, bringing her furniture which is stored in the 'other house'.
  - **Late October:** the tables and chairs are exchanged, beginning a complete change of the furnishing of Grandma's house.
  - **Christmas Eve:** Grandma's table and chairs are restored to her house.
  - **Christmas Day:** Alec weakens briefly but Aunt Ina fails to win him over and the whole family stands firm in loyalty to Grandma.

# Activity 1 [ T ]

*Summarising characters'*
*thoughts in relation to key events*

### Learning objectives
- to identify key events in the story
- to empathise with characters
- to use skills of inference and deduction to look at key events from multiple viewpoints

### Introduction
- As a general introduction to what the story is about, pose the following question: 'Not a great deal happens in the story: a rather domineering, widowed great-aunt moves in with relatives. She gradually changes the furniture, replacing it with her own, but at Christmas the family make it clear they liked things as they were, and she moves out to a place of her own. So what is the story *really* about?' Steer the children towards considering the **relationships** in the family and their background, and the **thoughts and feelings** of the main characters: Grandma, Aunt Ina and Alec, who is caught up in an adult drama which he doesn't really understand at the time.
- Ask the children to think of one event in the story which they think is important to Grandma, to Aunt Ina or to Alec. Get a range of responses and record them on the board or flipchart.

### Development
- Using the diagram on **activity sheet 1** as a model, choose one of the key events of the story and write it in the central box. Then ask the children how they think each of the four main characters views that event, recording a summary in each box. An example is given below.
- Brainstorm a list of 'significant events' for the children to choose from. This might include the day of Ina's arrival; the setting up of her furniture in the 'other house'; Ina's taking over the cooking; the fact that Ina is not house hunting; the exchanging of the table and chairs; the exchange of all the furniture; the return of Grandma's table and chairs on Christmas Eve; the serving of Christmas dinner in the 'other house'; Alec's apparent siding with Ina; his last-minute change of heart; Ina's moving out.
- Give out **activity sheet 1**. Working in pairs, the children should choose one of the significant events from the list and summarise the characters' thoughts about it in the way you have demonstrated.
- In the first instance the work should be based on recall. Make copies of the book available, though, for children who need to check parts of the story.

### Review
- Compare charts featuring the same event and discuss their similarities and differences. Encourage the children to give reasons for the content of their summaries.

---

**Alec's thoughts**
He's indignant that Aunt Ina is to take over his beloved attic bedroom and he is therefore dismayed at the news.

**a significant event**
Aunt Ina's letter arrives saying that she is coming to stay and is bringing her furniture with her.

**Grandma's thoughts**
She thinks that her sister is returning to her childhood home because she is lonely after her husband's death and is looking for company.

**Aunt Ina's thoughts**
She is looking forward to moving back into the family house and making it her own. She is thinking mainly of her own needs, not those of her relatives.

**Grandpa's thoughts**
He is mainly worried about the practical problems Ina's move will cause, such as where to put the furniture. He cheerfully accepts that his sister-in-law has a right to stay.

# Activity 2 [ C ]

## Writing a profile of Aunt Ina

### Learning objectives
- to examine characterisation
- to practise the skills of inference and deduction

### Introduction
- Ask the children which of the main characters in the story we learn most about. (After a discussion, the children should settle on Aunt Ina.)
- Re-read the paragraph where Alec sees his great-aunt for the first time ('Great Aunt Ina stepped off the Wednesday bus a week later.' p. 82). What are his first impressions of her?
- Brainstorm what the children think about Aunt Ina.

### Development
- Explain that when drawing up a profile of a character, it is useful to break the description down into a number of different aspects.

Write the following headings on the board or flipchart and ask for brief explanations of what each would cover:

- family circumstances;
- appearance;
- personality;
- talents;
- weaknesses;
- religion and values;
- how she gets on with her relations;
- her intentions;
- how she views her future.

- Split the class into groups. Each group should have a copy of the book which can be passed round the group for reading aloud.
- As the story is read aloud, the group should listen for information on each of the points listed in the character profile.

### Review
- Compile a class profile drawn from the children's work.

---

## Comprehension questions

For suggestions on how to use these, see page 17.

# Heroes and Villains: Christmas in the Other House
## Comprehension questions

Before you answer the questions, draw a family tree to show how
Alec is related to the adults in the story.

**1**
Why did Alec like to spend so much
time at his grandparents' house?

**2**
Why did Alec dislike going into the
'other house' alone?

**3**
In what ways was Aunt Ina
different from her sister Jean?

**4**
'As the weeks passed, Aunt Ina showed
no sign of looking for a house of her own.'
Why do you think that was so?

**5**
Why was the change of furniture so
important to Aunt Ina and to Grandma?

**6**
Until Christmas Day, everyone seemed to
do as Aunt Ina wished. Why was that?

**7**
Alec almost had Christmas in the
'other house'. What made him change
his mind at the last minute?

**8**
What eventually persuaded Aunt Ina
to find a place of her own?

Name _____     Date _____

*Write a summary in each of the boxes.*

Alec's thoughts

Grandma's thoughts

a significant event

Aunt Ina's thoughts

Grandpa's thoughts

# Heroes and Villains

**Author**   *Paul Stewart*

**Short narrative**   *A contemporary war story*

## Synopsis

This is a powerful and hard-hitting story which explores the twin themes of heroism and villainy within the context of war. A group of homeless orphans are living together in a bombed-out hotel basement, surviving by stealing food. The city has been overrun by government forces, sent in to crush a revolution, and it is now in ruins, its inhabitants oppressed, hungry and miserable. 'Spooks' (i.e. government soldiers) patrol everywhere. Two of the children, Sprint (the narrator) and Bo-bo, get caught in possession of black-market cheese and are taken to a prison camp. There, Sprint glimpses an old friend and ally, Horse, who used to live with the orphans and who is now a terrorist. Sprint considers him to be a hero but he is in for a rude shock. Horse lobs a bomb into the room where the children are being interrogated ('There is no sacrifice too great for the cause!' Horse has said). The spook sergeant saves everyone's life by breaking the blast of the bomb with his own body, raising the question: Who is the hero and who the villain?

## Discussion points

### Before reading

- Sprint says, 'We're homeless orphans in the middle of a war,' which neatly sums up their situation at the start of the story. Describe the city (its geographical location is not given; the story stands for any modern city torn apart by civil strife), explaining why it is in ruins and who the opposing forces are. Explain that the story gives a vivid glimpse of what it might be like for an orphan in this situation. Round off by saying that the story tries to answer the question: 'In wartime, who are the heroes and who are the villains?'

### During reading

- Pause on page 112 at the end of the passage which outlines the political situation which led to the war: the burning of the opponents' flag, the raising of the victorious rebels' tricolour above the parliament building, and then the tanks rolling in. Make sure the children understand what is going on here and how it led to Sprint's situation as a homeless orphan.
- Pause on page 120 at the end of the passage which describes the camp that the children are taken to. Re-read it to make sure the children can visualise the scene and Horse's part in it.

### After reading

Focus on the 'heroes and villains' theme. It may well be too difficult for the children to work out for themselves the ambiguity of these two terms as presented in the story. You might like to describe it as follows and use the description as a basis for a discussion:

- **The children**: they see themselves as *heroes* because they are managing to survive in extreme hardship and are doing their bit to harass the opposing forces (the spooks).

They are *villains* in the eyes of those from whom they steal, including mothers struggling to find food for their families, and in the eyes of the spooks.

- **Horse**: the children see him as a *hero* because he is fighting the spooks, and they believe he is on the side of those who want freedom and self-determination.

He is eventually seen as a *villain* because he is willing to murder people on his own side, including children, to further the cause of freedom.

- **The sergeant**: the children eventually see him as a *hero* because he saved the lives of everyone in the cabin by shielding them from the bomb blast at the cost of his own life.

But he is still a *villain* because he is one of the spooks, part of the force that killed the children's families.

(Activities 1 to 3 are linked and are best done in sequence.)

# Activity 1  |C|

### *Examining characterisation; compiling fact files*

> #### Learning objectives
> - to collaborate in a group to examine characterisation
> - to scan for relevant information
> - to represent this information in a fact file

### Introduction
- Write the following items on the board and, after each one, ask the children what first springs to mind about them: the city; the war; Sprint; Neck; Bo-bo; Nutter; Horse.

### Development
- Split the class into groups and give each group one of the above to gather information on (the city and the war could be done as one topic).

- Make sure each group has a copy of the book. It should be passed round the group so each member takes a turn at reading aloud extracts relevant to their area while the rest of the group make notes.
- When the group has gathered all the information they can find, they should organise it into a fact file (i.e. a list of bullet points). You may have to show the children how to do this. For example, for Sprint, the fact file might begin:

  - orphan, aged 12
  - lives in the basement of a bombed-out hotel
  - cohabits with a number of other orphans
  - family killed by a bomb on their apartment 18 months before the story begins
  - survives by scrounging and thieving
  - best friends are Neck and Bo-bo
  - models himself on Horse, an older terrorist who once protected him...

### Review
- Each group should report back on their findings.

# Activity 2

### *Hot-seating the main characters*

> #### Learning objectives
> - to use the information gathered in *Activity 1*
> - to develop oral skills
> - to empathise with characters and explain their actions and motivation

### Introduction
- Ask the children to work in the groups they were in for *Activity 1*. Ask each group to recap on what they discovered about their area of enquiry.

### Development
(This activity assumes that the children have had some experience of hot-seating and know how it works.)

- Ask each group (excluding the city and war group) to nominate one person to hot-seat the character they have investigated.
- Then ask the group to come up with some questions to ask about one of the other characters. Make sure all of the characters are covered in this way.
- Call the first role-player forward. Use the questions framed by one of the groups to begin the hot-seating process. Encourage other groups to join in.
- Proceed until all the characters have been hot-seated. (Some may have to be recalled if new questions emerge after they have stepped down.)

### Review
- Reflect upon the hot-seating process. Ask the hot-seaters how they felt. Ask which kinds of questions created the best responses. Ask what the children think of hot-seating as a learning process.

# Activity 3

*Writing a case-study report (for able writers only)*

---

### Learning objectives
- to project beyond the story
- to practise report writing using a framework
- to examine characterisation

## Introduction
- Recap briefly on the first two activities, focusing on the characters of Sprint, Neck and Bo-bo.
- Ask the children to project the story a year on: the war is over and the children are settling into an orphanage. What would life be like for them? What psychological scars and problems might they have?

## Development
- Ask the children to imagine that they are a doctor in the orphanage responsible for the care of Sprint, Neck and Bo-bo. They are writing a report on each of the children to explain their situation, their problems and their suitability for adoption. The children's task is to write one of these reports.

- Give the children a framework and discuss what the headings mean, for example:
  - name, age, family background;
  - situation during the war (Speculate with the children about what might have happened to Sprint, Neck and Bo-bo in captivity. Did they escape?);
  - problems he now faces (e.g. readjusting to adult supervision, nightmares and traumatic flashbacks, fear, contempt for rules and procedures, loneliness);
  - his hopes for the future;
  - the doctor's recommendations for the boy's treatment and their predictions for the boy's future.

- Discuss with the children the style of the language they will need to adopt for an official report. It may be helpful to write a few sample sentences in this style as a model for the children.

## Review
- Discuss the similarities and differences between the doctors' reports.

# Invisible

**Author**   *Richard Brown*
**Short narrative**   *A contemporary story*

## Synopsis

Ten-year-old Denny is going through a crisis in his life. Dad left home some time ago and has now stopped visiting. Denny becomes depressed and loses all his confidence. Mum, unhappy herself, cannot give him the support he needs; only his eleven-year-old sister Lena understands what he is going through. Denny pretends to be invisible; he barely functions at school and is uncommunicative at home. The turning-point in his fortunes comes when he and Lena stay with their Aunt April, an artist, in her country home. April's dog Kip, a favourite of Denny's, gets trapped in a rock fissure and the boy carries out a difficult rescue. The ordeal brings a psychological shift and, through the medium of April's art – her photo-montage and portrait painting – Denny begins to reassemble his shattered self.

## Discussion points

### Before reading

- Explain that this is a serious story about a boy who is going through a crisis in his personal life, triggered by the splitting up of his family.
- Towards the end of the story, the art form known as **photo-montage** becomes an important part of the story. It consists basically of photographs of the picture's subject cut up and rearranged to give multiple viewpoints, creating a 'fractured' effect. This form has become well known recently through the work of David Hockney. It would help the children to visualise the form if you were able to show them pictures of his (or another artist's) work in this form.

### During reading

- Pause at the end of part 6 (p. 31) and review Denny's situation. Ask the children:
  - Why is he unhappy?
  - Why does he pretend to be invisible?
  - Why does Mum appear to be so unsympathetic?
  - Why does he run away?

### After reading

- Discuss the personality change in Denny indicated clearly at the end of the story. What caused it? How hopeful a sign is it? In rescuing Kip, Denny is also, in a psychological sense, 'rescuing' himself. He learns that he will achieve nothing by being 'invisible'; that, like Kip, he'll need help to get better; and that, like the rescue, it will be a struggle.
- Discuss what part the following played in Denny's crisis: the game of invisibility; the mirrors; the television; the bolt hole in the woods; Dad's portrait; Kip; the photo-montage of Denny.

## Activity 1  [ T ]

*Discussion and writing about
the main characters' relationships*

### Learning objectives
- to use inference and deduction to describe the relationships between characters
- to scan for detail and recall evidence
- to develop a vocabulary to describe how people relate to one another

### Introduction
- To sort out initial ideas about the four main characters, brainstorm a spider-chart for each of them with the group or class. Concentrate on the personality and inner lives of the characters.

### Development
- Split the class into pairs or groups of three and ask each to write the names of the four main characters on four separate slips of paper.

- They should then select two slips at random and discuss how these two characters relate. Key questions are:
  - What do they think about each other?
  - What do they feel about each other?
  - How do their thoughts and feelings about each other change during the course of the story?
- The children should record their ideas in the following form: 'What _____ thinks and feels about _____.'

- Have copies of the story available for reference, but the work should be based on recall in the first instance.

### Review

- Compare what the pairs or groups say about the same combination of characters. Base your discussion around the similarities and differences.

---

# Activity 2

*Assembling evidence for character development*

### Learning objectives
- to examine the idea of character development within a narrative
- to develop empathy with the main character

### Introduction
- Discuss in general terms how Denny's personality has changed over the year since Dad left. (We can infer that he was originally a normal, happy boy with no real problems.) Introduce terms like 'a crisis in his life', 'family fracture', 'personality change' and 'depression' (which was in fact what he was suffering from, although no-one took sufficient notice of this). Ask the children how Denny's physical appearance changed, indicating changes in his inner life.

### Development
- Give out **activity sheet 1**. It asks the children to develop this discussion in more detail.
- Briefly help the children to recall the parts of the story indicated by each box.
- Remind the children of what is meant by the term 'personality change'.
- Have copies of the book available for reference, although the work should be based on recall in the first instance.

### Review
- Let pairs discuss their work before a general review of the children's responses.

---

# Activity 3

*Looking at the story's structure; assembling evidence*

### Learning objectives
- to examine the basic problem/solution structure of the story
- to gather textual evidence about the main character's state of mind in the first half of the story

### Introduction
- Write the following framework on the board or flipchart (omitting the text in brackets):

**the problem**
- cause (*Dad leaving home*)
- effect (*Denny's and Mum's unhappiness*)
- evidence (*for Denny's depression*)

**the turning-point**
- cause (*rescuing Kip*)
- effect (*Denny finds new confidence and begins to emerge from his depression*)
- evidence (*of his recovery*)

- Explain that this is the underlying structure of the story. The task is to see how the main elements of the story fit into the structure.
- Begin by discussing **the problem**.
  - Cause: Dad leaving the family and failing to visit them.
  - Effect: the family is fractured; Denny in particular feels rejected, loses his confidence and undergoes a personality change; Mum changes too.

### Development
- Split the class into small groups.
- The group should brainstorm evidence for Denny's depression. You can start them off with: 'He pretends to be invisible; his work at school is now very poor...'.
- Make sure each group has a copy of the book from which group members can take turns to read aloud appropriate passages, when asked to do so by the rest of the group.
- Here is the kind of thing that should emerge from the brainstorming: poor personal appearance and hygiene; does and says little at home; stays in bed a lot; doesn't have much appetite; keeps out of the way; keeps irregular hours; dislikes seeing himself in mirrors; watches television without seeming to take it in; acts like a zombie; the acrostic; hiding in the bolt hole; paints over his father's portrait; cries at night.
- Having shared the results of the groups' brainstorming session, move on to **the turning-point**. The children should readily identify this as the rescue of Kip.
- The groups should now brainstorm the evidence for a change in Denny's thoughts and feelings about himself from this point (i.e. for the start of his recovery). Their findings should include the fact that Denny laughed at himself in the mirror; he's started to spike his hair again; he helps Lena assemble her photo-montage; he works on his own photo-montage; he agrees to have his portrait painted, thereby tacitly agreeing that he is no longer 'invisible'.

### Review
- If there is time, the children could write the results of their brainstorming into the framework given in the introduction. If there isn't time, return briefly to the framework and show how what you have discussed fits into the basic structure of the story.

Name _____    Date _____

How did Denny's appearance and personality
change during this crisis in his life?
Fill in the boxes.

| **before Dad left**<br>appearance<br><br><br><br><br><br><br><br>his personality | **after Dad left**<br>appearance<br><br><br><br><br><br><br>How did his personality change? |
|---|---|
| **just after rescuing Kip**<br>**(still looking like a scarecrow)**<br>appearance<br><br><br><br><br><br><br>What were his feelings? | **when Denny was assembling the**<br>**photo-montage of himself**<br>appearance<br><br><br><br><br><br>What changes do you think will develop in<br>Denny from this point? |

# Making Rain and Other Magic

**Author**   *Monica Furlong*

**Short narrative**   *A contemporary story*

## Synopsis

This story is set in a vast, hot desert and is told by a girl called Blossom. She gets caught up in the deadly rivalry between two 'clever men' (magicians) – Mosquito, whom she respects; and Sunfly, whom she fears. There is a terrible drought and Mosquito inexplicably puts off the rainmaking ceremony, thus undermining his authority. Blossom's family, along with the rest of her community, are forced to go to the Christian Mission to seek food and shelter. However, the way of life is not to her liking. In the camp, Mosquito wastes away and seems near to death. He reveals to Blossom that someone has put a fatal spell on him which only another 'clever man' can lift. Sunfly, Mosquito's rival, is the only other 'clever man' available and Blossom, despite her fears, goes looking for him. In his tent she discovers a wooden doll representing Mosquito stuck with splinters. She secretly removes the splinters from the doll and Mosquito is soon on the mend. He convenes a rain ceremony at last and, as he chants, the rains come pouring down. Blossom decides to become a 'clever woman' and goes to ask Mosquito if she can become his pupil.

## Discussion points

### Before reading

- Orientate the children to the unusual background to this story and the identity of the narrator, Blossom. She is a black girl living in a nomadic community in a country where hot, dry seasons alternate with rainy seasons, radically affecting the way the people live. Belief in ancestral spirits and 'natural magic' inform the lives of the villagers. Blossom herself has nascent special powers and is likely to become a 'clever woman' (a magician and healer, one who can apparently influence the forces of nature) as she grows older.

### After reading

- Focus on Blossom. Discuss what she felt for and thought about Mosquito, what changes life in the Mission entailed for her, and the way she approached the matter of the wooden doll.
- Talk about the rivalry between Mosquito and Sunfly. How does the author make us respect Mosquito but disapprove of Sunfly?

## Activity 1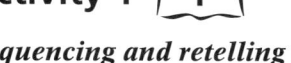

*Sequencing and retelling the story; thought-tracking*

> ### Learning objectives
> - to recall and sequence the main events of the story
> - to use the sequence to retell the story orally
> - to empathise with characters' thoughts and feelings

### Introduction

- Ask the children which parts of the story stand out in their minds. List these on the board or flipchart. Ask the children to speculate on why they recall those parts of the story and not others.

### Development

- Give out **activity sheet 1**, one between two. It lists events in the story which the children have to cut out and sequence.
- The correct sequence is as follows:
  - Blossom is bitten by a snake and becomes seriously ill.
  - Mosquito cures Blossom's snake bite.
  - There is a prolonged drought.
  - Sunfly challenges Mosquito to make rain.
  - The family are forced to take refuge in the Mission.
  - Mosquito becomes very ill and seems to have lost his powers.
  - Mosquito reveals to Blossom that a fatal spell has been put on him.

- Blossom plucks up courage to ask for Sunfly's help.
- In Sunfly's tent, Blossom discovers the truth about Mosquito's illness.
- Blossom removes the splinters from the wooden doll, washes it and hides it.
- Blossom asks Grandma if she has behaved correctly.
- Mosquito conducts the rain ceremony.
- Rain falls at last.
- Blossom asks Mosquito if she can become his pupil.

- Once the children have completed the sequence correctly, they should consider the feelings and thoughts of the characters who take part in the events featured on each slip of paper. They can note these on the back of the slips or list them separately if you wish to reuse the slips.
- The children should now retell the story in pairs, taking each episode in turn. They should make a point of including the characters' thoughts and feelings in their retelling.

### Review
- Retell the story in a class circle, discussing the characters' thoughts and feelings as you do so.

## Activity 2

### Finding and classifying information; note-taking within a framework

#### Learning objectives
- to scan for information
- to practise classifying information and note-taking
- to consider the major influences on the main character's life

### Introduction
- Ask the children to say in general terms in what ways Blossom's life is different from their own. Record the best of the children's ideas on the board or flipchart.
- With the children's help, begin to classify these ideas (perhaps by underlining in different colours) in terms of climate, living conditions, food, magic, celebrations and beliefs and so on.

### Development
- Split the class into groups and make sure each group has a copy of the book. The book should be passed round the group so that each group member can read aloud from it in turn.
- Give out **activity sheet 2**, one between two if you prefer.
- Talk about each of the questions on the sheet to make sure that the children understand them. Explain that the groups' task is to note in each box information gleaned from the story to answer the questions.

- Model the first example, about climate, showing how to answer in note-form. (You are not looking for complete sentences.)
- Talk about reading aloud, making sure that the children know they have to pause whenever anyone in the group thinks that some relevant information has been given. The reader could also take a lead, asking questions to prompt the rest of the group to think about whether what has just been read is relevant to the task.
- Make sure the children know that the boxes are in no particular order and do not have to be completed in sequence.

### Review
- Run through the answers with the whole class. They should come up with something like the following:

**What climate was Blossom used to?** Periods of extended sunshine with no rain, drought, rainy season.

**What were living conditions like in Blossom's community?** Families lived together. Clothes weren't important. Men went hunting for big animals. Campfires.

**What were living conditions like in the Mission?** Crowded. Some adults lived in tents. Children slept in dormitories and went to school. Old people had their own communal room. There was clean water and clean linen for some.

**What did Blossom's people eat?** Lizards, snakes, roots, tubers, wild honey, bread made from seeds.

**What was medicine like in Blossom's community?** Healers or medicine men/women were called to the sick. Used natural potions and objects such as leaves, crystals, bones, wands, lizards, herbs. Name was sung or yodelled.

**What 'good magic' did Blossom encounter?** Ritual for rainmaking. Healing of her snake bite.

**What 'bad magic' did Blossom encounter?** 'Sung me' – an evil spell put on Mosquito: a wooden doll pierced with splinters and smeared with green slime.

**What happened at celebrations and ceremonies?** Feasting, dancing, singing, story telling, performances by magicians, rituals and chants for rainmaking.

**What religious beliefs did Blossom encounter?** Belief in the spirits of her ancestors. Christianity in the Mission.

**Who had special skills and powers?** 'Clever' men or women such as Mosquito. Rainmakers. People who talked to the spirits of the ancestors.

# Heroes and Villains: Making Rain and Other Magic Activity sheet 1

- Cut out these events from the story and put them in the right order.
- Write on the back of each slip (or separately) what you think the characters involved in each event are thinking and feeling at that point in the story.
- Use the sequence of events to retell the story with a partner.

✂ - - - - - - - - - - - - - - - - - - - - - - - - - - - - - - - - - - - -

Blossom removes the splinters from the wooden doll, washes it and hides it.

Mosquito becomes very ill and seems to have lost his powers.

Blossom is bitten by a snake and becomes seriously ill.

Blossom plucks up courage to ask for Sunfly's help.

Mosquito conducts the rain ceremony.

Mosquito cures Blossom's snake bite.

There is a prolonged drought.

Blossom asks Mosquito if she can become his pupil.

Rain falls at last.

Sunfly challenges Mosquito to make rain.

The family are forced to take refuge in the Mission.

Mosquito reveals to Blossom that a fatal spell has been put on him.

In Sunfly's tent, Blossom discovers the truth about Mosquito's illness.

Blossom asks Grandma if she has behaved correctly.

Name _____      Date _____

Record in each box what you learn about Blossom's way of life.

| | | |
|---|---|---|
| What climate was Blossom used to? | What were living conditions like in Blossom's community? | What were living conditions like in the Mission? |
| What did Blossom's people eat? | What was medicine like in Blossom's community? | What 'good magic' did Blossom encounter? |
| What 'bad magic' did Blossom encounter? | What happened at celebrations and ceremonies? | What religious beliefs did Blossom encounter? |
| Who had special skills and powers? | | |

© Cambridge University Press 1999   Original artwork by Tony Kerins

# Tags

**Author**   *Ben Bo*

**Short narrative**   *A contemporary fantasy*

## Synopsis

This is a story with a strong, contemporary message. Big Greg, Tommo, Ned and Duncan are the Tag Squad – a gang of boys dedicated to the art of graffiti. Duncan is a reluctant member though, needing peer group approval. The boys pride themselves on their daring feats. One day, they discover a cave whose walls are covered with beautiful, mysterious primitive paintings. In the cave they encounter supernatural forces which shift the balance of power within the gang and force them to rethink their values. Greg, the leader, insists that they all sign their graffiti names – or 'tags' – on the walls of the cave. Duncan senses that this would be a violation of a sacred place, and there is talk of curses, but the boys all have to do as Greg says. Duncan is right: supernatural forces are unleashed, the boys get sucked into the walls and whirled about in a terrifying way. The wall-paintings come alive, dancing and chanting to ancient music. Finally, in a whirlwind, the boys are ejected from the cave but Ned is missing. Greg insists that they leave at once, but the gang sides with Duncan when he defies Greg, saying he won't leave until Ned is found. Greg's dictatorial hold over the group is broken and the gang's *raison d'être* is fatally undermined.

## Discussion points

### Before reading

- If possible, show the children some pictures of ancient cave paintings, emphasising how precious and delicate they are and how some may have had powerful religious significance. At this point you need not say what part such paintings play in the story.
- Talk about the children's experience of graffiti. Are there examples around the neighbourhood? What do the children think of it? Do they know who does the graffiti? Can they speculate about the intentions of the graffiti artists? How are graffiti viewed at home and in the community?
- The author of this story is a successful cartoonist. How might this affect his approach to the theme of graffiti?
- Make it clear that the story is told in the first person by Duncan (graffiti name – or 'tag' – SLAM), a boy of about twelve who is a member of a graffiti gang.

### During reading

- The story features a lot of non-standard terms. You may need to gloss some items as they come up if the children cannot work them out from the context:

  **bug-eyed:** eyes popping or bulging out;
  **grubber:** stupid; only clever enough to grub around on the ground;
  **jinking:** dodging this way and that;
  **made the hit:** the 'hit' is another word for tagging or spraying the walls with graffiti;
  **stompie:** feet-stamping angry;
  **twister:** a whirlwind;
  **twonker:** fool, idiot;
  **tags:** graffiti;
  **woosie:** a wimp, a 'chicken'.

- Pause after the paragraph which ends 'Well, what a surprise – Duncan is wrong again.' (p. 67) Discuss what the children think of Greg so far. Why is he the leader of the gang? Try to bring out the fact that Greg rules by force and ridicule, not because he is the most respected, and that Duncan suffers most from this dictatorial leadership.

### After reading

Discuss two key questions:
- Why were the supernatural forces in the cave so hostile to the boys?
- How have Duncan and Greg's positions in the gang changed by the end of the story?

# Activity 1

## Class debate on the ethics of graffiti

### Learning objectives
- to define aspects of graffiti and classify them
- to develop opinions in speech and writing
- to participate in a class debate

### Introduction
- Begin by helping the children to define various different kinds of graffiti (a drawing or words scratched, drawn or sprayed on a surface, usually a wall), its different purposes and the different attitudes towards it. Through discussion the following types of graffiti should emerge:

  1. Graffiti as urban pollution, consisting mainly of names and slogans. (This is the kind of graffiti the boys in the story produce.)
  2. Graffiti as an urban art form, often pictures or designs, sometimes having a political message, drawn by artists who are not paid or commissioned to do them.
  3. Graffiti which are commissioned and paid for, such as wall-paintings in communal areas, playgrounds, commercial premises and so on.
  4. Graffiti with a religious significance, such as in ancient ceremonial places like tombs or caves (as in the story).

- Having defined the types, discuss the purposes of each, or the intentions of the graffiti artists, and ask the children to rate them ethically.

### Development
- This debate about graffiti concerns mainly the first and second types. Ask half the class, working in small discussion groups, to set out arguments in favour of type 1 and against type 2. The other half of the class should do the reverse. The groups should note their main arguments in preparation for a formal class debate.
- You can have speakers for and against if you wish, or hold a less formal class debate. You might like to list on the board the main arguments put forward for and against the two types of graffiti.
- The children will probably vote for their own side, so it may not be appropriate to have a vote. You could try a secret ballot!

### Review
- Ask the children what they think they have learnt during the course of the debate, not just about the subject but also about developing and defending a point of view.

# The Visitor

**Author**  *Keith Ruttle*

**Short narrative**  *A science-fiction story*

## Synopsis

Billy and Steve are natural rivals and enjoy arguing with and insulting one another. When their science teacher, Doc Beasley, sets the class a half-term competition – to present a scientific report on Hawes' Comet, which will pass close to Earth during the week – they see it as an opportunity for further rivalry. But Hawes' Comet is not what it seems; although the scientific community regards it as a comet, it is in fact an automatic probe sent by another civilisation to gather samples of life forms at fixed sample points, using a beam of light to transport them into the probe for analysis. The boys wonder whether it might be a UFO; certainly Billy's Gran's stories about mysterious disappearances each time the comet comes to Earth (every 112 years) seem to suggest this. The boys, keeping up their friendly rivalry, keep track of the comet's progress from their vantage point on High Tor, near where they live. On the night of the comet's closest approach to Earth, the boys narrowly escape being beamed up into the probe. Billy's pet mouse, Butch, doesn't escape, giving the boys the essential clue to the comet's real nature. Brought together by their discovery, the boys present a report to Doc Beasley. She admires the scientific element of the report but scorns the legends and UFO theory, and Steve has a horrible suspicion that the whole thing is a trick played on him by Billy.

## Discussion points

### Before reading

- Having explained that this is a science-fiction story set in a familiar home and school setting on Earth, brainstorm with the children what the story might be about. Give them the following clues: a legend about people disappearing, a UFO, a mouse, and two boys who are always arguing with each other.

- The opening passage in italics about the probe and its mission uses many abstract terms and has a high readability level. The children will need to study it closely to understand what it says. It is important that they do understand this passage in order to get the most out of the story. So before reading the story, you may wish to do *Activity 1*.

## Activity 1

### *Reading and understanding the complex language of the prologue*

> **Learning objective**
> - to use a dictionary effectively

- Give out **activity sheet 1**, one between two if you prefer, and read aloud the two descriptive passages. Ask the children to underline words and phrases in the passages which they do not understand. They should then list them in the right-hand column and use dictionaries to help discover their meaning. It is likely that in some cases the dictionary will not be a great help to the children as the definition may be just as abstract and obscure to them as the word they are looking up. Acknowledge this difficulty and ask the children to tick the words which they do come to understand through their dictionary work. Then gloss the passage together.

### *After reading*

- Discuss what the probe will make of Butch. Will it, for example, understand that it has picked up a different life form this time? Or will it deduce a sudden mutation in the human form?
- Discuss which got closer to the truth and why: Gran's tales and the old legends, or Hubble and NASA.

## Activity 2 [T]

### *Drawing information from the text to create a fact file*

#### Learning objectives
- to scan for and extract relevant information
- to practise using inference and deduction

#### Introduction
- Activity sheet 1 gives adequate preparation for this activity; recap on the children's work. They will need activity sheet 1 to help them carry out the task.

#### Development
- Give out **activity sheet 2**. Explain what is meant by each of the headings. The final heading acknowledges that some important information is not given, leaving it open for speculation. Tell the children to list here any information which they think is important but is not given, for example who sent the probe, why they sent it, why they chose Earth, why it takes 112 years to orbit, where else the probe goes, how it sends back messages to its own planet, what happens to those messages.

- Copies of the story should be available for reference. Most of the information, however, can be found in the passages on activity sheet 1.

#### Review
- Here are the kind of responses you are looking for:
  - **The probe's mission:** to monitor the evolution of intelligent life on Earth over a long period of time.
  - **The purpose of the core:** to store the life samples and to house and protect the automatic control systems.
  - **The purpose of the outer layer:** to protect the core and to disguise the probe, making it look like a comet.
  - **The planet being studied:** Earth.
  - **The method of study:** to gather samples of intelligent life forms and to analyse them in the core.
  - **The purpose of scanning for samples:** to collect appropriate higher life forms and screen out lower ones or inanimate objects.
  - **The method of sample collection:** a beam of light which instantly transports (how, we are not told) the life form to the probe.

## Activity 3 [T]

### *Interviewing; story recall in pairs using prompts*

#### Learning objectives
- to recall the main elements of the story
- to practise interviewing
- to develop skills of inference, deduction and reasoning

#### Introduction
- Give out **activity sheet 3**, one between two. Working as a whole class, ask the children to come up with one sentence for each box to explain what part each item played in the story.

#### Development
- Explain the activity to the children. One of the pair selects a box and asks the other child questions about its subject, using question words like 'who', 'when', 'what', 'where', 'why' and 'how', and phrases like, 'Do you think...?', 'What is your view of...?' and 'If I said that...?'

- After several questions and answers, the second child takes over the role of questioner. The children should alternate roles as they proceed from box to box.
- Make the book available for those who need to check their answers.
- If you want the children to develop writing through this activity, they can record some of their answers on a separate piece of paper.

#### Review
- Check through the items with the class.

#### Further idea for writing
- Steve contacts the local paper and is interviewed about what he and Billy saw. The children should write the newspaper article that appeared. Apart from marshalling the key events and background information, the children will need to decide at the outset the reporter's slant (serious or tongue-in-cheek?) and what attitude Billy takes when interviewed.

Name _____     Date _____

To understand what happens in the story, you need to know
what these two descriptions are about. Underline all the words
you are not sure about, list them in the right-hand column,
then look them up in the dictionary.
Tick the ones you then understand.

**Words to be looked up**

The inner core of the massive probe machine is a
hollow metallic sphere about one hundred metres
across, densely packed with sophisticated
automatic control systems. An outer layer of
compacted ice about ten kilometres thick
surrounds the core to shield it from collision with
meteorites and other space debris.

　The machine's continuous mission is to monitor
the evolution of intelligent life within one sector of
the galaxy. It is currently studying the progress of
life on one of the inner planets of an otherwise
insignificant solar system situated near the edge of
the sector. To achieve this, the machine has placed
itself in an orbit around the solar system's sun,
which takes it close to the subject planet at regular
intervals. During each orbit, the machine must
collect for analysis a variety of life forms from a
variety of locations on the surface of the planet.

(page 7)

As it approaches the subject planet, the machine
activates its sensor system and begins to scan the
various sample collection zones on the planet's
surface. Scanning will continue until the precise
moment of sample collection. This must occur at
the exact moment when the machine and the
planet are in closest proximity.

(page 14)

# Heroes and Villains: The Visitor  Activity sheet 2

Name _____   Date _____

In the box, draw a cut-away diagram of the probe and put in the measurements.

What information is given about the following? And what other information can you deduce?

| the probe's mission | the purpose of the core |
|---|---|
| the purpose of the outer layer | the planet being studied and the method of study |
| the purpose of scanning for samples | the method of sample collection |
| information not given (e.g. where the probe comes from) ||

© Cambridge University Press 1999

Name _____   Date _____

*In pairs, take turns asking each other questions about the events in the story.*
*Frame several questions around each of these items.*

| | | |
|---|---|---|
| the probe/Hawes' Comet | High Tor | Billy's gran |
| Doc Beasley | Butch | Steve's personal radio |
| NASA Web site | Hubble space telescope | brilliant blue probe light |
| wooden cigar box and elastic band | the legend of High Tor | Billy and Steve's joint school report |

# Whitney Snow

**Author**  *Richard Brown*
**Short narrative**  *A comic fantasy*

## Synopsis

The story takes as its starting-point the traditional story of Snow White and puts it in a modern setting, with a computer standing in for the mirror, high-rise blocks instead of palaces, and the independent young businesswomen Goldie and Red visiting from other traditional tales!

## Discussion points

### Before reading

- Explain that this story gives a modern setting to the tale of Snow White. Briefly, get the children to retell the traditional story in a story-telling circle and ask them to keep it in mind as they read/hear the new story.

- If you want to share the reading of the story, appoint two confident readers to take the parts of Whitney and Queenie; there are smaller parts for Dr Wright, the computer, Red and Goldie.

### After reading

- Discuss the intertextual element of the story (i.e. how the traditional story was used to develop a new one). What is borrowed? What has changed? What is completely new?

- Explore some ideas about the use of stereotypical characters. Brainstorm words to describe the traditional Snow White character, and then do the same for Whitney Snow. What are their similarities and differences? Which is the stereotype and which is original? Does Whitney have any stereotypical features? Do the same for a traditional queen and then for Queenie. Is Queenie a stereotype of the wicked stepmother? What about the Henchmen? Are they stereotypes or do they have some original features?

---

## Activity 1

*Using a writing framework to examine characters' actions and their consequences*

### Learning objectives
- to examine and make moral judgements about characters' actions
- to practise writing persuasively, drawing upon textual evidence

### Introduction

- Explain that the focus of this activity is to think about characters' decision-making. Decision precedes action: it may be instant or long deliberated; it may be a trivial decision (such as talking to the computer) or an important one (deciding to drive Whitney mad) – the importance often lies in the consequences of the decision rather than in the original intention. Ask the children to think of a trivial decision they have made recently and a more important one, and to share these. Did any seemingly trivial decision turn out to be important because of its consequences?

### Development

- Give out **activity sheet 1**. It is an open-ended writing framework.
- Model the activity for the children. Read out some of the questions on the sheet and then decide with the children which character is going to be put under the spotlight and which decision is going to be examined. Then work your way through the questions with the children, recording the most persuasive answers on your copy or on an OHP.
- The children should now choose another decision for the same character or a new character and fill in their framework in the same way.
- The work should be based on recall in the first instance, but make copies of the book available for reference.

### Review

- The framework and the children's answers could be used as the basis for hot-seating a character.

# Activity 2 T

### Looking at the use of metaphor and cliché

## Introduction

- Explain that you are going to look at a particular feature of the language used to tell this story, one which heightens the drama and gives textual colour and comedy to the telling; namely the use of common metaphors and clichés.
- Make sure the children know that a **metaphor** is a comparison which doesn't use 'like' or 'as', and that a **cliché** is a phrase which is used so often as to lose all freshness and vitality.

- Read out the first example of a clichéed metaphor in the story, from the first paragraph: 'That girl was getting above her station.' Ask the children what they think it means and then explain what 'station' means in this context. Give another example from later in the story: 'Her hands clawed the air' (p. 59). What does this metaphor tell us about Queenie's state of mind at this point?

## Development

- Give out **activity sheet 2**. It lists further examples of metaphors and clichés taken from the story. The children have to give their own translations of their meaning in the right-hand column.

## Review

- Compare the children's responses. Compile a class list from the best suggestions.

# Activity 3 T

### Vocabulary extension; dictionary work

## Introduction

- Ask the children what strategies they use when they come across a word in their reading which they have not met before or are unsure about. Brainstorm a list of such strategies and then, with the children's help, number them in order of best practice.
- Point out that the author of 'Whitney Snow' likes to make use of a wide vocabulary. For example, within the first couple of pages, he uses words like 'luxurious', 'wretched', 'grimaced', 'cackle', 'raving', 'cowering', 'pursued', 'resident'. The children's task is to try and write definitions of such words.

## Development

- Give out **activity sheet 3** and ask the children to read through the sentences. Make sure they know how to pronounce the key words.
- Make sure the dictionaries the children are going to use are comprehensive enough to contain all the words, and check that the children know how to use them efficiently.
- Model a response for the first example if you think the children need it.

## Review

- Check the results. Discuss the children's definitions, highlighting or recording on the board or flipchart those you think get nearest to the precise meaning in the context.

# Heroes and Villains: Whitney Snow    Activity sheet 1

Name _____    Date _____

Choose a character from the story and a scene in which that
character makes a decision. Then answer these questions

Character: _____

in the scene in which _____

1.  What decision did the character make?

2.  Why did the character make that decision?

3.  Do you think it was the right decision for the character in the circumstances?

4.  Are there any other decisions the character could have made at that point
    which would have been just as good or better?

5.  What were the immediate consequences of the decision?

6.  What long-term consequences can be traced back to this decision?

7.  Did the character's original intentions match the outcome?

# Heroes and Villains: Whitney Snow    Activity sheet 2

Name _____    Date _____

In the right-hand column,
write what you think these
metaphors and clichés mean.

| metaphor or cliché (in italics) | what you think it means |
|---|---|
| 1. Queenie *fixed him with burning, black eyes.* <br>(page 43) | |
| 2. Dr Wright felt his sturdy knees *turn to jelly.* <br>(page 44) | |
| 3. . . . Queenie *glowed with satisfaction.* <br>(page 48) | |
| 4. . . . even the toughest Henchman was *reduced to rubble . . .* <br>(page 49) | |
| 5. . . . Dr Wright . . . , *throwing caution to the wind,* flew over to White Tower in a taxi. <br>(page 55) | |
| 6. They . . . *racked their brains.* <br>(page 56) | |
| 7. Her pulse was beating, *her head was whirling.* <br>(page 57) | |
| 8. Queenie would dearly have loved *to scratch out those eyes . . .* <br>(page 61) | |

Name _____    Date _____

Complete the middle and right-hand columns.

| unusual word in the story | what you think it means | the dictionary definition |
| --- | --- | --- |
| 1. Queenie *grimaced*. (page 41) | | |
| 2. Dr Wright . . . had been dazzled – no, *stupefied* – by her beauty. (page 43) | | |
| 3. But his excitement *evaporated* when he saw his patient. (page 43) | | |
| 4. Queenie . . . flapping her arms like a *demented* bat. (page 44) | | |
| 5. Dr Wright spent the night *concocting* an antidote. (page 45) | | |
| 6. Dr Wright could only stammer some *inanity*. (page 45) | | |
| 7. Whitney wandered the streets for a while, full of *exhilaration*. (page 46) | | |
| 8. The grateful and *bedazzled* Dwarf took her straight to his home . . . (page 47) | | |
| 9. When the Dwarfs understood her *plight*, they gave her the top flat . . . (page 47) | | |

If you have access to the book, collect other words from the story
and see if you can work out their meaning in the same way.

# In the Court of the Jade Emperor

**Retold by** *Rosalind Kerven* (see author profile on p. 147)

**Illustrator** *Bryna Waldman*

**Short narrative** *A collection of traditional Chinese stories*

## Description

The author has retold 15 traditional Chinese tales including myths, legends and folk tales. The stories are all self-contained, although some – like the four Monkey stories which begin the collection – use a recurring character. The stories are short enough to be read and discussed, and for follow-up work to be well underway, in one session.

## Before reading

- The notes at the end of the collection (pp. 85–91) contain background information about the nature and origin of these stories. It is worth reading these and extracting points which you think will help the children to put the stories in a historical and geographical context, and which will explain some of the religious and philosophical ideas they contain. You will almost certainly want to return to the notes as you share the stories with the children, so initially you need to extract only a few key points from each section.

- Ask the children to find China on a globe and in atlases, and to locate Beijing, Hong Kong and the Gobi Desert.
- You might like to use pictures and books to help share ideas and knowledge about ancient and modern China. However, this is not a project on China; you should simply be aiming to give an impression of Chinese culture, ancient and modern.
- As the stories are rooted in the Buddhist tradition, it would be a good idea to use them alongside a study of Buddhism.

## A choice of literacy activities

| Activity | Focus | Page |
|---|---|---|
| 1. | Retelling the story; chanting a verse; compiling a list of Monkey's transformations. ('In which Monkey proves that nothing is impossible') | 60 |
| 2. | Sequencing; retelling; thought-tracking. ('In which Monkey gets too big for his boots') | 61 |
| 3. | Recall; retelling. ('In which Monkey takes a giant leap to nowhere') | 62 |
| 4. | Identifying within the story recurring elements of traditional tales. ('Darkness') | 62 |
| 5. | Retelling the story; describing the settings. ('The Golden Key') | 63 |
| 6. | Identifying colloquial language; quiz. ('The Man Who Did Dragons' Work') | 64 |
| 7. | Story telling in a circle; improvised drama. ('The Hot Pig and the Dragon Princess') | 65 |
| | Comprehension questions. ('In which Monkey tastes the Peaches of Immortality') | 67 |

# Part One: The Extraordinary Adventures of Monkey

These four stories tell of Monkey's assumption of supernatural powers, his growing sense of mischief and arrogance, how he angered the gods and defeated all their attempts to destroy him, and how the Buddha Himself finally tamed and converted him, turning him from an unstoppable, if likeable, tyrant into a god who introduced the holy scriptures of Buddhism to China.

---

## Activity 1

***Retelling the story; chanting a verse; compiling a list of Monkey's transformations***
***Story to use:*** '*In which Monkey proves that nothing is impossible*'

> ### Learning objectives
> - to explore the character of Monkey
> - to practise oral retelling in a group
> - to practise speaking and learning a verse
> - to use imagination to draw up a list

### Introduction

- Brainstorm with the children words and ideas to describe the character and nature of Monkey. He's a complex character, so break the story down into stages:
  - when Monkey was happy to be king of the monkeys;
  - when he became sad at thoughts of mortality;
  - when he travelled the world looking for Immortals;
  - when he worked humbly for Father Subodhi for seven years;
  - when the magic verse exerted its power on him and he assumed great powers;
  - when he feels himself to be invincible, at the end of the story.
- How does Monkey's view of himself change at each of these stages?

### Development

- Give out **activity sheet 1**, one between two. The main part of the sheet contains a brief summary of Monkey's journey to supernatural power. Pairs, small groups or the whole class can use this as a prompt for recall and oral retelling of the story.
- Let pairs or groups contribute part of a retelling to a whole-class story-telling session.
- Discuss with the children the meaning of the verse which Monkey is taught by Father Subodhi. Then ask them to chant it and learn it themselves.
- You might like to put a time limit on the listing of some of Monkey's transformations; ten minutes, for example. Insist that the suggested transformations are consistent with the world Monkey inhabits; thus, a dragon would be appropriate but not a car.

### Review

- From the children's suggestions, compile a long class list of transformations (72 of them, ideally!). This can then be displayed. Ask the children in what circumstances Monkey might wish to transform himself into some of the incarnations they have come up with.

### Extension

- Some children could make a collage of Monkey to display alongside the '72 transformations' list. Monkey could be surrounded by words from the brainstorming session. Other children may wish to write a Monkey story of their own about one of Monkey's 72 transformations.

# Activity 2 [T]

*Sequencing; retelling; thought-tracking*
*Story to use: 'In which Monkey gets too big for his boots'*

### Learning objectives
- to recall the sequence of the story
- to retell the story orally and in writing
- to infer characters' thoughts

### Introduction
- Discuss with the children what this story adds to their knowledge of Monkey.

  - Is Monkey still an attractive figure?
  - What does he do that the children admire?
  - What does he do that is thoughtless or arrogant?
  - What new powers has he got?
  - What danger might he be in?

### Development
- Give out **activity sheet 2**, one between two. The children have to cut up the sentence strips and sequence them correctly.
- Check the sequence with the whole class. It should be as follows:

  **o.**  An evil demon storms Monkey's palace and kidnaps the monkey children.

  **d.**  Monkey fights the demon who is wielding a powerful sword.

  **m.**  Monkey transforms hairs into tiny Monkeys.

  **f.**  He frees the monkey children and takes them back to his palace.

  **c.**  Neighbouring kings, wild beasts and even demons pay homage to him.

  **j.**  Monkey bores everyone with his boasting.

  **n.**  Monkey wants a powerful and magical weapon.

  **l.**  The Dragon King welcomes Monkey to his sea-kingdom.

  **a.**  Monkey is disappointed at all the weapons he is shown.

  **h.**  The Dragon Mother Queen offers him the Golden Clasped Wishing Staff.

  **e.**  He threatens the sea monarchs with the magical staff.

  **b.**  He is given magical shoes, a cap and a jerkin of exceptional quality.

  **k.**  In a rage at Monkey's rudeness, the Dragon King complains to the Jade Emperor in Heaven.

  **g.**  Monkey dreams that he is being judged by Yama, the grim King of Death.

  **i.**  The King of Death hands in a complaint about Monkey to the Jade Emperor.

- Ask each pair (or make up groups of three if you have more than 30 in the class) to practise retelling one strip of the story in a story-telling style, adding plenty of detail. Make sure somebody is working on every strip.
- As the children finish, ask them to turn over some of the strips and write on the back what they think Monkey or one of the other main characters is thinking at that point in the story.
- Bring the children together in one large story-telling circle and ask each pair (or group of three) in sequence to retell their bit of the story.
- Share the thought-tracking ideas written on the back of the strips.
- Each child should now write up their bit of the story in their own words.

### Review
- Join all the parts of the written story into a single retelling. Read it – or let the children read their section – aloud to the class.

### Extension
- Give some children the class story and the original, and ask them to compare the two versions. Were any bits left out? Was anything added?
- Other children could write the three spells which Monkey used to free the monkey children, bring them home and transform his palace.

# Activity 3 |C|T|

*Recall; retelling*
*Story to use: 'In which Monkey takes a giant leap to nowhere'*

## Learning objectives
- to recall parts of the story orally
- to retell in writing the climax of the four Monkey stories

## Introduction
- To do this activity the class needs to have read and discussed the information about Buddhism given at the end of the book (p. 87).
- The story falls into three parts:

  1. Monkey's battles with the forces of Heaven, in which he ultimately proves the stronger;
  2. the Buddha's challenge, which he fails;
  3. Monkey's transformation into a god.

  To help the children grasp this structure and recall what happened, ask some questions about each part of the story.
- Re-read the last part of the story, which begins, 'But don't shed any tears for him, reader.' (p. 29) Within the context of the four Monkey stories, and drawing on what the children have learnt about Buddhism, discuss briefly concepts such as repentance, rebirth, self-control, extraordinary powers, pilgrimage, holy priests, holy scriptures and wisdom – all of which appear in this short passage.

## Development
- Give out **activity sheet 3**, one between two. The children should work in pairs, recalling the part each item in the top half of the sheet played in the story and recording this information in writing. Once the children have finished, some can check their answers by referring to the book; others can go on to the second half of the sheet until a copy of the book becomes available.
- The short dialogue is a direct transcription of part of the conversation between the Buddha and Monkey. It should be read aloud by the children, working in their pairs.
- Each pair should discuss what they recall of the end of the second part of the story when the Buddha teaches Monkey a lesson, and the third part when Monkey becomes a god.
- The children should then work individually on their own written account.

## Review
- Share the children's responses to the first part of the activity.
- Talk with the children about their impressions of Monkey at the end of the four stories.
- Ask one or two children to read out their retellings of the end of the final story.

# Activity 4 |C|T|

*Identifying within the story recurring elements of traditional tales*
*Story to use: 'Darkness'*

## Learning objectives
- to analyse the story into elements common to many traditional tales
- to see how many of these elements apply to another traditional story
- to retell the story orally or in writing

## Introduction
- The first part of the story describes a world plunged into never-ending night. Brainstorm with the class what such a world would be like. What would be missing? How many things would be affected by the loss of light? With the children contributing as much as possible, write a free verse class poem about life in a land of darkness. You could begin each line with the word 'No'; for example:

  No light shone from the stars,
  No sunlight fell on the withering leaves,
  No reflection in the dark lakes...

## Development

- Give out **activity sheet 4**, one between two. Talk in general terms about recurring elements in traditional stories, using some of the items on the sheet as examples. Drawing upon the children's recent experience of traditional stories, ask for examples of some of the items on the sheet. For example, Snow White is a heroine, and in 'Rumpelstiltskin', sorting the pile of grain is a seemingly hopeless task.

- The children should work together in pairs, listing (on a separate sheet) what each of the items refers to in the story 'Darkness'.

- Advise the children that if they get stuck on one item, they can move on to others and come back to it. As a last resort, give the children a copy of the book to look up the reference.

- Pairs who finish quickly can be asked to compare their answers with another pair. They can then look at another story in the book or in another collection of traditional stories and search for further examples of the items on the sheet. (This is also a good activity for homework.)

- Check with the whole class that their answers are similar to the following:

  a calamity = darkness;
  a hero and heroine = Dajian and Shejian;
  a quest = to find the sun and the moon;
  arduous travels = the long journey over mountains and plains;

a wondrous and beautiful sight = the sun and moon bobbing on the lake;
villainous creatures or the enemy = the two dragons;
a special sign of help = pale smoke behind the boulder that covered the entrance to the cave;
a guide or helper = the old woman;
a punishment = the old woman's fifty-year imprisonment;
powerful objects that defeat evil = the magic golden axe and scissors;
an arduous or seemingly hopeless task = digging in the earth for days;
a transformation = the axe becomes a streak of lightning;
something inanimate comes alive = the scissors when hurled at the dragons;
something living turns into something inanimate = the pieces of dragon turn into stones and rocks;
food which gives supernatural strength = the dragons' eyes.

## Review

- All the pairs should now search for examples of these items in other traditional stories. Set the pairs targets according to their abilities – for example, lower ability should find and report back on three examples, middle ability on six, and top ability on eight examples.

---

# Activity 5

*Retelling the story; describing the settings*
*Story to use:* 'The Golden Key'

### Learning objectives
- to retell the story prompted by a pictorial map of its setting
- to describe in writing the story's settings

### Introduction
- Ask the children what the main theme of the story is. Is it greed, drought, bravery or friendship? (The children may come up with some other suggestions.) Brainstorm ideas which support each theme and then take a vote on which the class thinks is the main theme and which are the subsidiary ones.

### Development
- Talk about where the story is set. Ask the children to imagine one scene from the story and get some of them to describe it to the class.
- Give out **activity sheet 5**, one between two. It is a pictorial map which represents all the settings in the story. Ask the children to check that all the places featured in the story are represented on the map.
- In pairs, the children should recall the story, saying what happened at each of the numbered places.
- If you want the children to rewrite the story in their own words, they can do so at this point, using the map as a guide.
- Alternatively, you can do as the instructions suggest and ask each child to write a description of each of the six numbered places. This will give

them practice in writing descriptively and evocatively. It may help the quality of the writing if the class begins by brainstorming a list of words appropriate to each place, focusing separately on nouns, verbs, adjectives and adverbs.

## Review

- Compare the children's descriptions.

---

## Activity 6 |C|T|

*Identifying colloquial language; quiz*
*Story to use: 'The Man Who Did Dragons' Work'*

### Learning objectives

- to look at colloquial English in a first-person account
- to scan a text for evidence
- to give opinions

### Introduction

- This is an example of a Creation story. Ask the children how this story explains the origin of weather.
- Ask the children if they noticed whether the way this story is told (the style of the language) is in any way different from the other stories in the book. They may not be able to give a clear explanation, but their answers should allow you to point out two features of the retelling: it is in the first person and it is told in an informal, conversational style. Colloquial phrases are used to convey a sense of immediacy. Usually, the convention is that formal language is used in the narrative (the author's voice, in effect) and colloquial language in the dialogue (the voices of the characters). In a first-person account these distinctions can get blurred – as in this example.
- Give out **activity sheet 6**, one between two. Ask the children if they can find six colloquial phrases in the extract. These are: 'There's this friend of mine'/'Li Jing his name is'/'he couldn't for the life of him'/'his horse could hardly keep on its legs'/'he went blundering about'/'this really amazing house'. Can the children say why the phrases are colloquial and what they mean?

### Development

- Ask the children to write a more formal version of each of the phrases.
- Ask an able group to look through the rest of the story to find further examples of colloquial language.

- The rest of the class can get on with the 'True'/'False'/'Maybe' quiz, which is based largely on recall. Explain that sometimes there is no evidence for an answer and that, therefore, two or even three answers are possible. For example, question 2 could be 'False' or 'Maybe' because there is no evidence that the pearls are dangerous. However, they are given by a grateful dragon so the likelihood is that the pearls are good.

### Review

- The group looking for colloquial phrases should report back on their findings. They should read their examples in the context of the whole sentence so that the rest of the class can discuss formal versions.
- Possible answers to the quiz are as follows:
  1. False. He was lost in the forest.
  2. False/Maybe. No evidence. Given by a grateful dragon so we can expect them to be good.
  3. True/Maybe. Dragon carvings in house/seems to be half-dragon/sons seem to be dragons.
  4. True/Maybe. The story says 'That's how the weather happens.'
  5. True/False/Maybe. No evidence that he was a particularly good man. But perhaps the Jade Emperor had chosen him for some reason.
  6. False. Li Jing showed him the pearls.
  7. True. The title of the story and the message from the Jade Emperor reveal this.
  8. Maybe. No evidence for this but it is but quite probable since he rules the universe.

# Activity 7 ☐ T

*Story telling in a circle; improvised drama*
*Story to use: 'The Hot Pig and the Dragon Princess'*

## Learning objectives
- to recall the story and develop story-telling skills
- to work collaboratively in small groups to dramatise a scene from the story

## Introduction
- In a large space such as the school hall, arrange the class into a story-telling circle and get them to retell the story so that the children are all familiar with what happens.
- Explain that you want them to to adapt the story into an improvised dramatisation, with small groups contributing short scenes in sequence. Groups can work as follows:

  - **Group 1** (4 members): Narrator, Baldhead, pig and traveller (p. 61 to line 25).
  - **Group 2** (4 members): a new Baldhead, Dragon King, pig and someone to do wave effects (p. 61, line 26, to p. 62, line 16).
  - **Group 3** (4 or more members): Baldhead, Dragon King (showing off his imaginary palace), servants (p. 62, lines 17 to 33).
  - **Group 4** (2 members): Baldhead and Princess (mysteriously appearing from the vase) (p. 62, line 34, to p. 63, line 21).
  - **Group 5** (2 or more members): Baldhead, Princess, a priest to marry them? Show their happy married life and imagine their amazing mansion (p. 63, line 22, to p. 64, line 8).

  - **Group 6** (2 or more members): Zhang and servant(s) who invent absurd and malicious stories about the Princess (p. 64, lines 9 to 21).
  - **Group 7** (3 or 4 members): Zhang, Baldhead, Princess (and servant) (p. 64, lines 22 to 31).
  - **Group 8** (4 members): Princess (who becomes Dragon), Baldhead, Zhang, servant to plant trees (p. 64, line 32, to p. 65, line 12).
  - **Group 9** (4 members): Princess, Dragon King to give pot, Baldhead, Zhang (p. 65, lines 13 to 34).
  - **Group 10** (4 members): Princess, Baldhead, Zhang and the weird voice in the pot (p. 65, line 35, to end).

The narrator from Group 1 can close the play with the last two lines of the story.

## Review
- Each group should perform what they have rehearsed. Encourage the rest of the class to comment positively and constructively with prompts such as: 'What did you like about it?', 'What did you think worked well?', 'It might be improved if...'
- Perform the whole play with the groups working in sequence.

## Extension
- Groups could write a play script based on their improvisation. These could be assembled into a class script which could be read in group reading sessions or performed on tape.

# Comprehension questions
The comprehension questions are on the third of the Monkey stories, 'In which Monkey tastes the Peaches of Immortality'. For suggestions on how to use them, see page 17.

## For stories without suggested activities

- Ask each child to write a question about the story to ask the rest of the class. It can be a question which requires a factual answer or one which requires an opinion in response.
- Hold a question-and-answer session.
- Devise activities for the stories yourself, drawing on the bank of ideas in part 3 of this book.

### 'Woman-of-the-Moon, Man-of-the-Sun' (pp. 33–36)

This myth explains the origin of *yin* and *yang*, the 'female' and 'male' aspects of the universe. The equilibrium that must be maintained between *yin* and *yang* is an essential part of Tao philosophy (see p. 86 of the notes).

### 'The Farmer and the Goddess' (pp. 37–40)

This is a friendly little story about a poor farmer who needs a wife. His humble ox turns out to be a god in disguise and he tells the farmer how he can marry a beautiful goddess.

### 'The Palace of Boundless Cold' (pp. 45–48)

This is a cautionary tale about a boy who is punished for his greed and cruelty by being condemned to labour for ever at an impossible task in an icy palace on the moon.

### 'The Girl Who Went Her Own Way' (pp. 69–72)

This is a serious story about Buddhist beliefs. A virtuous princess outrages her parents by becoming a nun and her father has her murdered for her defiance. The king of Hell can't cope with her virtue and sends her off to Buddha in Heaven, where she becomes the Goddess of Mercy.

### 'Cakes and Kitchens' (pp. 73–75)

A poor, starving stonemason is forced to give up his wife to a richer man. Later, when she smuggles some gold out to him, it is stolen from him. However, after his death, the Jade Emperor makes him the Kitchen God so that he need never feel the pangs of hunger again.

### 'Storm Girl' (pp. 77–79)

A little girl is born with strange powers. Her spirit leaves her body to rescue her brothers from a shipwreck. When she dies she becomes the Empress of Heaven.

### 'The Boys Who Lost Their Time' (pp. 81–84)

This is a mysterious story about two boys who jump into the future. They find that everything in their village has changed and nobody recognises them.

**1**

What did the Jade Emperor want of Monkey on his first visit?

**2**

How did the Jade Emperor react when Monkey issued a proclamation saying he was equal to Heaven?

**3**

What was the second job given to Monkey in Heaven?

**4**

How did Monkey become 'an absolute super-being'?

**5**

What did Monkey do at the Peach Banquet?

**6**

Who was Laozi and why should Monkey fear him?

**7**

What did Monkey drink in Laozi's laboratory and why?

# In the Court of the Jade Emperor: In which Monkey proves that nothing is impossible    Activity sheet 1

Name _____    Date _____

Retell the story using this flow chart as a prompt.

Monkey is made King Monkey and he is very popular and happy.

He becomes sad at the thought that he will grow old and die.

He sets off on a quest to find the Immortals.

Father Subodhi reveals the path to supernatural power and Monkey becomes more like a god.

He discovers from a woodcutter where an Immortal may be found.

He spends seven years with Father Subodhi.

Say the verse together.
Try to learn it.

All magic grows within you: deep.
Spirit, breath and soul are all your own.
Coil them like a spring, then keep
them tightly. They will yield the strongest powers known.

What do you think Monkey might change himself into?
Make a list of some of Monkey's 72 transformations.

# In the Court of the Jade Emperor: In which Monkey gets too big for his boots    Activity sheet 2

Cut out these sentences and put them in the right order.

✂ - - - - - - - - - - - - - - - - - - - - - - - - - - - - - - - - - - - - - - - - - - - - - - - -

**a.**   Monkey is disappointed at all the weapons he is shown.

**b.**   He is given magical shoes, a cap and a jerkin of exceptional quality.

**c.**   Neighbouring kings, wild beasts and even demons pay homage to him.

**d.**   Monkey fights the demon who is wielding a powerful sword.

**e.**   He threatens the sea monarchs with the magical staff.

**f.**   He frees the monkey children and takes them back to his palace.

**g.**   Monkey dreams that he is being judged by Yama, the grim King of Death.

**h.**   The Dragon Mother Queen offers him the Golden Clasped Wishing Staff.

**i.**   The King of Death hands in a complaint about Monkey to the Jade Emperor.

**j.**   Monkey bores everyone with his boasting.

**k.**   In a rage at Monkey's rudeness, the Dragon King complains to the Jade Emperor in Heaven.

**l.**   The Dragon King welcomes Monkey to his sea-kingdom.

**m.**  Monkey transforms hairs into tiny Monkeys.

**n.**   Monkey wants a powerful and magical weapon.

**o.**   An evil demon storms Monkey's palace and kidnaps the monkey children.

# In the Court of the Jade Emperor: In which Monkey takes a giant leap to nowhere     Activity sheet 3

Name _____          Date _____

What part did each of these things play in the first part of the story (pages 25–26)?

the Wishing Staff

transformations

the Diamond Snare

the executioner's block

cosmic fire

a thousand million thunderbolts

the Crucible of the Eight Trigrams

the forty-ninth day

Read this conversation between Monkey and Buddha.

**BUDDHA** (*shaking his head*): Monkey, do you really think you are clever enough to rule over Heaven? After all, the Jade Emperor has been perfecting himself and gathering wisdom for over two hundred million years.

**MONKEY** (*guffawing*): What a slow-coach! Goodness me, I'm already much cleverer than him, and I've only been around for a fraction of the time.

**BUDDHA:** Is that so, Monkey? Well then, let me challenge you to a wager. All I want you to do is this: jump across the palm of my right hand. If you succeed, the Jade Emperor's throne shall indeed be yours. But if you fail – oh, then Monkey, you must agree to a long and lonely punishment.

**MONKEY:** Great. I accept, Buddha old chap. Ohoh, this is too easy! But just a minute – are you quite sure that you're really in a position to give me what you've promised?

**BUDDHA** (smiling): Absolutely certain.

Now write in your own words what happened next – how Monkey was tricked and punished and how, at the end, he became a god.

Name _____ Date _____

*Find an example of each of these things in the story.*

| | | |
|---|---|---|
| a calamity | a hero and heroine | a quest |
| arduous travels | a wondrous and beautiful sight | villainous creatures or the enemy |
| a special sign of help | a guide or helper | a punishment |
| powerful objects that defeat evil | an arduous or seemingly hopeless task | a transformation |
| something inanimate comes alive | something living turns into something inanimate | food which gives supernatural strength |

# In the Court of the Jade Emperor: The Golden Key    Activity sheet 5

Name _____

Date _____

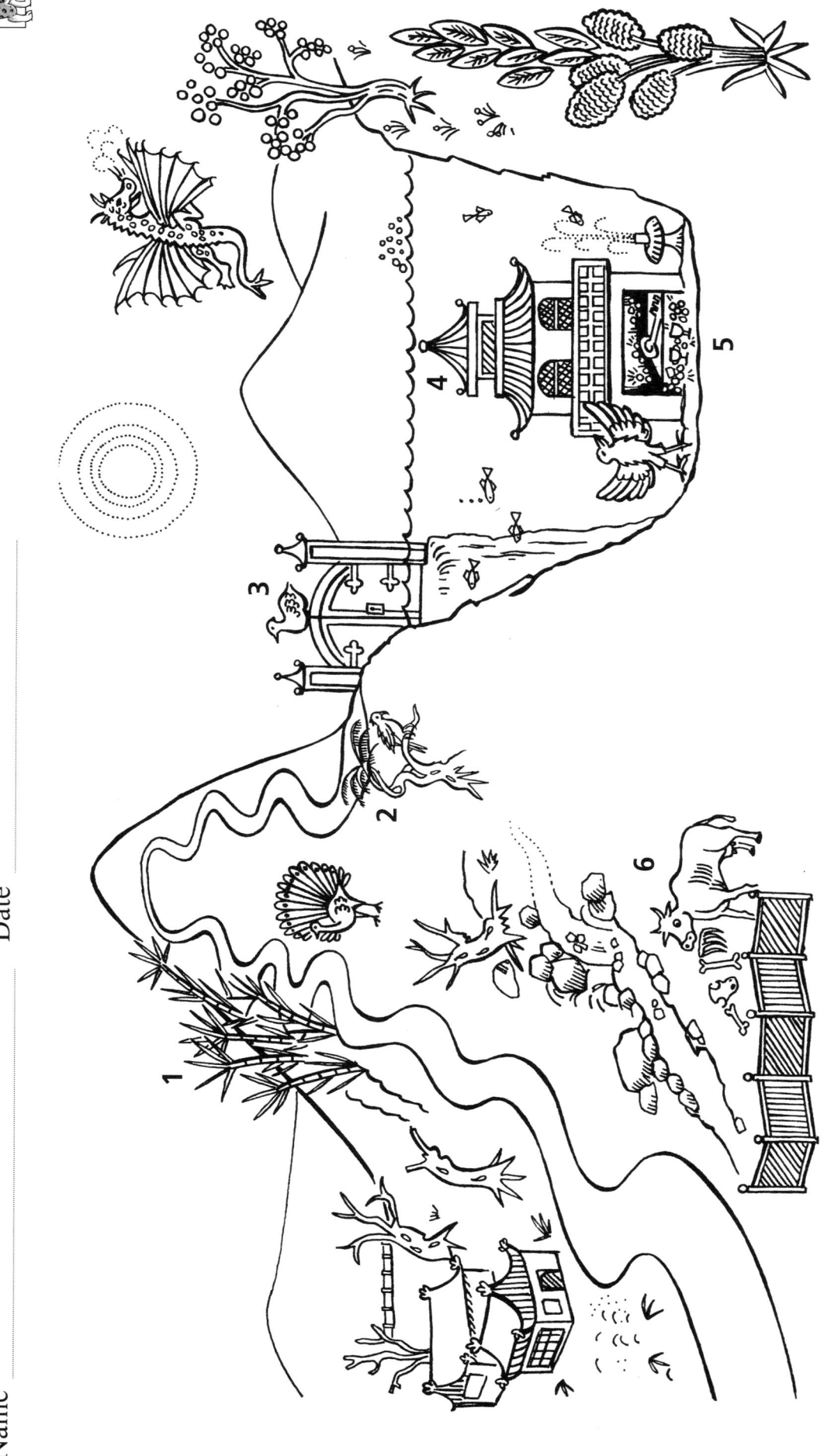

The story's settings. Use the map to help you retell the story, perhaps to someone who hasn't heard it or read it before. Then write a descriptive sentence or short paragraph about each of the numbered places on the map.

Name _____    Date _____

Underline the phrases in this passage which you think are **colloquial**; that
is, the kind of phrase you think would be used in everyday conversation.

There's this friend of mine – Li Jing his name is – and one day he was out hunting deer in the forest when he got separated from the rest of the party and realised he was completely lost.

It was turning dark, and he couldn't for the life of him remember the way home.

He was tired out and starving, and his horse could hardly keep on its legs. Anyway, he went blundering about among the trees and was just short of panicking when he suddenly came to a big clearing with a river running through it; and on the bank he saw this really amazing house.

Fill in the boxes with your opinions.

|  | True/False/Maybe? | What makes you think that? |
|---|---|---|
| 1.  Li Jing came to the palace on purpose. |  |  |
| 2.  The pearls were dangerous and would bring him bad luck. |  |  |
| 3.  The old lady was a dragon in disguise. |  |  |
| 4.  The Chinese believe rain is caused by a rider sprinkling the clouds. |  |  |
| 5.  Li Jing was a very good man and deserved what happened to him. |  |  |
| 6.  The person telling the story had never met Li Jing. |  |  |
| 7.  The brothers were really dragons. |  |  |
| 8.  The Jade Emperor had planned it all so that Li Jing would ride the horse. |  |  |

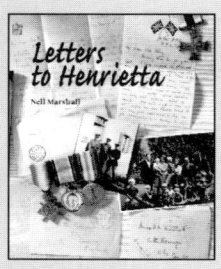

# Letters to Henrietta

**Author**   *Nell Marshall* (see author profile on p. 148)

**Illustrated**   *with early twentieth-century photographs and illustrations, and with artwork by Sam Thompson*

**Picture/Cartoon**   *An illustrated history of one family's experience of the First World War*

## Synopsis

This book is based closely on letters and other family records belonging to the author's family. With the help of these records, Nell Marshall has re-created the childhood of Henrietta Marshall and her brothers and sister in a country vicarage at the end of the nineteenth century. The story moves on to cover their young adulthood working in various parts of the British Empire, and their experiences in the First World War. Throughout the book, the family's particular experiences are related to the wider historical context, and the book is extensively illustrated with contemporary material.

## Before reading

- Make sure the children are aware that the stories in this book are true and that the letters which appear really were written at the time by members of the Marshall family. The book needs to be set in its period context, so have books on the late Victorian period and the First World War available for the children to read and refer to. Spending some time at the outset exploring the history and the social conditions of the period will enrich the children's understanding and enjoyment of the book.

## A choice of literacy activities

| Activity | Focus | Page |
|---|---|---|
| 1. | Writing a letter in the character of Henrietta or one of her brothers. | 75 |
| 2. | Collecting and scribing family stories. | 75 |
| 3. | Listing the advantages and disadvantages of various types of schooling. | 76 |
| 4. | Writing a description of life in the trenches. | 77 |
| 5. | Comparing definitions from various dictionaries; writing definitions. | 77 |
|  | Comprehension questions. | 78 |

# Activity 1

*Writing a letter in the character of Henrietta or one of her brothers*
*'How can we know about our families in the past?'*
*to 'Activities and adventures'*

### Learning objectives
- to scan for relevant information
- to use inference and empathy
- to write a letter creatively and in character

### Introduction
- Ask the children to imagine that they are Henrietta, Jack, Henry or another member of the Marshall family, and that they are writing a letter to a newly acquired pen-pal in another part of the country. Remind the children how long journeys took in those days and that the only way to communicate with a friend in another county would be by letter.
- Give out **activity sheet 1** and read it with the children. Ask the children to say what the new pen-pal wants to know, and where in the book they might find that information. Some of the information is given; some may need to be inferred. For example, to answer the question: 'What do you like to do?' the children will have to use their imagination to empathise with Henrietta and her brothers. The children will have to make some decisions – do the servants count as people in the family? As well as answering Alex's questions,

the children may want to respond to other information which he gives in his letter. How does the Marshall family's life differ from that of the Pollocks?

### Development
- Encourage the children to scan the book for information they can use in their letters. They could work collaboratively in groups of up to four, sharing a book.
- Help the children plan their letters. Do they know the conventions of letter writing? What will their opening and closing paragraphs say? What questions will they ask their new pen-pal? The children might find it helpful to base the structure of their letters on Alex's letter.
- More able children should be able to imagine how their chosen character might react to Alex's letter. How might Henrietta's reaction differ from Jack's, for example? Can the children convey this reaction in their replies?

### Review
- Display the finished letters. Which ones do the children think are most like something the Marshall children might have written? Why?

### Extension
- This activity could be linked with novels that are written in letter form, for example Jacqueline Wilson's *Cliffhanger*. Some children might like to write an extended piece of work in letter form.

# Activity 2 [ T ]

*Collecting and scribing family stories*
*'How can we know about our families in the past' to 'Activities and adventures'*

### Learning objectives
- to draft pertinent questions for an interview
- to select relevant and appropriate material
- to identify elements of spoken and written language and transform one into the other

### First session
### Introduction
- Re-read the stories about the boys skating off across the fens (p. 15) and about their long journey

to school in Wales (p. 16). Ask the children if they have ever done anything which is memorable for being funny, scary or adventurous, or for which they were praised or got into trouble! It might help to give a couple of examples from your own childhood.

### Development
- Ask the children to share some of their stories with the class. If possible, make a recording of some of the children's stories.
- Now ask the children to write their stories down, first in rough and then in a polished form.
- Compare the first, spoken version of the story with the final written version. What differences do the children notice?

### Second session

- Ask the children to work in small groups of three or four. They should draw up a list of questions they would need to ask in order to elicit a family story from someone else. They should consider how to open the interview, for example: 'Can you remember an event in your life which was funny, exciting or frightening?'
  They might continue with:

  – How old were you?
  – Who else was involved?
  – Where did the story take place?
  – What did you feel while this was happening?
  – What happened afterwards?
  – How did other people react?
  – Why do you think you remember this story?

- For homework, the children should use these questions to help them elicit and summarise a story from a family member, friend or acquaintance.
- Talk to the children about how best to prepare for the story telling – for example, describing the story-telling at school and retelling one of the stories from the first session; getting the setting right; making sure the story teller feels comfortable when telling the story.
- Talk about how to record the story so that it can be easily remembered. The options are to jot down the main events of the story, to retell it to oneself or to record it on audio or video tape.

### Third session

- The children should write up their stories as well-shaped narratives.
- Any children who did not manage to elicit a story from home could listen to a classmate's story on tape and use that as the basis for their written work.

### Fourth session
### Review

- Share the spoken and written stories in a story-telling session with each child introducing their own contribution.

---

## Activity 3  |C|T|

*Listing the advantages and disadvantages of various types of schooling*
*'School – at home and away'*

---

**Learning objectives**
- to scan for information
- to use skills of empathy and imagination
- to write persuasively

### Introduction

- Ask the children to scan the text to see how many kinds of schooling are referred to (being taught at home; the boys' prep and public schools – both boarding schools; the village school; Henrietta's boarding school in Winchester).

### Development

- With the children's help, divide this list into three types of schooling: boarding schools which you leave at eighteen; day schools which you leave at fourteen; learning at home.
- Now ask the children to say what they think are the advantages and disadvantages of each type of education. They should scan the text for evidence to support their arguments, but they may need to use a little inference and empathy and their own imaginations. For example, is it fun to be at boarding school because you're with lots of people your own age, or is it horrible because you miss your family?
- When the lists are complete, ask the children to pick one form of education and write a paragraph arguing for or against it. (Alternatively, you may wish to divide the class into six groups and allocate the tasks.) Remind the children that they can use the pros and cons from lists referring to other types of education – for example, if going away from home is a disadvantage for boarding schools, the fact that you don't have to go away from home is an advantage for the village school.

### Review

- Share and discuss the various responses.

### Extension

- The children's written work could be used to inform a class debate. Propose the following motion: 'This class believes that every child should attend boarding school.'

## Activity 4 |C|T|

### Writing a description of life in the trenches
### 'Jack's War', 'Evelyn's War', 'Henry's War'

**Learning objectives**
- to skim and scan for information
- to use skills of inference and empathy
- to extend vocabulary
- to write imaginatively

### Introduction

- Ask the children, in groups, to find and skim the relevant sections in the book, and to draw on other sources if appropriate, to build up an initial impression of life in the trenches. To get them going, you could read one or two of the letters from the sections on Jack, Evelyn or Henry.

### Development

- Remind the children of the five senses. Ask them to brainstorm in their groups what they could feel, see, smell, hear and taste if they were in the trenches. They should scan the relevant parts of the text for this information. They will need to use inference to decide, for example, what they can smell – gunpowder? smelly people who haven't been able to wash for weeks? Collect this information on the board.
- At this point, the children could use a thesaurus to gather alternative words for 'smell' ('stink', 'stench'), 'cold' ('freezing', 'chilly'), 'frightened' ('terrified') and so on.
- Now ask the children to write in the first person a short description of life in the trenches, based on the information gathered on the board and using the wider vocabulary they have found in the thesaurus. They might wish to begin:
'It is midnight. It has been quiet for over an hour now and I've been sitting here afraid to fall asleep...'

### Review

- Share and discuss the various responses.

## Activity 5 |C|T|

### Comparing definitions from different
### dictionaries; writing definitions
### Glossary

**Learning objectives**
- to practise using dictionaries
- to extend vocabulary

### Introduction

- Divide the children into groups. Each group should have access to a copy of the book and to a dictionary. Try to have several different dictionaries – for example, Oxford, Collins and Chambers.

### Development

- Give out **activity sheet 2**. Ask the children to find each word in the book and then look them up in the glossary, and in the dictionary.
- The groups should record the definitions given in the dictionary and the glossary and then think about the questions at the bottom of the worksheet before filling in the comments column.
- 'Home front' may not appear in some dictionaries. Point this out to the children and use it to demonstrate that all dictionaries are selective and may therefore not contain the word they are researching.

### Review

- Finally, compare all the definitions from all the groups, and ask why dictionaries differ from one another, which dictionary the children like best, and why. Together, write the 'best' definition for each word on the board, drawing on all the definitions.

### Extension

- Ask the children if there are any words in the book which do not appear in the glossary and which they think should (e.g. 'barbed wire', 'rivals'). Use the dictionaries and the context of the word in the book to write glossary entries for these new items.

## Comprehension questions

For suggestions on how to use these, see page 17.

**1**

Who was fighting whom in the
First World War?

**2**

Why do you think the declaration of
war was 'greeted enthusiastically'
by most people in Britain?

**3**

The British had not fought a major war
for 50 years. What were the main differences
between the way the war was fought in 1914
and the war 50 years earlier?

**4**

The Americans joined the war later.
How did they help to win the war
for the Allies?

**5**

What is a 'conscript'?

**6**

Why didn't Britain introduce
conscription until 1916?

**7**

What did Henrietta's seven brothers
do to help the war effort?

**8**

What did Henrietta do during the war?

# Letters to Henrietta       Activity sheet 1

Name _____       Date _____

Imagine you are one of the children in the Marshall family. You have
just received this letter from a boy who would like to be your pen-pal.
What will you say in your reply?

15 Melvin Street
Kelvingrove
Glasgow

28th November 1897

Dear Friend

I am so pleased you are going to correspond with me. I think it will be A1 to have a
friend in England!

I live in Glasgow and go to school at the Academy here. My two sisters don't go to
school and they think I am lucky. But I think I have to work very hard! Jean and
Mary only do lessons with mother but I have to learn mathematics and Latin and
Greek. It is prime playing rugger with the other boys though.

I am glad I can go to school in the city because I would miss mother and father
and my sisters if I had to go away to school. But I wouldn't tell Mary and Jean that!
How many people are there in your family? Do you go to school near your home?

My home is a tall thin house in a row of other houses. We only have a little
garden, not big enough to play football in. It is all full of mother's flowers so we have
to be careful. Is your garden big enough to play in?  What is your home like?

Mary and Jean like the shops but I would rather go to the docks and see the ships
coming in from all over the Empire. Sometimes I go there with my father, who works
in an office near the docks. I think his job is boring. I would rather sail the ships
myself! What does your father do?

Mostly after school I have to go home and do my lessons, but sometimes I go to
places with my friends or we play football in the park if we don't get caught by the
park keeper. I read a lot too. I hope you like reading. I can get a lot of books from the
masters at school and from the free library, so I'm lucky. Mary and Jean like reading
too and sometimes I play with them as well, but only if I can't see my school friends.
Mary and Jean play boring things like dolls' houses and board games, and do drawing
and needlework. Sometimes mother lets them play tennis at our friends' house. That's
only in the summer though. What do you like to do?

Well, I must stop now because I won't have anything to write in my next letter!
Write back soon. I want to hear all about your family and home and what you like
doing. I hope you are a boy. If you are a girl, I hope you don't mind what I said
about girls and write back anyhow.

Your affectionate pen-friend

Alex Pollock

Name _____    Date _____

Find each of these words in the book and then look it up in the glossary and in a dictionary. Record the definitions in the second and third columns. Then look at the questions at the bottom of the sheet. When you have thought about them in relation to each word, write in the 'Comments' section what you think about the different definitions.

The dictionary we used was _____

|  | **The glossary says** | **The dictionary says** | **Comments** |
|---|---|---|---|
| home front |  |  |  |
| reconnaissance |  |  |  |
| censor |  |  |  |
| sniper |  |  |  |
| missionary |  |  |  |
| volunteer |  |  |  |

- How does the dictionary definition differ from the definition given in the glossary?
- Why do you think it is different?
- Which is better? Is one definition good for one reason and the other for another reason?
- Does the dictionary definition make sense in the context of the book?

# Sandstorm

**Author**   *Judy Cumberbatch* (see author profile on p. 146)
**Illustrator**   *James Bartholomew*
**Extended narrative**   *A time-slip fantasy*

## Synopsis

The action takes place mainly in modern Egypt, in a village not far from Cairo. It centres on Rashida, who lives with her grandmother. Rashida's father is dead and her mother works in Cairo. While walking home from school with her best friend Iman, Rashida gets caught in a sandstorm. When the storm abates, she finds an ancient mirror buried in the sand at the foot of a tree. In it she sees a girl from the time of the pharaohs, Teti, who is in great distress because her father, Ani, has been arrested for stealing a mirror from the temple. He faces the death penalty. Rashida gets emotionally caught up in Teti's plight and feels that, because she alone sees in the mirror what is happening to Teti, only she can help the girl from the past to prove her father's innocence.

Parallels begin to emerge between the two girls' lives. Rashida's mother returns to the village with Sami, whom she is intending to marry. Rashida does not trust him. She has an ambivalent relationship with her teacher, Abla Selma, too – just as Teti has with her father's cousin, Opet. Sami is very interested in the mirror, which proves to be valuable. Rashida fears that Sami will steal it, take it back to Cairo, sell it and desert her mother. If that happens, she won't be able to help Teti and her father.

However, Rashida proves to be wrong about Sami, and about her teacher too. Teti's situation reaches a climax, in parallel with Rashida's own flight from Abla Selma, and both are rescued in the nick of time. The mirror proves to be a mysterious catalyst in the lives of both the girls.

## Background information

- The novel is set in modern Egypt with mysterious flashbacks to Ancient Egypt.
- **Modern Egypt:** the setting is an imaginary but typical village on the Nile. Agriculture is the main activity in the narrow area between the river bank and the desert. The great majority of country people are devout Muslims, the men (but not women) attending prayers in the mosque on Fridays. The country men generally wear traditional long cotton tunics (*gallabias*) but many of the women now wear long, western-style dresses. Schoolchildren wear western clothes.

- **Ancient Egypt:** the parallel story is set in the same area, but the period is the Middle Kingdom (2052–1786 BC), several centuries after the building of the Great Pyramids. There was huge expenditure on furnishing tombs to provide comforts for the dead in the Underworld. Robbery from tombs was a perennial problem, punishable by death. Literacy was confined to the religious élite; the scribe (Nakhte in this story) was a very powerful official.

## Introducing the book

### Before reading

- Have a brainstorming session on Ancient Egypt. List everything the children know on the subject. This will probably include mummies, pyramids and hieroglyphics. Make sure the children know

that the Ancient Egyptians believed that embalming the body enabled the soul to inhabit it again in the Underworld.
- Locate Egypt on a map. Identify the Nile, the Sahara Desert and Cairo.

- Carry out a brainstorm on deserts. The children are likely to come up with 'sand', 'Bedouin', 'oasis', 'camels', 'thirst'... Get the children to consider what happens when the wind blows over the sand.

### Library research (extension)

- Allocate to each child or to pairs of children one of the following topics: life in modern Egypt, Islam, mummification, the Nile, crocodiles, the Sahara, Ancient Egyptian art. The children have to come up with five interesting facts (stress 'interesting'!) about their topic to share with the rest of the class.
- Each child should find and copy an Ancient Egyptian picture or statue of an important man, and of a woman. They should pay particular attention to hairstyle and personal ornaments. (This is specially relevant to the early chapters.)

## A choice of literacy activities

| Activity | Focus | Page |
|---|---|---|
| 1. | Discussion to clarify what happens at the beginning of the story. | 82 |
| 2. | Thought-tracking the main character. | 83 |
| 3. | Illustrating a descriptive passage. | 83 |
| 4. | Writing a letter from a character in the story. | 83 |
| 5. | Identifying textual clues about school and Abla Selma, the teacher. | 84 |
| 6. | Exploring characters' points of view. | 85 |
| 7. | Setting out arguments for and against a course of action. | 85 |
| 8. | Group or class discussion. | 86 |
| 9. | Group or class discussion. | 86 |
| 10. | Writing the end of the story. | 86 |
| 11. | Discussion. | 87 |
| | Comprehension questions. | 88 |

# Activity 1 T

### Discussion to clarify what happens at the beginning of the story
### Chapter 1

#### Learning objectives
- to evaluate different interpretations of events
- to discuss the genre of the story

- The following questions may be discussed in pairs or groups first and then as a whole class:

  - What might have happened to Rashida once the sandstorm had died down and before Iman reappeared? (pp. 9–10)

  - Is there a suggestion here that, for a brief time, Rashida slipped back into the past?
  - What might have happened to Iman during the storm?
  - What kind of novel do you expect this to be? a historical novel? a thriller? a time-slip story? a fantasy which includes magic?
  - What clues do you base your answer on?

# Activity 2  |C|T|

*Thought-tracking the main character*
*Chapter 2*

## Learning objectives
- to develop understanding of the main character
- to empathise with her feelings and thoughts

## Introduction
- With the children's help, recall everything that has happened to Rashida in the first two chapters, in particular the sandstorm, Iman's temporary disappearance, seeing the strange old woman, finding the mirror, coming home after the storm, clearing up with Grandma, remembering her trip to Cairo to see her mum, and seeing the girl in the mirror. Ask what Rashida might have been thinking and feeling at each of these points. How did she try to make sense of what was happening to her?

## Development
- Give out **activity sheet 1**, one between two if you wish the children to discuss their responses in pairs before writing them down.
- Explain to the children that they can focus on feelings or thoughts or combine them in one response, depending on what they think is most appropriate.
- Talk about the possible styles of the reponses. They can be done as reported speech (e.g. 'I think she must have been feeling...') or as a direct reflection of Rashida's own thoughts (e.g. 'Oh, it's wonderful to be home again...').

## Review
- Let the children compare their responses in pairs and groups.
- Collect the most persuasive answers to build up a class account of Rashida's thoughts and feelings in chapter 2.

# Activity 3  | C |

*Illustrating a descriptive passage*
*Chapter 2*

## Learning objectives
- to extract relevant information accurately from a short text
- to transform written information into graphic information

- Ask the children to draw Rashida's house, using the first paragraph of chapter 2 (p. 12) as their reference.
- When they have finished, the children should compare their drawings and discuss any differences.

# Activity 4

*Writing a letter from a character in the story*
*Chapter 3*

## Learning objectives
- to develop an understanding of the relationship between two principal characters
- to write in a personal style, using the conventions of letter writing
- to fill in a narrative gap using inference and deduction

## Introduction
- In this chapter, Rashida receives some unexpected news in a stressful context and is upset by it. In discussion, explore with the children why Rashida is upset and why she rejects the idea of a step-father.

## Development
- Rashida might have been helped by her mother's letter, but she doesn't actually read it at this point. Ask the children, 'What might Rashida's mum's letter have said?' The aim is to get the children to

explain things from Mum's point of view – for example, putting the past behind her, starting a new life, how she met Sami, what he's like, her thoughts on how their marriage will benefit Rashida.

- Some children may find it helpful to have some suggestions for the opening of paragraphs in the letter, for example:
  - 'It's such a long time since I've seen you and...'
  - 'Now I have some very good news to tell you...'
  - 'Sami is such a...'
  - 'I did not tell you about this before because...'
  - 'I told Grandma because...'
  - 'I know you will feel...'

Don't restrict the children to these suggestions; they are simply prompts for those who need some help.

- Alternatively, for children who may find writing such a letter too demanding, try a discussion based around this question: 'If you were a close friend or relative of Rashida, what help and advice would you give her at this point in the story?'

### Review

- The letters should be passed around and read.
- Ask children to read out to the rest of the class extracts from their letters on particular points. Compare the differing views expressed.

---

## Activity 5  |C|T|

*Identifying textual clues about the school and Abla Selma, the teacher*
*Chapter 5*

### Learning objectives

- to visualise Rashida's school
- to build up a picture of a principal character
- to understand how authors create impressions of places and people

### Introduction

- Read from the beginning of chapter 5 down to '... drifted in through the window.' (p. 32) (You can omit the middle section on pp. 29–30 where Rashida is absorbed in her history book.)
- Ask for the children's general impressions of the school and of the teacher, Abla Selma.

### Development

- If you are doing this as a class activity, explain that you (or another fluent reader) are going to read the passage again. Ask half the class to put up their hand every time they hear a specific piece of information about the school which they think is worth recording. Ask the other half to do the same with references to Abla Selma. Record the information on the board or flipchart. (You can either do this yourself or ask two competent children to do it for you.)
- Alternatively, split the class into groups. Give each group a copy of the book and ask a couple of members of each group to read the passage aloud in turn. The group has to record in two columns specific items of information about the school and about Abla Selma.
- Here are some examples of the kind of information you are looking for:

| the school | Abla Selma, the teacher |
| --- | --- |
| – the bell had already gone | – she's rude to Rashida for being late |
| – there's a peanut seller under a mango tree by the school gate | – Rashida thinks she's the strictest teacher in the school |
| – 'sandy netball pitch' | – Iman hates her |
| – long, single-storey, brown building | – she was the only one who talked straight about Rashida's father's death |
| – covered verandah | – she's 'crazy about the past' |
| – girls in blue tunics and trousers with white head scarves | – Rashida's punishment is after-school detention |
| – Rashida shares a desk with Iman | – her mouth is a 'thin scarlet line' |
| – dog-eared book without a cover | – she 'slashed across a page with her red pen' |
| – there's a blackboard | |

- Pool the groups' responses.
- Ask the children what they have learnt about the author's skill in conveying impressions. What nouns, adjectives and verbs can they pick out which convey a mood or atmosphere? For example, why is Abla Selma's mouth described as 'scarlet', rather than simply red? Why is 'slash' a good verb to use? What impression of the school do the words 'dusty', 'brown' and 'dog-eared' convey?

## Activity 6

### Exploring characters' points of view
### Chapter 7

### Learning objectives
- to explore each character's view of two key points, using inference and empathy
- to scan for textual clues
- to use textual evidence to support a point of view

### Introduction

- As you read chapter 7, pause to ask the children to comment on Sami's European clothing, which contrasts with the local style of dress. Is this difference significant? Ask if the children can pick out some phrases which make clear Rashida's first unfavourable impression of her future step-father.
- Comment on the fact that the characters leave their shoes outside the door before entering a room. Make sure the children know that this is polite and customary.

### Development

- Two key points in Rashida's story are covered in this chapter: her first meeting with Sami and the family's reaction to the mirror. Everyone present has a different view of these two moments. Ask the children to speculate on Rashida's thoughts in both situations. Then remind them that there are three other people present – Sami, Mum and Grandma. They will each have a different angle on what is going on. The children's task is to speculate on what these three people are thinking.
- Give out **activity sheet 2**.
- Re-read the two relevant passages (pp. 40–41 and 41–42), or ask the children to re-read them in groups.
- Encourage the children to discuss their responses first and to write them in draft before filling in the thought-bubbles. They should be able to refer to the text to justify their answers.

### Review

- Share some of the thought-bubbles for each character, noting the similarities and differences in the children's responses. Ask them to justify any response which is not immediately obvious by referring back to the text.

## Activity 7

### Setting out arguments for and against a course of action
### Chapters 7 and 8

### Learning objectives
- to consider alternative plot-lines
- to marshall arguments for and against possible actions

### Introduction

- The second half of chapter 7 (pp. 43–46) contains a lot of dialogue. It provides a good opportunity to allocate children character parts for reading aloud in an ensemble. You will need readers for Iman, Rashida, Mum, Abla Selma and Sami (the last two are very small parts).
- Now read chapter 8. The children should begin to consider the emerging parallels between the lives of Rashida and Teti.

The main parallels are:
- both are mistrustful of adults (especially Sami and Opet);
- both have lost, or are about to lose, a father;
- both are mysteriously linked to the mirror;
- both are approaching a dramatic crossroads in their lives.

Is this why Rashida is the only one who can see Teti in the mirror?
- Ask whether there is anything Rashida can do to help Teti prove her father's innocence.

### Development
- Brainstorm with the children what Rashida could do with the mirror at this point in the story, given that it is creating such problems for her.

- Give out **activity sheet 3**, one between two. Compare the options listed on the activity sheet with the ones the class came up with in their brainstorming session.
- One child in each pair could write the argument for option 1 while the other writes the argument against. They can then change around for the next one. However, if you want to develop paired discussion, the children could work together on both sides of the argument. Give the children these two choices.

### Review
- Share sample arguments for and against each option. Praise particularly well-reasoned arguments and encourage the children to challenge poorly reasoned ones.

---

# Activity 8

*Group or class discussion*
*Chapter 11*

> ### Learning objective
> - to develop oral skills (discussion)

- Ask the children 'Is Rashida right in assuming that Sami searched her room for the mirror?'

- The children should scan the text for clues for or against their view.

### Review
- Do the children arrive at a consensus?
- Why do they think Rashida protected Sami?

---

# Activity 9

*Group or class discussion*
*Chapter 12*

> ### Learning objective
> - to develop oral skills (discussion)

- At the end of the chapter, Rashida is convinced that Sami (in the present) and Nakhte the scribe (in the past) are somehow one and the same person, and that it must have been Nakhte who stole the mirror from the temple. Ask the children why Rashida thinks this and whether it can possibly make sense.

---

# Activity 10

*Writing the end of the story*
*Chapter 15*

> ### Learning objectives
> - to practise discussion, looking at the links between the characters in the past and the present
> - to plan and write a piece of narrative

### Introduction
- At the end of this chapter, Rashida's misunderstandings fall away. She realises that she was wrong about Nakhte and Sami, that Opet was the thief and that Abla Selma is not the friend she seems. Explicit links are now drawn between the characters from the past and those in the present. Draw these links up on the board and discuss with the children how each pair is similar in certain key respects:

- Teti is linked with Rashida (some work has already been done on this in activity 7);
- Ani is linked with Mum (both are trusted parents; Rashida wants to 'save' her mum from Sami, thinking he is a thief, just as, in more dramatic terms, Teti wants to save her father);
- Sami is linked with Nakhte, the scribe (both wrongly suspected; both eventually prove to be honourable);
- Opet is linked with Abla Selma (both prove to be cruel and unscrupulous).

### Development

- At the end of this chapter, Rashida is fleeing from Abla Selma. She is heading for the river, to the spot where she found the mirror, thinking that this might be where she can meet Teti. Ask the children to write the next part of the story, setting out what happens next. They can plan their chapter(s) around the following questions:
  - What is Rashida doing? Where is she going?
  - What is Abla Selma doing?
  - Who comes to Rashida's rescue?
  - What happens at the spot where Rashida found the mirror?
  - What happens to the mirror?
- The children may need more than one writing session for this. Some of the work can be done as homework.

### Review

- If possible, share some of the stories before you read the final chapters of the book. The children's versions can then be compared with the original.

## Activity 11

*Discussion*
*Chapter 16*

### Learning objective
- to develop oral skills (discussion)

- Discuss with the children:
  - how Rashida throwing the mirror into the river might have helped Teti;
  - what Abla Selma is guilty of;
  - how Rashida's view of Sami has changed.

## After the reading of the novel

### Extension ideas
### A letter from Rashida to Sami

- Rashida has a lot of explaining to do! In particular she will need to:
  - thank Sami for saving her life;
  - apologise for accusing him of stealing;
  - explain why she lied about finding the mirror;
  - say how pleased she is that he's marrying her mother – and explain why.
- Alternatively, the same ideas could be covered in a role-play between Sami and Rashida: 'Sami, can I have a word with you?...'

### The trial of Abla Selma

- This is a complex undertaking but well worth while. The key to success is thorough research and preparation by all participants. The children must all plan carefully what questions they are going to ask and what evidence they will give, probably working in pairs or for homework. You may need to discuss each role privately with the individual concerned.
- The prosecution must:
  - decide what charges to bring (attempted theft? assault?);
  - compile a list of incriminating evidence with which to confront Abla Selma;
  - prepare questions to ask her and the other witnesses.
- The defence must plan their arguments to show that:
  - it is a trumped-up charge;
  - Abla Selma was attacked by Rashida;
  - Rashida has lied in the past;
  - the evidence that Abla Selma stole anything is very weak.
- Witnesses must be prepared to explain exactly what they did at each stage of the story (e.g. Rashida must say why she ran to Abla Selma's house and then changed her mind about her).

- The trial: you will probably need to be court usher to control proceedings! The most successful performers will be those who can listen to their opponents and counter their arguments effectively.

### A newspaper report

- Ask the children to write a newspaper article based on the story. Here are some possible headlines:

SCHOOLTEACHER ACCUSED OF STEALING FROM CHILD

HISTORIC TREASURE THROWN INTO RIVER

SCHOOLGIRL CLAIMS SHE COULD SEE INTO PAST

## Comprehension questions

The comprehension questions are based on a short passage from chapter 4 which is reproduced on the sheet.

For general suggestions on how to use comprehension questions, see page 17.

Read this passage carefully, then answer the questions about it.

The girl sat with her back to the wall, listening to the pounding feet outside and the confused jumble of voices.

She carefully filled a pot with the sour-smelling dough, coughing as a wave of smoke drifted in from the oven, her ears straining to hear what was going on outside. Even Opet, her father's cousin who worked with her, had stopped talking, stopped her constant angry complaining about her feet and her back and the laziness of the other workers.

The noise from the street grew louder.

The girl stood up and went to the window. She could see a crowd gathering outside, near the carpenter's shed where her father worked. For a moment, she imagined him bending over the coffin he was carving, smiling as he rarely did at home, now that her mother had left them for the Underworld.

The crowd of people parted and fell silent as a tall man elbowed his way to the front. She recognised him. It was Nakhte the chief scribe, and he was followed by the medjay-police. They walked past the bakery and on towards the carpentry shed.

"What's the matter?" asked the girl.

"The tombs have been robbed," said Opet. "They are going to arrest the thief."

The girl shivered, despite the clammy warmth of the bakery.

"What's your father been doing?" Opet nudged her as the scribe made his way into the carpenter's workshop. "Not robbing the dead, I hope." She sniggered at her own joke.

The girl turned away. Sometimes she hated Opet. A stir of excitement among the crowd made her look up again. The medjay-police had re-appeared, pushing a man in front of them.

The girl craned her neck to see better, then cried out in dismay.

It was Ani, her father, and he was being held like a prisoner.

"What is it? What are they doing with him?" she gasped.

"They say your father's a thief," said Opet, her eyes gleaming maliciously. "They say he's broken the seal of the dead and stolen from the tombs."

The girl shrank back.

"No," she screamed. "It's not true, it's not true."

1. What is the girl's job and where does she work?
2. Who is Opet and what is she like?
3. What is Ani's job, and what is he making at the time of the arrest?
4. What is meant by 'her mother had left them for the Underworld'?
5. When the girl was looking out of the window, whom did she recognise in the crowd?
6. What is Ani being arrested for?

When you have finished, think about this:

When Rashida tells Grandma what she has seen in the mirror, Grandma says: "I expect it was just a dream".

What do you think of Grandma's answer?

Name _____   Date _____

What might Rashida have been thinking and feeling at these
points in chapter 2? Thought-track her, writing your responses
in the right-hand column.

| what happens | Rashida's likely thoughts and feelings |
| --- | --- |
| Rashida arrives home after her strange experience in the sandstorm. | |
| Rashida visits her mum in the tiny crowded flat in Cairo where she has to live. | |
| Grandma at first shows no interest in the mirror and Rashida has to help her do the cleaning. | |
| Instead of her own reflection, Rashida sees the face of a strange girl in the mirror. | |
| Rashida tries to wipe away the mirror-girl's tears. | |

# Sandstorm: chapter 7    Activity sheet 2

Name _____    Date _____

What do you think is going on in each character's mind in these two situations? Fill in the bubbles. (Two have been done for you.)

**When Rashida first meets Sami (pages 40–41).**

Sami

Mum

She looks like a nice child but she's very nervous. I hope we're going to be friends.
I wonder whether she'll like her present.

Rashida

Grandma

**The family's reaction to the mirror (pages 41–42).**

Sami

Mum

Rashida is not telling the truth. Why is she pretending she bought it in a shop? She told me she found it by the river.
Oh dear, I hope she didn't steal it!

Rashida

Grandma

Name _____     Date _____

What should Rashida do with the mirror?

| Rashida's options | arguments for | arguments against |
|---|---|---|
| 1.  throw the mirror away | | |
| 2.  let Sami have it | | |
| 3.  tell Mum all about it | | |
| 4.  tell Abla Selma (her teacher) about it | | |
| 5.  tell Iman about it | | |
| 6.  stop looking in the mirror | | |

Do you have any other advice for Rashida?

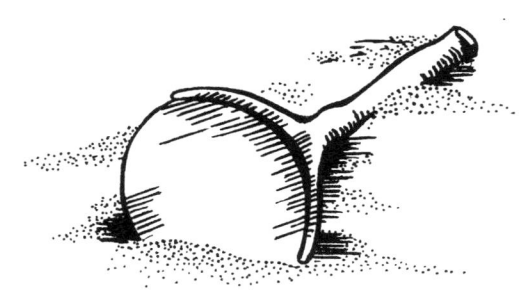

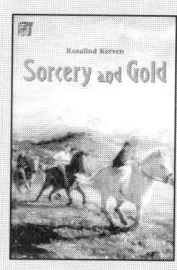

# Sorcery and Gold

**Author** *Rosalind Kerven* (see author profile on p. 147)
**Illustrator** *Simon Brett*
**Extended narrative** *A historical novel*

## Synopsis

This story is set in Iceland during the Viking age – about a thousand years ago. It is told by a Viking girl, Ingrid, who lives on a farm with her Aunt Thorhalla and Uncle Egil Olafsson. All is not well on the island: the sheep and cattle are sick and dying and newborn babies are dying too. The people believe that an evil sorcerer is to blame. One snowy night the household is disturbed by a band of men hunting for the Sorcerer. The Olafssons are sheltering a weary traveller from Ireland called Ruadh, who is searching for his long-lost son, snatched years before by Viking raiders when the boy was only four. Ruadh is in danger of being mistaken for the Sorcerer. Luckily, he is not discovered and is soon sent on his way, out into the freezing night. Ingrid feels sorry for him – he is old and sick – and she sets out to help him. However, on the way, she encounters the real Sorcerer, who explains his evil motivation. Ingrid escapes with no more than a prophecy about her future. Later, Ruadh tells Ingrid his story – of a lost son and a lost kingdom – and she is more determined than ever to help him.

In Ingrid's household is a slave boy, Kjartan. He is not what he seems. He too is most anxious about the welfare of Ruadh. Kjartan enlists Ingrid's help in looking after the old man in a hut near the mountains. This involves Ingrid in secret excursions from the house, bribing three meddlesome old women not to reveal that she is riding out with a slave boy (a great disgrace for a young girl of good family). She has to arrange a sea passage to Ireland for Ruadh, stealing gold from her guardians to bribe the boat owner. She also has to put up with Kjartan's ironic and often cruel tongue.

In a thrilling climax, Ingrid helps Kjartan to defeat the Sorcerer and she discovers that the slave boy is in fact Ruadh's long-lost son. As Kjartan gets ready to leave for Ireland to reclaim his kingdom, Ingrid vows to herself that, when she is comes of age, she will set out for Ireland to find him.

## Before reading

- Refer to the author's notes at the back of the book (pp. 139–140) for the historical background to the story.
- Show the children the book, explain that it is a story of the Viking age, read the blurb and some of the chapter headings and discuss the expectations they raise. Summarise the points in the author's notes about the historical background to the story.
- You may be using this novel as part of a project on the Vikings. If not, it is worth having an introductory session in which the children find out or reacquaint themselves with some basic information on:

  - where the Vikings lived;
  - how they lived;
  - their religion;
  - their clothes;
  - their dwellings;
  - their means of transport;
  - what they did (war, leisure, hunting);
  - family and marriage customs.

Pairs or groups could choose one of these areas to research and then report back to the class.

# Activity 1 [C][T]

*Completing cue-question charts for*
*some of the main characters*
*Chapter 1*

### Learning objectives
- to explore characterisation
- to use skills of inference
- to practise note-taking

### Introduction
- Write on the board the names of the characters introduced in this chapter: Uncle Egil Olafsson; Aunt Thorhalla; Ingrid, their niece and foster-daughter; Kjartan, the slave boy; Ruadh, the visitor from Ireland; Grim Helgisson, acting as a law officer searching for the Sorcerer. Ask the children to recall any information about these characters and any impressions they may have formed of them.
- Ask the children:
  - Where is the story happening?
  - What is the Olafssons' house like?
  - How do we know that the Olafssons are fairly well-off? (e.g. servants)
  - Should they have let Ruadh in? Why did they?
  - What clues are we given that Ruadh might not be the Sorcerer?
  - What might have happened to all the characters if Grim had discovered Ruadh?

### Development
- Introduce the idea of cue questions (see part 3, p. 153) by writing this example up on the board:

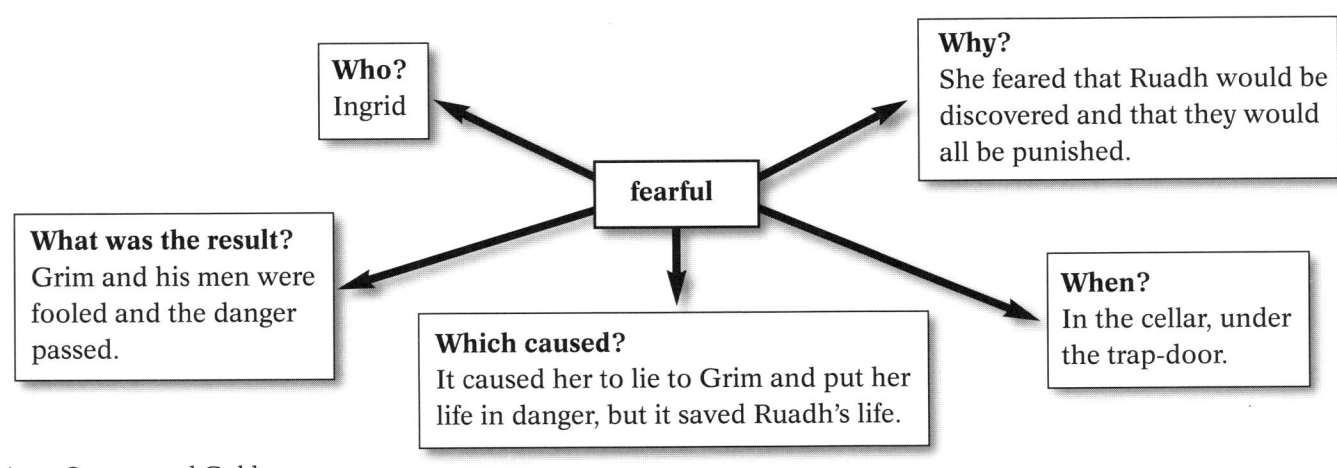

**Who?**
Ingrid

**Why?**
She feared that Ruadh would be discovered and that they would all be punished.

**fearful**

**What was the result?**
Grim and his men were fooled and the danger passed.

**Which caused?**
It caused her to lie to Grim and put her life in danger, but it saved Ruadh's life.

**When?**
In the cellar, under the trap-door.

- Give out **activity sheet 1**, which contains two similar charts, one for Ruadh and one for Grim. The children should complete them in the same way. Let them refer to a copy of the book if they need to.

### Review

- Their charts should contain the following information:

  **Lost and homeless**
  **Who?** Ruadh
  **Why?** He has been searching for his lost son.
  **When?** A year or more.
  **Which caused?** Much hardship; wandering in strange countries; a life of exile.
  **What was the result?** He came to iceland. He seeks food and shelter at the Olafssons' farm.

  **Determined**
  **Who?** Grim Helgisson
  **About what?** To rid the land of the Sorcerer.
  **Why?** Because the Sorcerer is doing so much damage. Because Grim wants to take the credit for it.
  **When?** In the spring; one freezing night.
  **Which caused?** He has to spend a long time away from home searching in the cold with his men, causing fear wherever he goes.
  **What was the result?** He meets the Olafssons but he does not find the Sorcerer.

- Compare and contrast the children's responses.

---

## Activity 2

*Exploring a key relationship;*
*looking at textual clues*
*Chapter 2*

### Learning objectives
- to develop understanding of two key characters and their attitudes to one another
- to scan the text for information about the relationship
- to practise oral skills (discussion and reading aloud)
- to summarise what has been learnt

### Introduction

- This chapter is important for the information it gives about the key relationship in the story, that between Ingrid and the slave boy Kjartan. It also presents a mystery about Ruadh: is he the Sorcerer that Grim is hunting for?
- Re-read the first section of the chapter (pp. 18–20) with the following question in mind: 'Is Ruadh the Sorcerer?' The author gives subtle clues – for example, Ruadh's gentleness, his bewilderment at

the change in attitude toward him, his sorrow rather than anger, his reference to Christian hospitality and, perhaps most significantly, Ingrid's sudden belief in his innocence. The clues should sow doubt in the children's minds; take care not to remove that doubt, as Ruadh's ambivalence is an important part of what is to come.

### Development

- Move on to the relationship between Ingrid and Kjartan. Ask the children to work in groups of three. Give each child a copy of **activity sheets 2a and 2b**.
- Read through the instructions on activity sheet 2b with the children to make sure they understand the task. In particular, talk about the different ways phrases can be expressed when read aloud to signal meaning, emphasis, attitude and emotion.
- Dictionaries might be useful for some words like 'tauntingly', 'impudence' and 'winced'.

### Review

- Ask groups to report back on at least one of the quotations.
- Share and comment on the summaries.

## Activity 3

**Class discussion about the Sorcerer; drawing**
**Chapter 3**

> **Learning objectives**
> - to practise oral skills
> - to scan a text for information
> - to transform written information into a visual form

### Discussion

- The Sorcerer is a key figure in the book, and the most mysterious one. We learn that he is an exile from his birthplace, 'a sinful corner of the Earth', and that to survive he has turned to 'wizardry' of an unpleasant kind. He makes no secret of the fact that people think he can poison sheep and spread disease, and that he sells evil spells for a living (pp. 29–30). Contrast the Sorcerer with Ruadh: what are the differences and similarities between them?
- Also ask why Ingrid feels sorry for the Sorcerer and why he decides not to harm her.

### Drawing

- The children could follow up this discussion by producing a drawing of the Sorcerer with a caption giving basic information about him.
  They should be able to find information in the text to justify their decisions in the drawing.

## Activity 4

**Summarising interactions between characters**
**Chapter 4**

> **Learning objectives**
> - to consider the extent to which information is given through dialogue
> - to consider characters' motives
> - to summarise the key events in – and the consequences of – each scene

### Introduction

- Discuss why the chapter is called 'Rumours'. Ask the children to think of some examples of rumours in this chapter (e.g. that the Olafssons harboured the Sorcerer, that Ingrid is implicated).
- Point out that most of the story is told through dialogue rather than as straight narrative. There are four scenes in this chapter:

- scene 1: Thorhalla, Egil and Ingrid (pp. 33–35);
- scene 2: Ingrid and Kjartan (pp. 35–36);
- scene 3: the old women, Thorhalla and Ingrid (pp. 37–39);
- scene 4: Ingrid and Grim (pp. 40–41).

- As an example of how dialogue is used to convey information (an important narrative device), re-read the short scene between Ingrid and Kjartan which begins, 'As I went, Kjartan happened to go past...' (p. 35). What does this scene tell us about their relationship? What secrets are they keeping from one another?

### Development

- Give out **activity sheet 3** and discuss the questions.
- Make sure copies of the book are available for those who need to refer to the text.

### Review

- Pairs can compare their responses before a whole-class reporting-back session.

## Activity 5

**Discussion**
**Chapter 5**

> **Learning objectives**
> - to develop understanding though group discussion
> - to skim and scan the text for evidence

- Discuss the following questions, either all together or in small groups first and then as a whole class:
  - Why is Egil so happy when he returns from the Great Assembly?
  - Why are his family fearful for his safety?
  - How is Grim soon to be related to the Olafssons?

- How might this change Grim's attitude towards them?
- What did Ingrid's dream foretell?
- How might Kjartan have known what the dream meant?
- How has Kjartan's position in the family changed by the end of the chapter?

- Rather than presenting all the questions at once, they could be written on separate pieces of paper and distributed one at a time for the groups to discuss. This approach encourages in-depth discussion rather than a desire to 'get through' all the questions as quickly as possible! Whatever your approach, make sure all the questions are covered in class.

# Activity 6

***Summarising what the characters think about one another***

### Learning objectives
- to look at characters from different points of view, using inference and deduction
- to practise summarising skills, using key relationships at a particular point in the story
- to use textual evidence to support a point of view

### Introduction
- Explain that different people may have different views of the same person. Illustrate this by taking the character of Kjartan and asking the children to say what Egil thinks of him, what Ingrid thinks of him, what Grim thinks of him, and possibly also what Ruadh thinks of him. What does Kjartan think of himself?

### Development
- Ask the children to write the names Kjartan, Egil, Ingrid, Grim and Ruadh on small strips of paper.

- They should then write the following on separate pieces of paper:

'What _____

thinks of _____.'

- Working in pairs, the children should take two name slips at random and fit them into the boxes to complete the above sentence.
- They should then discuss what the first character thinks of the second, referring to the text for evidence wherever possible.
- The children should then summarise their conclusions.
- Let the children work through as many different combinations of characters as there is time for.

### Review
- Draw out pairs of characters' names and ask for corresponding examples of the children's writing. Can they refer to incidents in the story to back up their assertions?

# Activity 7

***Cloze procedure; looking at descriptive language; drawing***
***Chapter 7***

### Learning objectives
- to use contextual clues to find missing vocabulary
- to examine descriptive language
- to transform written language into a visual form

### Introduction
- Before you begin this activity, discuss what we learn about Kjartan in this chapter. Ask the children if their view of him is changing. Does Ingrid have anything to fear from him?
- Ask the children what images they have of the landscape Ingrid rides through in this chapter.
- Give out **activity sheet 4** and gloss the meaning of any of the words in the list of nouns which the children may not know. Alternatively, ask the children to look up unfamiliar words in the dictionary.

### Development

- The children can work in pairs if you wish. They should cut up the words in the noun box and move them around the cloze passage until they find the right arrangement.
- Check through the answers with each pair, or, alternatively, leave this until you can go through the answers with the whole class. Children who finish quickly can begin to plan their drawings.
- The answers are:

| | |
|---|---|
| 1. grasslands | 13. cracks |
| 2. desert | 14. hills |
| 3. rocks | 15. valley |
| 4. lava | 16. slopes |
| 5. mountains | 17. wilderness |
| 6. fortress | 18. dust |
| 7. sky-line | 19. stones |
| 8. crystals | 20. horizon |
| 9. smoke | 21. flowers |
| 10. blow-holes | 22. earth |
| 11. boulders | 23. wind |
| 12. gullies | 24. spiders |

- When you have agreed on the correct answers, the children can write them into the spaces on the activity sheet.
- Point out some examples of adjectives used to describe the nouns – for example, 'bleak, pocked-marked', 'smooth, ochre-coloured'. Ask the children to underline other examples.

### Review

- As you check through the adjectives with the children, point out also the very precise, detailed, descriptive language used; the care with which the author paints the scene with words; and the wide vocabulary used. It is a very fine descriptive passage, so try to get the children to engage with it and appreciate its quality.

### Extension

- The drawings should be planned in outline and checked by you. You can help children with their planning by asking them to note first what should be included in the foreground (e.g. the grasslands, flowers), the middle ground (e.g. boulders, gullies, cracks) and the background (e.g. the track through the valley, hills, mountains).
- The drawings can be done in the children's own time.

Note that there is a set of comprehension questions on **chapter 8** (see p. 101) which should be completed before moving on to chapter 9.

---

# Activity 8 |C|T|

*Completing a chart of Ingrid's fears*
*Chapters 9 and 10*

---

> ### Learning objectives
> - to consider the main character's fears at crucial points in the narrative
> - to use the skills of inference and deduction

### Introduction

- Summarise, or ask the children to summarise, what happens to Ingrid in these two chapters.
- Give out **activity sheet 5**. Discuss what is happening to Ingrid in each of the six boxes in the left-hand column, reading the relevant sections from the book.

### Development

- Discuss what the children might write in the first box – for example, 'She was afraid that the old women would tell her uncle and aunt that she had been out with the slave boy, that she had slipped away from the wedding, even perhaps that she had been seen with the Sorcerer. She would be severely punished.'
- Ask each child to give this information in their own words. Discuss what the children have written, checking that they have understood the task.
- Make copies of the book available for reference.

### Review

- Discuss variations in the children's responses to each box.

# Activity 9

*Recall; prediction*
*Chapter 11*

## Recall
- Ask the children to recall the three conditions that Ulf Whitebeard sets Ingrid (in writing if you prefer) and what difficulties they are likely to cause her.

## Prediction
- Ask the children what they think will happen to Ingrid in the next chapter. A key question would be: 'What will Ingrid have to do to get Ruadh to the ship and to pay for his passage?' (e.g. find more gold; get ponies for Ruadh and Kjartan; make a long, dangerous journey to Ruadh's camp; disguise Ruadh; journey back to the ship across land where the Sorcerer lurks)

---

# Activity 10

*Sequencing; group recall; role-playing*
*Chapters 12 and 13*

## Introduction
- To help the children reflect on what is happening in these two chapters, ask them to say what part in the story the following items played: the golden chalice, the blanket, the gold bracelet on Groa's arm, Ruadh's coughing, the Thor's Hammer necklace.

## Development
- Divide the class into groups of three and give each group a copy of **activity sheet 6**.
- The groups' first task is to cut out the boxes and sequence them correctly. You may wish to impose a time limit on this – ten minutes, for example.
- Give the correct sequence at the end of the session or time limit, as follows:

1. Ingrid steals a golden chalice.
2. She sets out from the farm on her aunt's pony, Spinner, and with two other ponies for Kjartan and Ruadh.
3. Kjartan demands to see what Ingrid is hiding under her cloak.
4. Ruadh makes a disguise and Kjartan cuts off the old man's beard.
5. They camp for the night by the river and eat roasted birds.
6. They skirt Ingrid's farm and join the road.
7. They meet the three old women.
8. Ingrid's identity is discovered.
9. They gallop to the sea.
10. Thurid is insolent to Kjartan; he hurls a boulder into the sea.
11. Ingrid offers the chalice.
12. Ingrid offers her golden Thor's Hammer necklace.
13. The Sorcerer appears.

- Each person in the group now has to role-play one of the three main characters (i.e. Ingrid, Ruadh and Kjartan). Working through the boxes in sequence, they should say what they were thinking and feeling at that point in the story.

## Review
- Choose volunteers to hot-seat any of the three characters.

# Activity 11

*Recalling the whole story*
*Chapters 14 and 15*

---

### Learning objectives:
- to recall the main plot of the whole story
- to consider the importance of places and objects in a story
- to write summaries of parts of the story, based on recall

### Introduction
- Discuss the climax of the novel, using questions such as:

  - How did the Sorcerer show his villainy?
  - Who showed real courage?
  - Whose actions were disappointing? (e.g. Grim)
  - Was the revelation of Kjartan's identity well prepared for?
  - Should Ruadh have died?
  - How did Ingrid feel about Kjartan at the end?
  - Will their paths cross again?

### Development
- Give out **activity sheet 7**, one between two. Explain that it contains 12 pictures of places and objects which played a significant part in the story.
- To demonstrate how the activity should be done, ask the children what part a castle played in the story. You are looking for a retelling of Ruadh's story – the Viking raid on his Irish kingdom; the kidnapping of his son, Kjartan. Model a written summary of this, for example: 'At one time, Ruadh was a king in this Irish castle. It was raided by Vikings. His son was kidnapped. Eventually he abandoned his kingdom to find his son.'
- Having discussed what part each item or place played in the story, the children should write their own summaries.

### Review
- Ask a child to read out a summary for a picture, then ask if anyone has written something containing different information. If they have, discuss the differences. Work through all the pictures in this way.

---

## Comprehension questions

The comprehension questions focus on Ruadh's story from chapter 8. It is important to a proper understanding of the story that the children know Ruadh's history and his reason for being in the land of the Vikings. These eight comprehension questions should help the children understand Ruadh's position more fully and give them a clear pointer to the relationship between the ex-king and Kjartan.

For general suggestions on how to use comprehension questions, see page 17.

**1**

What was life like for Ruadh before
the Vikings raided his castle?

**2**

What caused his wife's death?

**3**

How did the Vikings treat the Irish?

**4**

What happened to Ruadh's son when
the boy was four years old?

**5**

What was life like for Ruadh after
the Viking raid?

**6**

Why did Ruadh set out in a little
boat to the northlands?

**7**

When the boat landed in Iceland, Ruadh
was mistaken for someone else. Who?

**8**

What might Ruadh have meant when he
said to Ingrid, "I am no longer in darkness
now, for truly the sun has come to shine
on me again"?

# Sorcery and Gold: chapter 1    Activity sheet 1

Name _____    Date _____

Complete these two charts.

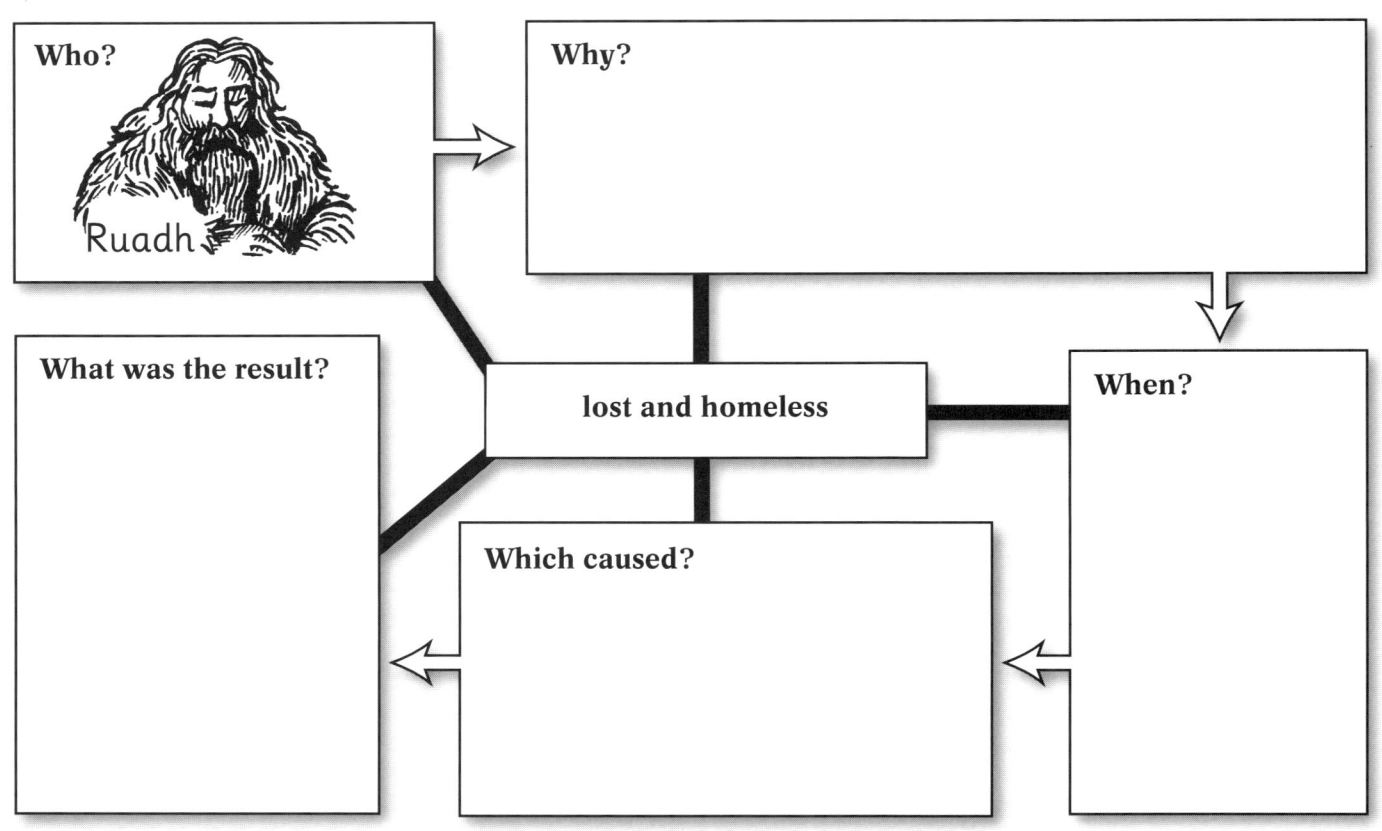

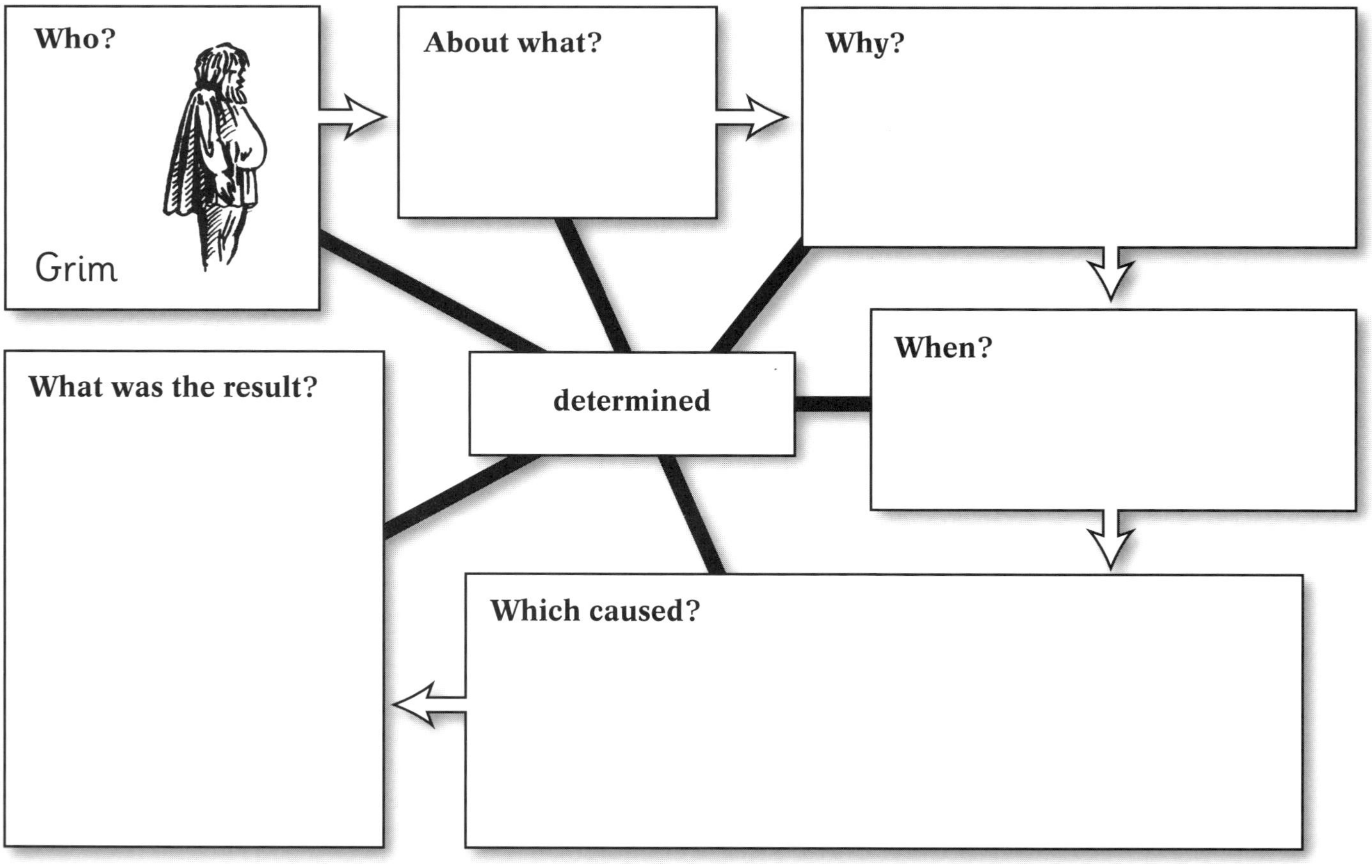

**Who?** Ruadh

**Why?**

**What was the result?**

lost and homeless

**When?**

**Which caused?**

---

**Who?** Grim

**About what?**

**Why?**

**When?**

**What was the result?**

determined

**Which caused?**

Name _____    Date _____

Read this extract from pages 22–24.

By the light of a small candle that he shielded with his cupped hand, I saw Kjartan.

"What's the matter, young Mistress?"

I took a deep breath to steady myself.

"Open the door for me since you're here," I whispered as haughtily as I could.

He made no move.

"Please open the door for me."

"Where are you going?" he asked slyly. He knew he had me cornered: I would get into as much trouble as he for wandering around at this time of night. I dared not strike him or make a fuss, for fear of waking my uncle and aunt.

"Don't ask questions, slave boy. Do as you're told."

He edged round to block my way and stared at me full on.

"You're going to follow the Irishman, aren't you?" he said tauntingly.

He played teasingly with the bolt. My uncle was right: he was strong. He pulled back the great iron bar as easily as a feather; and then at once rammed it shut again.

"That's an odd thing for a high-born young lady to do," he said, imitating the way that Aunt Thorhalla spoke. He even had the cheek to wag a reprimanding finger at me. "Off in the night after a foreign sorcerer, eh? Whatever would your foster parents think of that – Ingrid?"

He wasn't supposed ever to address us by our proper names: it was the height of impudence.

"Open the door at once, you nasty little slave," I hissed. "Then go away – and mind your own business."

"Don't call me that," he snarled back. "I'm too good to be a slave. Better than you are." He grasped my arm so hard that I winced. "Give me my freedom, Ingrid."

"Don't be stupid, how can I?" I said, slapping him away. "And why should I want to? Just wait till the morning – I'll see that you're whipped!"

"But what about you?" he said. "Creeping up in the night like a thief, eh?" He stared pointedly at the bread in my hand. "Taking food to an outlaw who's condemned to death. What will happen when they hear about *that*?"

We glared hatefully at each other in the flickering candlelight, while the silence grew into a stony wall between us. At last, to break the tension, I said, "Anyway, I don't believe he is the Sorcerer."

To my surprise, Kjartan softened at once.

"No," he said. And then, "I wondered, when you said it before, whether you really meant it."

He slid back the bolt and stepped politely aside. "If you like, I'll tell you which way he went."

"But . . . why?"

"Your people should never have sent him away like that," he said. "He told me he's been really ill. He badly needs help. He hasn't got a single friend in Iceland." He cleared his throat. "He's gone south – along Trout River, heading towards the Smoky Mountains."

**Sorcery and Gold: chapter 2     Activity sheet 2b**

Name _____          Date _____

1.  Read aloud the passage on activity
    sheet 2a, one of you taking Ingrid's
    spoken part, one taking Kjartan's part
    and the third taking the narrator's part.
    As you read, pause to discuss how best
    to express the dialogue to bring out the
    feelings of the characters.

2.  When you have finished reading, look
    closely at the clues the author gives us
    about the characters' feelings and
    attitudes towards each other. Find
    these quotations in the passage,
    underline them and, as you do so, talk
    about what they tell us about how these
    characters relate to one another in this
    scene.

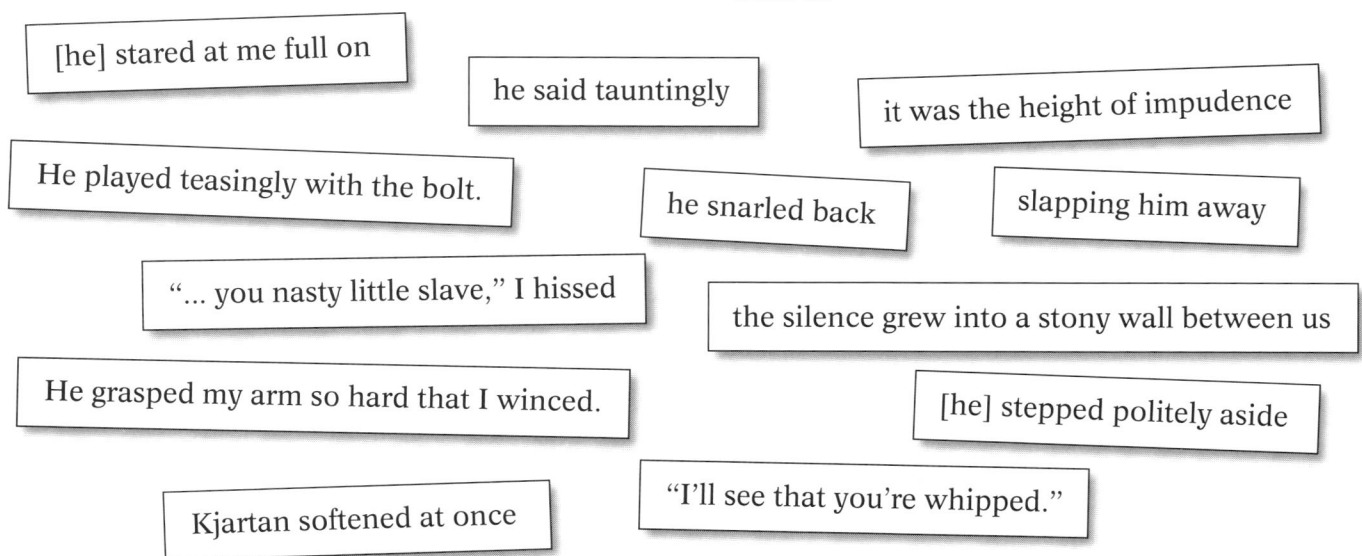

[he] stared at me full on

he said tauntingly

it was the height of impudence

He played teasingly with the bolt.

he snarled back

slapping him away

"... you nasty little slave," I hissed

the silence grew into a stony wall between us

He grasped my arm so hard that I winced.

[he] stepped politely aside

Kjartan softened at once

"I'll see that you're whipped."

3.  Now summarise your discussions.

    What does Ingrid think of Kjartan in this scene?




    What does Kjartan think of Ingrid in this scene?

Name _____          Date _____

Write your answers in the spaces provided.

| | |
|---|---|
| **Scene 1: Thorhalla, Egil and Ingrid**<br>What did Ingrid want?<br><br><br><br><br><br>What was Thorhalla's response? | **Scene 2: Kjartan and Ingrid**<br>What did Kjartan want?<br><br><br><br><br>What is Ingrid keeping secret and why?<br><br><br><br>What do you think Kjartan<br>might be keeping secret? |
| **Scene 3: the three old women,<br>Ingrid and Thorhalla**<br>What did the old women want?<br><br><br><br><br><br>What happened between them and Ingrid? | **Scene 4: Grim and Ingrid**<br>What did Grim want?<br><br><br><br><br><br>What might be the consequences? |

# Sorcery and Gold: chapter 7     Activity sheet 4

Name _____     Date _____

- Cut out the nouns in the box at the bottom of the page.
  Fit them into the right spaces in the passage below.
- Then underline the adjectives used to describe these nouns.
- Draw the scene described here.

The (1) _____ were thinning out rapidly now, and fairly soon we reached their end.

A vast expanse of grey, stony (2) _____ stretched ahead.

    "This is where I usually see him," said Kjartan, drawing Storm Cloud to a halt.

"When he's well enough, he walks to meet me here."

    I gazed at the bleak, pock-marked carpet of (3) _____ and ancient

(4) _____ flows. After a mile or so it rose into smooth, ochre-coloured

(5) _____, looming hard and barren like a giant's (6) _____ against the

(7) _____. Their upper reaches were encrusted with

(8) _____ and white, silent columns of (9) _____ rose from secret

springs and (10) _____ in their midst.

    "Which way?" I dared not look behind, in case I lost the courage to go on.

    "Just follow me."

    We began to ride carefully across the (11) _____, over dried-up water

(12) _____ and sudden gaping (13) _____ in the ground. In front, the

glistening (14) _____ grew steadily closer, until I saw that the track led into a sheer-

sided (15) _____ between their (16) _____.

    The silence became stronger as we penetrated the (17) _____. It seemed to whistle

in the ears, to cling at us and our surroundings, heavy as a formless layer of (18) _____.

    We were quite alone. Not even a single bird hung above us in the sky. There were only dry

(19) _____, cracked and crumbling to the jagged line of mountains on the (20)

_____. Occasionally we passed startling clumps of tiny purple (21) _____,

clinging to the (22) _____ in terror of the (23) _____; and scores of brown,

leggy (24) _____ scurrying across the desert on secret business of their own.

## Nouns

| blow-holes | mountains | valley  | lava    | hills    | horizon  |
|------------|-----------|---------|---------|----------|----------|
| grasslands | rocks     | cracks  | spiders | flowers  | gullies  |
| fortress   | desert    | stones  | earth   | boulders | wind     |
| crystals   | wilderness| dust    | slopes  | smoke    | sky-line |

© Cambridge University Press 1999   Original artwork by Simon Brett

# Sorcery and Gold: chapters 9 and 10    Activity sheet 5

Name _____    Date _____

Here are six crucial moments from chapters 9 and 10. Write in
the boxes on the right what you think Ingrid fears at each point.

| Crucial points in the story | What was Ingrid afraid of? |
| --- | --- |
| 1.  When Ingrid met the three old women. <br><br>(pages 80–85) | |
| 2.  When she arrived back at the wedding, having been out for most of the night. <br><br>(page 86) | |
| 3.  When Grim says that if anyone is caught helping the Sorcerer, they will die. <br><br>(page 87) | |
| 4.  When Gudrun tells her that she is pregnant. <br><br>(page 90) | |
| 5.  When she saw a thin, fleeting shadow on the way home from Gudrun's. <br><br>(page 92) | |
| 6.  When she knows she has to ride to the Fjords to arrange a sea passage for Ruadh. <br><br>(page 95) | |

Name _____    Date _____

Cut out the boxes and put them in the right order.
In groups of three, role-play Ingrid, Kjartan and Ruadh. Talk
about your view of each of these scenes and what you felt.

| | |
|---|---|
| They skirt Ingrid's farm and join the road. | Thurid is insolent to Kjartan; he hurls a boulder into the sea. |
| They gallop to the sea. | Kjartan demands to see what Ingrid is hiding under her cloak. |
| Ingrid steals a golden chalice. | Ingrid offers her golden Thor's Hammer necklace. |
| They meet the three old women. | Ruadh makes a disguise and Kjartan cuts off the old man's beard. |
| The Sorcerer appears. | Ingrid offers the chalice. |
| Ingrid's identity is discovered. | They camp for the night by the river and eat roasted birds. |
| She sets out from the farm on her aunt's pony, Spinner, and with two other ponies for Kjartan and Ruadh. | |

© Cambridge University Press 1999    Original artwork by Simon Brett

Name _____     Date _____

Talk about what part each of these places or items played in the story.
Then write a summary of this information for each picture

an Irish castle

a Viking longboat

a cross on a
leather thong

a Viking farmhouse

a mouse

dead sheep

a hovel

a blanket and a
fishbone needle

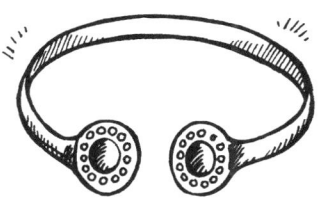

a golden bracelet

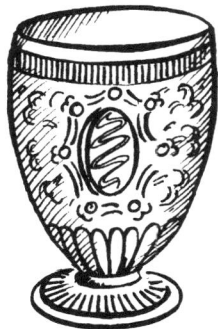

a golden chalice

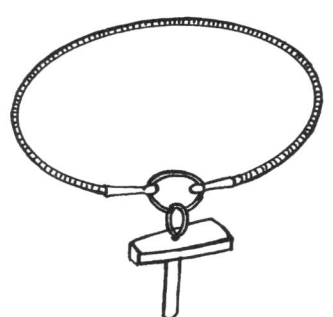

a Thor's Hammer
necklace

a bottle of poison

# Spindle River

**Author** *Judith O'Neill* (see author profile on p. 149)
**Illustrator** *Ian Stephens*
**Extended narrative** *A historical novel*

## Synopsis

In the summer of 1819, the Sinclair family arrive in New Lanark to seek work in Robert Owen's cotton mills. Mr Sinclair, a fisherman, has died at sea off Caithness. Christina, his widow, has an uncle working at the mills, so she and her five children make the long journey south in the hope of work. They are welcomed and hired by Mr Owen and settle in. Work in the mills is noisy, tiring and dirty, but Christina and her eldest daughter, Henny, get used to it. Jockie, aged eleven, gets work as a servant in Mr Owen's house; and the three youngest Sinclairs, Betty, Tam and Davie, go to the mill school. Henny and Jockie make friends with Rab Cunningham, a boy who works at the mill. Rab introduces them to the forbidden world of nature in Mr Owen's private park. At Braxfield House, Jockie comes into conflict with another servant boy called Dan Drysdale who, jealous that Jockie has taken a position he coveted, attacks and nearly kills him. Dan is banished to do menial work in the mills. Nursing a grievance against the Sinclairs, he pushes Betty into the river and she nearly drowns. Eventually, after an exciting denouement, his murderous actions are discovered and he is transported to Australia.

The story is about how the Sinclairs, in their different ways, adjust to their new situation; how some of them appear to put down roots while others look forward to returning home. It gives vivid insights into the effects of the Industrial Revolution on families and communities, and gives a clear idea of what life was like in Britain in the early part of the last century.

## Background information

- New Lanark is the famous cotton-spinning mill, built in the late eighteenth century in the deep valley of the River Clyde near the old town of Lanark. It is a place of great importance because it was here that the reformer Robert Owen (1771–1858) put into practice his pioneering ideas on the management of labour and his unusual social and educational theories.

The mill at New Lanark was begun by David Dale (1739–1806), with his partner Richard Arkwright, the English inventor and mill-owner, who regarded the site as perfect for the use of water power. The first mill was built in 1785 and spinning began there in March 1786. Several more large and handsome mill-buildings still standing today were erected in Dale's lifetime. He recruited impoverished Highland families and destitute orphans from Glasgow and Edinburgh to work for him and he provided them with housing. In the 1790s Robert Owen, a Welshman with several years' experience of managing cotton mills near Manchester, first visited New Lanark and met Dale and his daughter, Caroline. He married Caroline in 1799 and his company bought New Lanark from Dale soon afterwards. Owen began to manage the mill according to his own ideas: he improved the housing for workers; he employed no children under ten; all the hundreds of children, both those working in the mill and the younger ones, attended his unusual school – influenced by Pestalozzi's ideas – where lessons in geography, dancing, singing and natural science were added to the usual reading, writing and arithmetic. He founded a 'New Institution for the Formation of Character', largely for the education of his adult workers. He started a Sick Fund and a Savings Bank and ran a Co-operative Store in the village where the families could buy food more cheaply than in Old Lanark up the hill. The population of New Lanark in 1819 was 2,300. It was a little self-contained world, deep in the wooded valley, with the tremendous racket of water-wheels and spinning machines filling the air.

Owen delighted in his role as a kindly father-figure to all the hundreds of children and adults he employed and educated. But Robert Southey, who visited the place in 1819, wrote that 'Owen in reality deceives himself'. Southey thought the workers were under 'the same absolute management as so many negro slaves'. He saw the mill-operatives as far too passive and docile, as mere 'human machines', and he was critical of Owen's benevolent but manipulative system of control. This conflict of views about New Lanark underlies the story of *Spindle River*.

## Introducing the book

- Through a mix of teaching and research, the children need to fill in some of the above historical background to the novel.

- Discuss the title, the author (see profile on p. 149) and the cover. Get the children guessing about the content:
  - What clues do the cover and blurb give about the story, the genre, the themes and the setting?
  - What kind of book is it?

  After discussion, tell the children that you are going to read the first chapter and that, at the end, you will ask them the same questions again.

- Read chapter 1 but leave out the place and date given at the start of the chapter. What clues are given about the period and the setting? Return to the questions you asked at the outset.

## A choice of literacy activities

| Activity | Focus | Page |
|---|---|---|
| 1. | Looking for period clues; creating fact files; drawing the setting; compiling a glossary. | 112 |
| 2. | Discussion; writing from one character's point of view. | 113 |
| 3. | Completing a chart to compare nineteenth-century and modern views of the Sinclairs' new living arrangements. | 113 |
| 4. | Drawing and captioning a sequence of diagrams to illustrate work in the mills. | 114 |
| 5. | Devising and commenting on a 'silent monitor'. | 115 |
| 6. | Discussion; role-play. | 115 |
| 7. | Compiling a timetable of Jockie's day as a servant. | 116 |
| 8. | Improvised drama. | 116 |
| 9. | Discussion. | 117 |
| 10. | Writing a short novel based on an outline (*for able and motivated writers only*). | 117 |
| 11. | Shared reading of the chapter; discussion of historical references. | 118 |

# Activity 1

*Looking for period clues; creating fact files;*
*drawing the setting; compiling a glossary*
*Chapter 1*

### Learning objectives
- to scan for information
- to practise note-taking
- to use textual evidence to support a
  point of view

### Introduction
- A lot of information is worked into chapter 1 and
  some rich Scots is used to help convey it. The
  following tasks will help the children to:
  - develop an understanding of the historical
    period;
  - get to know most of the main characters;
  - empathise with at least one of the characters;
  - understand the use of dialect;
  - visualise the mills where much of the action
    takes place.

### Development
- Split the class into five groups. Each group should
  have at least one copy of the book which can be
  passed around the group for reading aloud. While
  the book is being read, the rest of the group should
  listen carefully for information relevant to their
  particular task.

- **Group 1** is looking for clues about the historical
  setting. To write this story the author had to
  imagine herself in another time. She had to
  research the period and the setting in order to
  provide authentic historical detail. The period
  detail had to be worked unobtrusively into the
  story; there are plenty of clues in the text to convey
  information about the period. The children should
  list relevant quotations and explain why each
  quotation gives a clue that the story is set in the
  past.
- **Groups 2 and 3** are drawing up fact files on the
  major characters: Henny, Jockie, Rab, Mr Owen
  and Christina Sinclair. What clues does the author
  give us about what each of these characters is
  like?
- **Group 4** is compiling a dialect glossary. They
  should look for unfamiliar words which they
  believe to be Scots and try to guess their meaning
  by looking at the context. They should be able to
  explain the reasoning behind their definitions.
  Scots words can be checked in the glossary at the
  back of the book.
- **Group 5** is drawing the setting. They should list
  quotations from the book which describe New
  Lanark, then draw the setting based on this list.
  They could annotate their drawing with the
  quotations they have found.

### Review
- The work produced by the various groups could be
  put together to form a display about the novel.
- Differentiation can be achieved by appropriate

# Activity 2 [T]

*Discussion; writing from one character's point of view*
*Chapter 2*

<hr>

### Learning objectives
- to examine characterisation
- to practise oral skills (discussion)
- to use empathy
- to write creatively

## Introduction
- Remind the children of the information they have already gathered about Robert Owen, the owner of the mills and an important character in the novel. More explicit information is given in the background information section above.
- Discuss what the characters in the book think of Mr Owen. Does Rab like him or not? Does he respect him, and if he does, what is that respect based on? Recall what Henny thinks of Mr Owen when she first meets him (p. 22). Is his appearance any clue to what he is like as a person?
- Ask the children to recall the ways in which the different characters show their respect for Mr Owen – for example, Rab gasps, whips off his cap and bows; Christina curtsies; Jockie calls him 'sir'. How do children show respect to authority figures such as teachers and police officers today?

## Development
- Make sure all the children can see a copy of the book. Turn to page 21 and read aloud the passage which covers the first few minutes of the Sinclairs' meeting with Mr Owen, a fateful meeting that will settle their future (from ' "It's the maister" ' on p. 21 to "We ken how to work hard" on p. 22).
- Discuss what each character might be thinking and feeling during this meeting. Ask the children to re-read for clues to the characters' movements and then to move beyond the text to use their own imagination. If the children have created fact files on the characters for *Activity 1*, they can refer to them for help.
- Ask each child to choose one character (other than Mr Owen himself) whom they would like to be.
- Put children who have chosen the same characters together to discuss what their character would think about Mr Owen, and what they would feel during the meeting.
- Ask the children to write, in character, a diary entry for that day describing the meeting with Mr Owen. They should try to convey a sense of the period as well as of the character's feelings about Mr Owen. Some more able children may even like to try writing in Scots.

## Review
- Ask some of the children to read their work aloud and ask the rest to guess which character's diary is being read. How did they know? Ask them also to choose one authentic historical detail which they particularly liked and to comment on it.

<hr>

# Activity 3 [C][T]

*Completing a chart to compare nineteenth-century and modern views of the Sinclairs' new living arrangements*
*Chapter 3*

<hr>

### Learning objectives
- to scan for relevant information
- to use empathy in considering the Sinclairs' view of their new home

## Introduction
- Ask the children what impression the author gives of the Sinclairs' previous living conditions in Wick, a coastal fishing village, and how these compare with the new accommodation at New Lanark. Do the Sinclairs welcome all the changes?

## Development
- Give out **activity sheet 1**, one between two if you prefer. Give out spare copies of the book to a few readers.
- Ask one of the readers to find the passage in chapter 3 which corresponds to the first item in the left-hand column on the sheet.
- The passage should be read aloud. Ask the children what the Sinclairs think about the whitewashed walls, the bare floors and the iron grate. How would the children feel if they had to live in such conditions? What are the differences of view and why?

- Let the other readers read their passages aloud. Pass the book on to new readers until all the passages have been covered.
- The children should now fill in the boxes. Make copies of the book available for reference.

### Review
- In a reporting-back session, highlight the different social expectations of the children today and of the Sinclairs in 1819.

---

# Activity 4

*Drawing and captioning a sequence of diagrams to illustrate work in the mills*
*Chapter 4*

> ### Learning objectives
> - to scan for information
> - to translate written information into a graphic sequence
> - to write explanatory captions
> - to collate information from several texts

### Introduction
- In this chapter we are given details of the repetitive, boring and dangerous work done in the mills. Christina, Henny and Jockie are given particular jobs which are carefully explained to them. Read aloud these passages. (Jockie's is on p. 50, Christina's on pp. 51–53 and Henny's is reproduced on activity sheet 2.) Ask the children what images these descriptions create in their minds. How would they react to that situation themselves if they were in the characters' shoes? Do they think it is right for children in particular to be doing such hard and dangerous work?
- Provide some information books on early Victorian factories and use them to fill in some background historical details concerning the move from agricultural to industrial work.

### Development
- Give out **activity sheet 2**. The children can work in pairs sharing their views before completing their own sheets. Six boxes have been provided to guide the children through the six-stage process:

1. splitting the bales;
2. 'scutching' to get rid of seeds and dirt;
3. spreading them flat;
4. feeding them into the carding machines;
5. straightening the fibres and binding them into long, soft ropes called slivers;
6. pulling the slivers into thinner ropes called rovins.

For those children who find it difficult to isolate these six stages, read the extract together and, with the help of the children, underline them in different colours.

- Refer the children to the glossary at the back of the book. It gives clear explanations of many of the technical terms (cop', 'rovin' and so on).
- Encourage the children to use information books, pictures, CD-ROMs and so on to make their diagrams more historically accurate.
- The children should write short captions in an appropriate style.

### Review
- Let groups and pairs compare their diagrams and make alterations if necessary.
- Choose some children to explain their graphic sequence.

### Extension
- Use the sequences of drawings as a basis for mime in drama, giving the children the opportunity to act out the sequence that Henny is involved in every day.

# Activity 5 T

*Devising and commenting on a 'silent monitor'*
*Chapter 4*

### Learning objectives
- to explore a philosophical idea through discussion and experiment
- to argue for or against a point of view
- to practise speaking and writing discursively

## Introduction
- Read aloud the passage about the silent monitor (pp. 56–57).
- Divide the class or group into two. Half the children should argue in favour of the monitor, half against. Brainstorm their views and record the most interesting in two columns on the board, 'For' and 'Against'.

## Development
- Ask pairs of children to devise their own monitor which could be used to record their own behaviour and that of their classmates during a day at school. They should then think up some examples of the kind of behaviour associated with each colour.
- Compare what the children come up with and then agree on how you – as the arbiter of behaviour – can make fair judgements.
- Ask the children to write a short piece (perhaps for homework) arguing for or against the use of the monitor in the mills.

## Review
- Try out a monitor for a day, or part of the day, in class and then discuss its flaws and benefits with the children. How did they feel about it? Did it give them an insight into how the millhands felt about it?
- Share the children's views of the use of the monitor in the mills.

# Activity 6 T

*Discussion; role-play*
*Chapter 5*

### Learning objectives
- to become familiar with a central experience in the Industrial Revolution
- to use empathy in role-play
- to argue for and against a position

## Introduction
- Re-read the passage in chapter 5 where Rab tells Henny and Jockie about the weavers in Lanark and the new looms which Mr Owen is thinking of bringing in (p. 61). It raises a central issue of the early industrial era: the threat to jobs created by the development of machinery.
- Ask these general questions:

  - Why does Mr Owen want to bring in new looms driven by water power?
  - Why does Rab's father say it could bring an awful lot of trouble?

Now develop the argument, recording the children's ideas in two columns on the board (the advantages/disadvantages of power from the water-wheel).

## Development
- Split the class into groups of four or five. Two children should role-play Mr Owen (the maister) and his manager, Mr Gillespie. Their task is to persuade the rest of the group, who role-play weavers, that switching to water power will benefit them and everyone else in the long run.
- Give each side of the group time to prepare their case, putting them together in one larger group to discuss the issues if you think this will help. The children may wish to jot down the main arguments in note form to act as an *aide-mémoire*.
- If a quiet area is available, tape one group's discussion to play back for the review.

## Review
- As a result of the role-play, are there any further points the class wish to add to the work you did on the board earlier?
- If a group's discussion was taped, play some of it back to the class.

## Activity 7  |C|T|

**Compiling a timetable of Jockie's day as a servant**
**Chapter 6**

### Learning objectives
- to use scanning, inference and deduction to compile a timetable
- to use reasons to support an argument

### Introduction
- Encourage the children to talk about the good and bad experiences that Jockie had on his first day at Braxfield House.
- Concentrate on first impressions of Dan. How does the author make us dislike him? Do we feel sorry for him because Jockie has dashed his hopes of working in the house? Is he likely to be an important character in the story? If so, what predictions can be made at this stage about his future behaviour towards Jockie?

### Development
- Re-read the passage on pages 82–83 which describes Jockie's duties, or ask a fluent reader to do so.
- Plenty of information is given about what Jockie has to do, but less on when he has to do it. The children's task is to work out the most sensible order of jobs, using clues in the passage as starting-points – for example, 'fires were lit each evening', chamber-pots are likely to be emptied first thing in the morning. Meals and rest times should also be included.
- Working in groups, the children should attempt to draw up a timetable of Jockie's day, referring to a copy of the book where necessary.

### Review
- Compare the groups' timetables.
- Hold a brief class discussion on which the children think is preferable – working in the mill or at Braxfield House. Encourage the children to give reasons for their views.

## Activity 8  |C|T|

**Improvised drama**
**Chapter 7**

### Learning objectives
- to adapt the text from prose to unscripted drama
- to use gesture, intonation and expression to rehearse and prepare a performance

### Introduction
- With the children, run through the sequence of events in chapter 7. Note the main events on a large sheet of paper as you do so. Ask how each character is feeling at different points, and encourage speculation about Dan's state of mind.

### Development
- The following improvisations need plenty of space; the school hall would be ideal. The children should work in groups of seven and play the parts of: Jockie, Dan, Mr Owen, Mrs Drysdale, Georgie/the surgeon, Christina, a gardener (one gardener will be enough).
- Make sure each group has a copy of the text from which the required references can be read aloud as the improvisations are being developed.
- Let the children sort out who's playing who.
- Suggest that the drama is divided into short scenes, for example:
  - **scene 1**: Dan's attack on Jockie and his discovery by Mr Owen (pp. 91–92);
  - **scene 2**: in the kitchen, with Jockie, Mr Owen, Mrs Drysdale and the surgeon (pp. 92–95);
  - **scene 3**: in the kitchen with Jockie, Georgie, Christina and Mrs Drysdale (pp. 96–97);
  - **scene 4**: carrying Jockie home, with Christina and a gardener (pp. 97–98).
- The conversations should be in the children's own words, not read from the text.
- Help the children with performance elements as they rehearse, in particular with the story line, with expression and dialogue, and with movements and gestures.

### Review
- Invite some groups to perform the four scenes and encourage positive and constructive comments on the performances from the rest of the class.

# Activity 9  |C|T|

*Discussion*
*Chapter 8*

### Learning objectives

- to practise oral skills (discussion)
- to practise text recall
- to use skills of empathy and prediction

## Introduction

- Re-read the first few pages of chapter 8, up to '"The maister's taken a likin to ye, laddie," they all said to him with friendly grins.' (p. 102)

## Development

- Head up two columns on the board and discuss what might go in each:

| How Dan's life has got worse | How Jockie's life has got better |
| --- | --- |
| He has lost his home at Braxfield House. | He is free of the mill. |

- Either complete the lists as a whole-class activity or do some of it together and then ask pairs to complete it, drawing upon their memory of the text.

## Review

- Finish by asking the class what they now think of Dan Drysdale. Do they feel any sympathy for him, given his background? What revenge might he take on the Sinclairs?

---

# Activity 10

*Writing a short novel based on an outline*
*(for able and motivated writers only)*
*Chapter 8*

### Learning objectives

- to develop the skills of story writing
- to write historical fiction
- to work to an outline
- to write in stages over a long period of time

## Introduction

- You may well have in your class a group of children who have the skills and motivation to attempt the writing of a longer piece of fiction. If this is the case, draw these children aside and sound them out about embarking on a longer writing project, much of which will have to be done in their own time.
- If they are enthusiastic about the project, give them a copy of **activity sheet 3** and read it together. The task is to write the story of the boy from Dundee.

## Development

- Decide as a group what action will take place in each chapter, for example:

**Chapter 1** The boy is working in the mill. He loses his finger in the machine. The pain. Instead of receiving sympathy, he is beaten by the overseer.
**Chapter 2** His mother throws the overseer down the stairs. She and the boy flee.
**Chapter 3** What happened to the mother.
**Chapter 4** The boy's journey on foot to Lanark. What happened on the way? How did he survive?
**Chapter 5** He arrives at Lanark and tells stories about the dreadful conditions in the Dundee mills.
**Chapter 6** Mr Owen gives him work and he finds good lodgings.
**Chapter 7** He gets restless and leaves. What happened to him next?

- You could give the children exercise books to write in. Alternatively, if any of the children have personal computers, they might like to compose their stories on screen.
- Illustrations can be added as the work proceeds.
- Monitor the work from time to time and let other children comment on the stories' progress.

## Review

- Let the children read their stories to the class. Put copies of them in the class and school libraries.

# Activity 11 [C][T]

*Shared reading of the chapter; discussion of historical references*
*Chapter 9*

### Learning objectives
- to understand historical and political ideas
- to understand how such ideas can be reflected in the events of a novel
- to practise oral skills (reading aloud and discussion)

- The whole chapter is a three-part conversation between Rab, Henny and Jockie which carries the narrative. This gives a good opportunity for shared reading. Choose three confident, fluent readers to take on the three parts. Give them each a copy of the book before the reading-aloud session so that they can practise their part first or at least read it through to themselves. Take the part of the narrator yourself and share the reading of the chapter to the class.
- There are some historical references in the children's conversation which will need to be glossed. They concern **Waterloo**, the **Peterloo Massacre** and **the franchise**.

  – **Waterloo, Battle of** (18 June 1815) *The final defeat of Napoleon I, ending the Napoleonic Wars and the Emperor's last bid for power in the Hundred Days. A hard-fought battle, in which Blucher's Prussian force arrived at the climax to support Wellington's mixed Allied force. A number of crucial blunders by the French contributed to their defeat.*

  – **Peterloo Massacre** (1819) *The name given to the forcible breakup of a mass meeting about parliamentary reform held at St Peter's Fields, Manchester. The Manchester Yeomanry charged into the crowd, killing 11 people. The incident strengthened the campaign for reform. 'Peterloo' was a sardonic pun on the Waterloo victory of 1815.*

  Chambers Dictionary of World History (1993)

  – **the franchise** Remind the children that most people did not have the vote in 1819 and were therefore not free in the political sense.

- When the reading is finished, discuss why the children's trips into the forbidden 'other world' of nature are so important to them and why they take so much trouble to free the badger.

Extraordinary session! Some of the most perceptive comments came from unexpected sources. Some of the most able children did not see the significance of the trapped badger being freed by Rab. Many of the poorer, more reluctant readers were 'spot on' in their assessments of the situation. I was very surprised and chastened to hear their sensitive and perceptive comments. Anne Fine says that literature is one of the most potent ways of conducting ethical enquiry. This discussion proved that point!

Contributor's comment

# Activity 12

*Writing the end of the chapter*
*Chapter 10*

### Learning objectives
- to draw on knowledge of the story to predict the next event
- to write in the style of the author

### Introduction
- This is an exciting and dramatic chapter in which

Betty is all but murdered by Dan. It begins with picturesque descriptions of nature and the school. It quickens when Betty plays truant to go down to the river, creating unease in the reader. For a while this unease is allayed with descriptions of the river, but it is then revived when Dan comes on the scene. The sinister element is only ever hinted at, but as soon as the children make the link between the boy and Dan (it is not stated explicitly in this chapter), it informs everything that happens. It is worth commenting on these deceptive shifts in pace and anticipation once the following work on this chapter has been completed.

## Development

- Read the beginning of chapter 12 and stop after the sentence 'Betty listened' (i.e. just before Dan tips her into the water p. 134). Ask the children to write the next few paragraphs of the story themselves.

> There will be a stunned silence and the children will urge you to continue with the reading, but insist that they write the next few paragraphs. The writing is so powerful at this point that you will not need to make many suggestions for ideas...
>
> This was an exciting session. The children returned to their places (they had been listening in the carpeted reading area) and were busy chatting about the story. Once they started writing the room fell silent and all the children were busy writing...

Contributor's comment

## Review

- After the writing session, read some of the children's work together. Then go back to the text to finish the chapter. Discuss similarities and differences between the text itself and the children's own ideas.

---

# Activity 13  C T

*Group discussion*
*Chapter 10*

### Learning objectives
- to practise oral skills (discussion)
- to use inference and deduction
- to give coherently argued answers

> The quality and interest level was high. The children experienced all kinds of emotional responses. They were very upset about Betty and indignant that Dan could treat her in this way. They were confused about Dan and felt angry and sorry for him. The discussion on responsibility was very good indeed and some children ventured personal experiences of encounters with unhappy, neglected children they had met at clubs and on holiday.

Contributor's comment

## Introduction
- Remind the class about what happens to Betty in this chapter.

## Development
- Split the class into small groups and give each group a copy of **activity sheet 4**. It contains questions about Dan Drysdale which the group should discuss. Make copies of the book available for reference.
- The children should make notes of the group's responses for the whole-class feedback session.

## Review
- Report back.

# Activity 14

## Writing song lyrics based on a model
## Chapter 12

### Learning objectives
- to write the lyrics of a song
- to use a rhyming verse form
- to appreciate the meaning of the song in relation to the story

### Introduction
- Give out **activity sheet 5** and read Betty's song with the children.
- Discuss the imagery and the form, making sure that the children understand that Betty is using the song to express her memories of her former home in the fishing village in Caithness. What does this tell us about Betty?

### Development
- Help the children to recall Henny's love of the 'other world' beyond the wall, where she has been with Jockie and Rab and where they rescued the badger. Ask the children what images from the wood might be used in a song composed by Henny. List the best ideas on the board or flipchart.
- Talk about the patterning in the verse form, particularly the simile in the second line signalled by the word 'like', the images of nature in the third and fourth line introduced by the word 'Where', and the rhyme scheme. (When the children begin to write, the rhyming can be dispensed with if you find that it is leading to doggerel.)

### Review
- Share the songs. Pay particular attention to weak or slack lines which could be sharpened up in a revision. Ask the rest of the children to help the writer with this process by suggesting better images or phrases.

### Extension
- Some children might like to compose a tune to go with the lyrics.

# Activity 15 [C][T]

## Hot-seating; interviewing; writing a newspaper report
## Chapter 13 (and the beginning of chapter 14)

### Learning objectives
- to use empathy, inference and deduction
- to scan the text for relevant information
- to write in a particular style

### First session: Hot-seating and interviews
### Introduction
- Read to the end of Mr Gillespie's letter to Mr Owen in chapter 14 (p. 173).
- Explain that an important event such as the mill fire would have been reported in the press at the time. Ask how it might be reported today. What would be the headlines in the local paper? What would the report focus on? Would there be a 'human interest' angle (e.g. the rescue of Dan by two children) or a mystery angle (e.g. Why was Dan in the mill? Was he guilty of arson? What were the rescuers doing out so late?)?

### Development
- Ask for three volunteers to hot-seat Rab, Henny and Mr Gillespie. Ask for a further three volunteers to help coach and question these three as they prepare for their roles. Mr Gillespie's role is the most difficult as most of it will have to be inferred, so reserve this for the most able pair. Send these six children off with a copy of the book each. They should work in pairs to commit to memory as much as they can about their role that night.
- The rest of the class can work individually or in pairs drafting interview questions to put to the three characters to elicit information for a newspaper report on the fire.
- When everyone is ready put the characters in the hot-seat and begin the interviews.

### Second session: writing newspaper reports of the incident
- Together, recap what happened that night (drawing on the accounts given by those who were in the hot-seat earlier) and note the main events on the board or flipchart.

- The children can work in pairs or small groups to plan the newspaper report.
- Read some examples of journalistic language from local papers to help the children write in the appropriate style.
- Make sure everyone understands that the reports should contain the essential information (i.e. the names and ages of those involved and what happened). Point out that most newspaper reports begin by stating the main event or outcome and are not usually told in a linear fashion. Illustrative quotes from Rab, Henny and Mr Gillespie can be made up. There can also be speculation about the cause of the fire, Dan's role in it, and the effect of the fire on morale and jobs at the mill in the immediate future.

### Review
- Reports can be revised on the word-processor and desk-top published.

## Activity 16

*Role-playing in group discussion to determine Dan's fate*
*Chapter 14*

### Learning objectives
- to use inference, empathy and deduction
- to argue a point of view
- to listen to and take account of differing points of view
- to reach a group consensus for action

### Introduction
- Much of this chapter concerns the fate of Dan. Before you embark on this role-playing activity, re-read the two paragaphs on pages 174–176 which begin 'Mr Owen had rather more difficulty in getting Dan Drysdale to talk,' and end 'Dan Drysdale might come to some good yet.' Ask for initial views of what should happen to Dan. What should be his punishment, given that he has seriously assaulted Jockie, nearly murdered Betty and set fire to the mill?

### Development
- Explain that you want the children to role-play a group of people closely concerned with Dan's crimes. They are meeting to discuss his behaviour and to decide on his punishment. This group will consist of Mr Owen (Dan's employer), Mrs Drysdale (his only relative and guardian), Christina (the principal injured party, representing both Jockie and Betty) and the Sheriff (the representative of the law).
- Brainstorm what position each of the four might hold at the start of the discussion and note the main points on the board or flipchart. We already have Mr Owen's view. Mrs Drysdale will plead extenuating circumstances and ask for leniency. Christina may temper her call for severe punishment with compassion. The Sheriff may demand the full rigour of the law, which at that time would probably have been the gallows.
- The children can now go off into fours, decide who is role-playing whom and begin their discussions.
- The outcome should be a recommendation for action, signed by all four members of the group.

### Review
- Ask the group to report back on their recommendation and the main reasons behind it.

## Activity 17

*Discussion and prediction*
*Chapter 14*

### Learning objectives
- to practise oral skills (discussion)
- to practise skills of prediction

- The children will probably enjoy holding a class discussion about what will happen to the characters next.
  - What stories might a sequel to *Spindle River* have to tell about Henny, Jockie, Rab, Betty and Dan?
  - Who would stay at New Lanark, and who would return to Caithness?
  - How would Dan get on in Australia?

Name _____     Date _____

What do the Sinclairs think about their new place?
What do you think? Fill in the chart.

| aspects of the new accommodation | the Sinclairs' view | your modern view |
|---|---|---|
| Whitewashed walls, bare floorboards, iron grate. | | |
| Curtained beds tucked into the wall ('hurlie-beds') with straw mattresses. | | |
| A 'chantie' or chamber-pot, to be emptied every day "in one o' the privies in yon row o' wee huts out the back". | | |
| Rubbish to be put on "the midden heap doun in the street". | | |
| Jockie reads the Bible to his family every night before they go to sleep. | | |
| They all have to wear cotton tunics in the mills. | | |
| Children working in the mills go to school after supper. | | |

Name _____     Date _____

Using the information in this extract, draw and caption a sequence of six
pictures to show what Henny has to do. Use information books to help you too.

"Right, Henny, I'm takin ye up to the top floor o' this grand mill o' mine. That's where we split open
the big bales of cotton that come over the sea in ships from Carolina and other faraway places. First
we do the scutchin to get rid of any seeds and dirt from the raw cotton, and then we spread it out
into a nice flat lap before we feed it into one o' the cardin engines. We've got whole rows o' splendid
cardin engines up there. Best in the whole world! Every one as big as an elephant! Well, near as big
as an elephant. The cardin engines straighten out the fibres and bind them into long soft ropes that
we call the slivers. Then the drawin machine pulls the slivers into thinner ropes that we call the
rovins, ready to be spun on the water-frames. Is that clear?"

|  |  |
|---|---|
|  |  |
|  |  |
|  |  |

In this extract, Judith O'Neill has sketched out a story line for a longer story. Can you write that story?

- Divide it into short chapters.
- Write it over a long period of time – and mostly in your own time.
- Show it to your teacher as you go along.

"There was a young laddie came here only last year from an awful mill in Dundee. He'd lost the wee finger off his left hand. Caught it in a machine when he was only eight years old, he told me. That poor bairn was beaten so hard with a thick stick by the overseer in yon Dundee mill that his mither went straight off in a fury to seek for the man. She found him at the top of the stairs so she grabbed him with both her hands and she threw him right down to the bottom! Then she had to run awa from the mill takin the lad with her. I dinna ken what became of her, poor woman. Perhaps she deed or went to prison but the bairn walked all the way here from Dundee, though he was only twelve and a wee laddie for his age. He told us such tales of the drunkenness and dirt in yon terrible mill, and about the rats runnin everywhere, and the shockin rude songs the poor women sang as they worked and the cruel maister and the rough overseers, and the lang hours and the bairns startin work at seven years old, and the ugsome food, and the damp cellars for sleepin. He couldna believe his luck when he came here and Mr Owen gave him work. A kindly family in Long Row offered the lad one end of a bed."

"Is he still here?" asked Henny with interest.

The woman shook her head.
"Na, he was too restless. His faither had been a souter – for mendin broken shoes, ye ken – and the laddie wanted to follow his faither's trade. So he walked off into Perthshire, hopin to find work with a souter. I often think o' him, poor laddie. He told me all about the mill-fever in Dundee. Children lying sick and shivering beside their machines, he said, and naebody to help them."

Name _____     Date _____

Discuss these questions about Dan's role in chapter 10. Make
a note of your responses for reporting back to the whole class.

1.  At what point in the chapter did you sense that something awful was
    about to happen?

2.  What clues were you given that something awful was about to happen?

3.  The author does not tell us who the boy is. Why do you think the boy
    must be Dan?

4.  What are Dan's motives for being so cruel?

5.  Could anyone have prevented this from happening?

6.  Did you expect this sort of behaviour from Dan? Why?

7.  Did Betty have any reason to be suspicious of him?

8.  Do you think Dan planned to harm the Sinclairs in some way?

9.  Did the event 'just happen' on the spur of the moment?

10.  Dan was very badly treated as a small child. Does this help to excuse
     how he has behaved towards the Sinclairs?

11.  When Dan is caught, how would you have him punished?

12.  How do you think Mr Owen will punish him?

Name _____     Date _____

Betty made up this song based on the movement of the spindles in the mills and on the things she loves and remembers about her previous home in Caithness. Compose a song for Henny, using the same words for the spindles but adding new ones to reflect her love of the woods where she saw the badger.

Spin, my spindles, spin,
Spin like the whirl o' the sea,
Where the fisherman lies asleep,
And never comes back to me.

Spin, my spindles, spin,

Spin like_____

Where_____

_____


Turn, my spindles, turn,
Turn like the swing o' the tide,
Where the herrin leap in the nets,
And boats to the harbour glide.

Turn, my spindles, turn,

Turn like_____

Where_____

_____


Fly, my spindles, fly,
Fly like the birds o' the wild,
Where the gannet dives to the wave,
And the kittiwake calls like a child.

Fly, my spindles, fly,

Fly like_____

Where_____

_____


Sing, my spindles, sing,
Sing like birds o' the land,
Where the women carry the peats,
And dream on the silvery sand.

Sing, my spindles, sing,

Sing like_____

Where_____

_____


Dance, my spindles, dance,
Dance in yer lang, white hair,
Till winter comes to its end,
And geese climb high in the air.

Dance, my spindles, dance,

Dance_____

_____

_____

# The Hermit Shell

**Author** *Frances Usher*

**Illustrator** *Liz Minichiello*

**Extended narrative** *A contemporary novel*

## Synopsis

This is the story of a boy called Neil, who runs away one January morning from the London Rest Home where he lives, from his parents who pull him in different directions, from school where he can't keep up, from boys who call him names – away from everything he can't cope with. He thinks he'll be safe in The Hermit Shell, his artist Aunt Tessa's small house in Cornwall, as safe as a crab in its shell.

But Tessa needs a shell, too, somewhere to be alone to paint. Why should she make room for Neil? And, as Neil starts to enjoy his new freedom, making friends and getting involved with the lifeboat crew, how can it be that all his old problems seem to have come with him, down there at 'the end of England'?

This is a thought-provoking story about running away and not running away; about dealing with other people's demands; and about having the courage to face your fear and come out of your shell at last and be happy.

## The contributor of this section

This section differs slightly from the other schemes of work in this book. The author of the novel, Frances Usher, is a highly regarded writer of novels and stories for children. She is also a teacher and is often invited into local schools to talk to the children about her work and sometimes to work with them on activities related to her books. She devised a scheme of work for *The Hermit Shell* and worked closely with a teacher at Wareham Middle School, Dorset, for half a term. This is her account of what happened.

## Introduction

The activities were tried out with 31 children of a mixed-ability Year-6 class, working closely with the class teacher, Miss Punter. The work was done in the children's English periods over half a term, and I was present at 15 sessions.

## Discussion points to follow each chapter

### Chapter 1

- What problems does Neil seem to have in London?
- Why is he so interested in the crab on Tessa's fax?
- Is Martyn and Lee's behaviour towards Neil really bullying?
- Should he tell someone about it before he runs away? If so, who?
- How do you think Tessa will react to Neil's arrival at The Hermit Shell?

### Chapter 2

- Talk about Neil's feelings when he first arrives in Cornwall that afternoon.
- Do you think Tessa should have been friendlier to Neil when he arrived at The Hermit Shell?
- What do you think Neil's parents did and said when they discovered he was missing?

### Chapter 3

- Tessa doesn't like being called 'Auntie'. Why not, do you think?

– Should Tessa have let Neil go out alone on his first morning in Portmartin? Are children generally safe on their own as long as they're sensible?
– How do you think Tessa gets on with Neil's dad, and with his mum? Look for clues in what they say and do when they're all together in The Hermit Shell.
– 'Would his dreams come true here?' Neil asks himself when his parents have gone back to London. What dreams do you think Neil has? And do you think they will come true?

## Chapter 4

– Neil's new friends call him 'Lofty'. Why does he like that, when he hated being called 'Nelly' by Martyn and Lee? What difference can a nickname make?
– Why do you think Neil's dad might have been 'secretly relieved' when Neil decides to stay in Cornwall?
– Annis doesn't seem to Neil the sort of person who would ever play truant. Who would be, do you think?
– 'He'd had enough females telling him what to do for a while.' Is it fair for Neil to feel that? Is Tessa right to be annoyed when Neil goes out without doing his chores, and comes back late?

## Chapter 5

– Does Tessa spend too much time on her painting? Should she behave differently towards Neil? If so, how?
– Why does Neil draw two fighting hermit crabs on his wrist during the maths lesson?
– Look again at what happens when Neil's friends come to Portmartin the second time. Should Neil have behaved differently at any point? If so, when? And how?
– 'They stared at each other for ten long seconds.' Time ten seconds of silence. While you're doing it, try to imagine what might have been going on in Neil's mind during that time.
– Why do you think Annis is angry when she hears someone saying the lifeboat crew are doing 'wonderful work'?

## Chapter 6

– Were you surprised to find Neil playing truant at the beginning of this chapter?
– 'Exactly the same things had gone wrong again,' Neil realises on the cliffs. In what ways is he in the same situation now as he had been in London?
– Neil promises not to tell Annis's secret to anyone, then changes his mind when he finds out what that

secret is. Should you ever tell anyone's secret? And would telling Annis's secret be different from Neil telling Wayne who vandalised the lifeboat house?

## Chapter 7

– Do you think Neil is brave to behave in the way he does when Annis falls over the cliff? How do you think you would behave in the same situation?
– 'I wanted to be with my mum, and I wasn't,' Annis tells Neil. Were people right to make Annis go to school on the day her mother died?
– Wayne tells Neil he reckons he'll go to school the next day and he'll be all right. Do you agree with Wayne?
– Are you surprised that Tessa has put Neil and Annis into one of her pictures?

## Chapter 8

– Danny and Pete are furious that Neil has 'grassed' on them. Are they right to be angry?
– Do you think it was difficult for Craig to become Neil's friend when other people at school were angry with him?
– 'Dozy old sheep,' Craig says about people who changed sides over Neil's 'grassing'. What do you think he means?

## Chapter 9

– When Neil's mother talks to him in St James's Park, she says the main trouble had been that she and his dad had 'just never stopped working'. Do you think parents sometimes spend too much time working? Why do they do it?
– Neil's father says that going to Cornwall has done Neil good. Do you agree?
– His mother cried a lot after he left, says Miss Cobham, perhaps because she felt she'd failed as a mother. Do you think she had? Whose fault was it that Neil left? Was it anyone's fault?

## Chapter 10

– Neil dreads going back to Cornwall after Wayne dies. So why does he do it?
– Watching the lifeboat go out, Neil thinks he just might be able to join the crew one day. What qualities do you think he'd need to do that?
– Tessa chooses to work in Penna's Café on carnival day instead of painting. Do you think she's changed at all since Neil came to The Hermit Shell?
– 'There were lots of different ways of living,' Neil discovers at the end of the story. What do you think he will decide to do next? What would you do in his place?

# A choice of literacy activities

| Activity | Focus | Page |
|---|---|---|
| | **During or after the reading of chapter 1** | |
| 1. | Discussion. | 129 |
| 2. | Research. | 129 |
| 3. | Discussion and personal writing. | 129 |
| 4. | Oral and written prediction. | 130 |
| | **During the rest of the reading and after** | |
| 5. | Writing diaries. | 130 |
| 6. | Writing letters. | 131 |
| 7. | Agony aunts or uncles. | 131 |
| 8. | Hot-seating. | 132 |
| 9. | Drama. | 132 |
| 10. | Artwork. | 133 |
| 11. | Sequencing; making a time-line. | 133 |
| 12. | Alternative plot-lines. | 134 |
| 13. | Imagining the future. | 134 |

# During or after the reading of chapter 1

(The reading may be broken off at certain points as indicated, or the whole chapter could be read first.)

### Learning objectives
- to help children follow chapter 1, and understand Neil's problems
- to help children begin to grasp the hermit crab analogy
- to develop oral skills and personal writing
- to develop predictive skills orally and in writing

## Activity 1

### Discussion

- Discuss what a Rest Home is, and what it would be like to live in one.
- Discuss Neil's state of mind that morning. If the children find this difficult, the following activity may help:
  In pairs or groups, children pick out suitable cards from a collection naming moods – for example, 'happy', 'excited', 'worried', 'frightened', 'hopeful', 'depressed', and so on. These ideas can then be shared by the class.

- Discuss as a class why Neil should feel like this. Make a list of the problems he seems to have.

## Activity 2

### Research

- Open the lesson by asking, 'What is a **hermit**?'
- In pairs or groups, the children should find out about the hermit crab, using books, pictures, the text (including the quotation from Ray Ingle's book on p. 6), the Internet and so on. Each group should present what it has discovered. Make sure illustrations of the crab, and the way it chooses an unused shell and enters it, are included.
- Round off the lesson by asking, 'Why do you think now that the hermit crab is so named?'

## Activity 3

### Discussion and personal writing

- Present the children with the following sentence:
  'He needed a place of his own away from everything, somewhere he could keep the entrance shut.'

- As a class or in groups, ask the children to discuss the following:
  - Why do you think Neil is interested in the hermit crab?
  - What are Neil's feelings at this point?
- When people feel like this, they sometimes need a place where they can get away from everything. Ask the children:
  - Do you have a place like that?
  - Would you like one?
  - If so, what sort of place would it be?

  Ask them to write about a time when they (or someone else) felt unhappy, and the place they went to – or would like to have gone to.

## Activity 4

### *Oral and written prediction*

- Ask the children: 'What do you think will happen when Neil arrives at The Hermit Shell?'
- Discuss this as a class, or in small groups. The children could then write the next part of the story as you think it might be.

The children were quick to pick up Neil's difficulties in the first chapter, many sympathising with the family strains, and his problems with school work and bullies. The 'mood cards' were scarcely needed as discussion groups came up with their own adjectives for Neil's feelings.

I was slightly chastened to find many children pitied Neil for having to live in a Rest Home among old people, when actually I'd put him there on purpose, thinking it interesting and out of the ordinary. Not to this age group, apparently.

However, the Underground scene with Martyn and Lee made a big impression, and was something the children were to return to again and again over the next few weeks. Generally, they seemed to understand Neil's need to get away from his London life, though they were also shocked that he didn't tell anyone he was going. Few anticipated any difficulty when he reached The Hermit Shell ('Tessa could move out and let Neil live there,' was one person's conjecture).

## During the rest of the reading and after

## Activity 5

### *Writing diaries*

> **Learning objectives**
> - to build empathy with the main characters
> - to visualise the narrative from a character's point of view
> - to practise writing autobiographically from multiple viewpoints

- Ask the children to focus on a character on a particular day and to write their diary for that day. They can begin, perhaps, with Neil's running away day, recorded both by Neil and by Tessa. Then Neil's dad or mum could write theirs for the day they visit Cornwall, Mat on the day of Annis's fall or Wayne's accident, Miss Cobham during her Cornish visit and so on.

- If possible, keep the diary going as the story continues, to explore how a particular character's thinking develops or changes.
- Different groups could work on one of the diaries, creating a whole range of diaries for one day when the class pool their results.

Some children enjoyed this activity particularly, welcoming the chance to get inside a character's skin. At first, many people setting out to write Neil's diary in the first person, but basing it on my third-person narrative, began slipping out of one into the other as they wrote. It often wasn't until the entry was read aloud that this was noticed. (Reading aloud helped punctuation, too, as it always does.)

As the children became more used to the diary form, the activity flourished. The diaries began to show how characters' thinking was developing – in Neil's case, illuminating his growing relationships with other people, and plotting his inner development. For Tessa, her diary pointed up her conflicting feelings about Neil's intrusion into her life, and how she began to resolve them.

# Activity 6

*Writing letters*

### Learning objectives
- to use knowledge of the story to create letters mentioned in the text
- to develop letter-writing skills, using different tones and registers

- The children could write letters mentioned in, or suggested by the text – for example:
  - the letter from Tessa that came by fax (chapter 1, section 2 [1.2]) with the crab drawing;
  - letters between Neil and his parents once he's in Cornwall;
  - letters between Tessa and Neil's parents once Neil is in Cornwall;
  - Annis's forged absence note to the school (chapter 6.4);
  - a letter of apology from the boys to Mat Boswell for damaging the life-saving equipment (chapter 8.1), and Mat's reply.

Some children did tackle this successfully, although many saw letter writing as a chore they'd rather avoid. We weren't able to try doing the letters on computer instead of by hand, which might have helped. And, while they always jumped at the chance of role-playing an adult, writing an adult's letter seemed much more inhibiting. Perhaps they'd never read an adult's letter?

# Activity 7

*Agony aunts or uncles*

### Learning objectives
- to explore characters' problems through a magazine format
- to encourage children to view conflict from both sides

- Ask the children to write (alone or in pairs) a letter to the problem page of a magazine from a character asking for advice about their difficulties, for example:
  - Neil, just before he runs away;
  - Neil's dad or mum, after Neil has moved to Cornwall;
  - Neil, after he's lived with Tessa for some weeks;
  - Tessa, after Neil has lived with her for some weeks;
  - Annis, around the time she's truanting;
  - Mat, asking for advice about Annis.
- The children can then write the agony aunt's reply.

If the previous activity made me think letter writing was almost a dead art, this one (which we first did at the end of chapter 4) changed my mind. The art is clearly alive, flourishing in the back pages of the mags.

The agony aunt formula worked; the children forgot they disliked writing letters and wrote freely and sympathetically. If once or twice I detected a parent's hand in the aunt's reply, written for homework, I was glad, liking to think the child and parent had talked over the problems together.

Once we had letters and replies, we could role-play, say, Neil or Tessa reading their letter to 'Aunt Betsy' and listen to her replies. The conflicts became very real to us all then; the different ways people can present the same facts, and the outsider's attempt to bring about a solution. This activity above all others got children seeing through adult eyes. We never again had the single 'Neil-view' we'd started with. Gone was 'Tessa could move out.' Tessa was seen to have opinions and fears too – just as Neil had, just as his parents had. I was moved to hear children write and speak so convincingly as Tessa or Mat, Dad or Mum, often unwittingly crossing barriers of sex or age to do it.

# Activity 8

## Hot-seating

### Learning objectives
- to explore motives for behaviour
- to help children develop a sense of justice

- Ask the children to question a character (in role) about their behaviour at a particular point in the story, for example:
  - Martyn and Lee, about how they spoke to Neil on the train;
  - Neil, about running away to Cornwall without telling anyone;
  - Annis, about truanting from school and forging notes;
  - Pete/Danny/Craig, about their vandalism.

This ongoing activity was seldom planned. The opportunities just arrived while we were reading. 'I think we'd better put so-and-so in the hot-seat about that,' was all the introduction it generally needed. A chair was put out in a prominent place, a volunteer was seated, and we were away. There were always volunteers ready to take the role, and try to defend the character's actions against sometimes hostile questioning.

A development, if children are experienced and confident enough, is sometimes to bring in a second or third character. They listen to the 'hot-seater's' explanation, and are asked if they're satisfied. If not, why not? For instance, Neil's mum and dad were called in to hear him explain why he ran away without telling them (chapter 3), and Wayne Penna to hear first Pete and Danny, then Craig and lastly Neil, taking turns in the hot-seat to talk about the vandalism (chapter 5). Towards the end, again, the gender barrier melted away. One of our best hot-seating times had a boy in the seat as Annis, talking about the need to forge her father's signature (chapter 6), and how it all tied in with her mother's death.

# Activity 9

## Drama

### Learning objectives
- to bring characters to life in a dramatic form
- to explore insights into situations and dilemmas in the story

- Among many scenes of the book suggesting themselves as a basis for improvisation are:
  - Neil's encounter with Martyn and Lee (chapter 1.4);
  - his arrival at The Hermit Shell (chapter 2.4);
  - his parents' visit to Cornwall (chapter 3.5 and 3.6);
  - Tessa and Neil's conflict over chores (chapter 4.2);
  - the vandalism at the lifeboat house (chapter 5.3);
  - the accusations of 'grassing' (chapter 8.1).
- Drama could also be improvised and developed on more general themes – hiding from stress in a hermit shell, and emerging from it; joining in with, or trying to stop, anti-social behaviour; facing the dangers of the sea, for example. This calls for discussion and careful build-up, and debriefing at the end, so it needs plenty of time.

Some scenes – the Martyn and Lee encounter, and the vandalism episode especially – were hard for the children to play out without descending to a brawl. In the end we devised a more stylised structure for both. For the Underground scene we had two children forming the train doors. Their opening and closing, and their intoned 'Mind the gap' marked the parameters of the scene very successfully, I thought. For the vandalism, we used a number of children to outline the lifeboat as the boys prowled round and round it. That not only gave the boat the centrality and stillness it deserved, but it also formed a good contrast with the boys' wild behaviour. And, of course, being a door or part of a boat was not too demanding for the shy.

# Activity 10

*Artwork*

---

### Learning objective
- to use knowledge of the story to make depictions based on it

---

- This work can be ongoing. There are many possibilities, for example:
  - a pictorial map of Portmartin, with beach, harbour, lifeboat station, Penna's Café, Ship Street;
  - a cutaway picture or model of The Hermit Shell, showing the rooms on three floors;
  - the view from Neil's attic window (chapter 4.2);
  - the helicopter rescuing Annis (chapter 7.4) (get facts from RNLI);
  - Miss Cobham's poster (chapter 1.1);
  - Tessa's painting of the undersea hunt (chapter 7.5);
  - a new poster captioned 'We Make All Your Dreams Come True', showing your own choice of 'dream'.

> Painting scenes from the book, or making collages, can help children absorb the story in a quite different way from reading it. Some of our children sent for excellent information packs from the RNLI, and talked to local lifeboat crew members, and were encouraged to get the details right. The RNLI also welcomes visits to lifeboat stations.

---

# Activity 11

*Sequencing; making a time-line*

---

### Learning objectives
- to see the structure of the story by arranging the plot chronologically
- to increase understanding of cause and effect

---

- There are several ways in which the activity can be carried out:

  1. Make several sets of small cards, each card in a set bearing a key event of the book (e.g. 'Annis falls down the cliff'). Small groups then sort their jumbled set into chronological order.
  2. Group these key events beneath the chapter titles – for example, 'Neil's parents go to Cornwall' = '**All your Dreams Come True**'; 'Neil and Tessa quarrel' = '**Hanging Day**'. Discuss the chapter titles with the children. Ask:
     - What do you think they mean?
     - Did some of the titles (e.g. 'Friends', 'Dead Calm') mislead you at first?
     - When did you change your mind?
     - Why might the author want to mislead you?
  3. Make one set of A4 cards, each card carrying a key event of the book. In a circle, children are each given a card, face down. At a signal, they look at their card, display it to the rest of the group and then, **in silence**, arrange themselves in the order in which the events occur in the book, beginning the sequence at a marked point in the circle.
  4. Hang the A4 cards in order from the ceiling or along a corridor to make a time-line. Add month cards (January to July) in a different colour at the appropriate places.
  5. Make storyboards showing a particular incident (e.g. Neil getting off the Underground train; Neil arriving at The Hermit Shell; the boys running riot in Portmartin) and join them into a frieze that tells some or all of the story.

> Once the reading is finished, doing any or all of these activities refreshes the memory and helps the children to see underlying patterns in the story. They enjoyed doing number 3 particularly; its enforced silence brought out all kinds of organisational skills and the right order was quickly achieved.
>
> Once achieved, it's a good idea to run through it again, to show the cause and effect of each link – Neil gets off the tube train **because** Martyn and Lee bully him… Wayne demands the names **and so** Neil truants from school **and so** he meets Annis on the cliffs…

# Activity 12

## Alternative plot-lines

### Learning objectives
- to develop skills of conjecture
- to deepen insight into character and motives

- Use 'What if…?' questions to prompt discussion and writing, for example:

  - What if Neil had stayed on the Underground train? (chapter 1.4)
  - What if Tessa had sent him back to London? (chapter 3.6)
  - What if Neil hadn't told Wayne the boys' names? (chapter 5.4)
  - What if Neil had run away when Annis fell? (chapter 7.1)

- Discuss these questions first as a class, or in small groups. Then ask the children to write the suggested alternative version as if it had happened. They can begin by copying a sentence or two from the text at the 'take-off point' – for example:

  "Now, tell me those names and for God's sake be quick about it."
  They stared at each other for ten long seconds.
  *"No," said Neil. "I'm not going to tell you."*
  (chapter 5.4)

This activity is best done at or near the end of the reading, when children know a lot about the characters and can try creating new, feasible, turns in the plot. I think it's not an activity for everyone. But, of course, that's what makes it excellent for stretching some people's creative abilities. To do it successfully, children need to be in tune with the story, the characters' feelings, and the story-teller's voice. With help, and – most important – enough time for writers to work over and improve what they first produce (my three golden rules are: Read it aloud/Read it aloud/Read it aloud) some good efforts will appear.

# Activity 13

## Imagining the future

### Learning objectives
- to reinforce knowledge of the story
- to practise skills of conjecture

- Ask the children to talk or write about how they think the characters would be a few years after the end of the book, for example:

  - Who's living in The Hermit Shell now?
  - How are Pete and Danny, and Martyn and Lee behaving now?
  - Did Annis ever play truant again?
  - Did Tessa and Mat get married?
  - How do Neil and his parents get on now?
  - Did Neil and Craig join the Portmartin lifeboat crew when they were old enough?

Time ran out here, though we spent a few minutes discussing a possible sequel to the book, and what ought to be in it, partly because some people were a bit disturbed by my open-ended conclusion to the story. I think many children would find a lot of satisfaction in pondering some of these questions.

# Twinkle, Twinkle, Planet Blue

**Compiled by**   *Morag Styles*

**Illustrated by**   *Mario Minichiello*

**Poetry**   *An anthology on the theme of conservation*

## Description

This is a thoughtful collection of traditional and modern poetry on the theme of nature and conservation. The collection contains some poems of celebration, but most focus on preserving what is fragile and irreplaceable in the natural world. The poems take many forms: laments for what has passed; anger and defiance against unthinking destruction; telling observations and descriptions of what might be lost through negligence; songs, chants and prayers to invoke conscience and healing. Children of this age are becoming very aware of the threats to their environment, not just headline subjects like exotic endangered species but issues concerning their own neighbourhoods. These poems will chime in with their concerns, sharpening and developing them.

## Introducing the book

- Stimulate a general discussion around the terms 'conservation', 'pollution', 'green', 'endangered species', 'eco-warriors', 'global warming' and so on to share general concerns and develop key ideas and concepts within the subject.

- Explain that a book of poems such as this one contributes many different voices to the subject. These voices celebrate nature, describe it, express anger and sorrow at its destruction, tell stories about it; sing chants, hymns and songs about it; all showing how universally important the 'green' theme is.

## A choice of literacy activities

Five types of activity are suggested here. They can be used with a variety of different poems from the collection.

| Activity | Focus | Page |
|---|---|---|
| 1. | Group reading and discussion. | 136 |
| 2. | Classifying the poems in terms of their form and their approach to the 'green' theme. | 136 |
| 3. | Looking at the language of poems which use non-standard English. | 137 |
| 4. | Using some of the poems as models for the children's own poems. | 137 |
| 5. | Annotating more challenging poems. | 138 |

## Activity 1

### *Group reading and discussion*

> **Learning objectives**
> - to explore and consider a variety of styles in poetry
> - to practise oral skills (discussion and reading aloud)

- For group reading and discussion, the children will need to have the poems in front of them. If you do not have a class set of the book, the following applies only to one or two groups of up to six children.
- The poems have been grouped into eight sections. For each group reading session, ask the children to concentrate on the poems in one section. Give them **activity sheet 1** to help them frame their responses.

- If you think it is appropriate, ask the groups to prepare a presentation of the poems in the section. The children's presentations might include:
  - reading the poems aloud;
  - taking parts;
  - choral reading;
  - mime and movement.

The children could preface each poem with, 'This is a poem about...', 'It is written by...', and they could round off their presentation with an open-ended question about its content for the rest of the class to respond to.
- The audience could use the questions on **activity sheet 1** to ask the group about the poems they have presented.

---

## Activity 2

### *Classifying the poems in terms of their form and their approach to the 'green' theme*

> **Learning objectives**
> - to develop a vocabulary with which to discuss poetry
> - to understand that one poem can contain many ideas

- It will help the children to understand the poems – and the variety of poetic forms used – if they can develop a vocabulary to describe the poet's approach. **Activity sheet 2** lists 16 different words or phrases which sum up the kind of approach, language and form used in most of the poems in this collection. It will help the children to talk about the poem's purpose and the author's intentions, and will develop their knowledge of poetic forms.
- Give out activity sheet 2, one between two. Explain the following to the children:
  - notes can be made on a separate sheet of paper;

  - the activity sheet is to be used as part of the group discussion to help the children understand the poems and to learn about different language forms;
  - poems do not often fall neatly into one category but will have elements of several.
- Spend at least one whole session simply reading the following poems with the children to illustrate each of the language forms on the activity sheet (if 16 poems are too many for one session, split it into two shorter ones):
  - **a lament for things lost or passing:** 'Morning Has Broken' (p. 8); 'The Village Shop' (p. 15);
  - **a complaint; an expression of anger:** 'Song of the City' (p. 11);
  - **a private world; thoughts confided:** 'I Have an Oasis' (p. 13);
  - **a thoughtful question:** 'Landscape' (p. 12);
  - **defiance:** 'I Won't Hatch' (p. 9);
  - **enjoyment; fun; delight in nature:** 'Raw Food' (pp. 16–17);
  - **a telling observation or description:** 'Haiku Moment' (p. 18);
  - **advice:** 'Be Like the Bird' (p. 20);
  - **a celebration:** 'Thrush' (p. 21);

- **an atmospheric description (usually of a place):** 'The Way through the Woods' (p. 27);
- **contains a powerful image:** 'The Rainflower' (p. 26);
- **contains a powerful idea:** 'The Whisper' (p. 32);
- **a prayer, hymn, song, chant or rap:** 'A Bright Future?' (p. 38);
- **amazing metaphors:** 'Whale Poems' (pp. 48–49);
- **a story:** 'My Mother Saw a Dancing Bear' (p. 57);
- **a plea to preserve:** 'Chicken Dinner' (p. 58).

- To illustrate how poems may include elements from more than one category, read 'Space Dog Remembers' (p. 65) and point out – or ask the children to point out – that it is a story, confides thoughts, has a powerful image (the first dog in orbit) and a thoughtful question (i.e. 'Was it worth it?').

# Activity 3

***Looking at the language of poems which use non-standard English***

### Learning objectives

- to understand that there are many dialects of English and that poetry can be written in any dialect
- to appreciate the sound values of non-standard dialects

- The following poems are written in non-standard English: 'For Forest' (p. 29); 'A Song for England' (p. 35); 'Up in the Morning Early' (p. 36); 'Baby-K Rap Rhyme' (pp. 40–41); 'All You Sea' (p. 44); 'Jamaican Song' (p. 54); 'Chicken Dinner' (p. 58); 'Christmas Wise' (p. 64); 'Blowin' in the Wind' (p. 68).

- For pronunciation, native speakers or those with an intimate knowledge of the accent and dialect are the best people to read these poems aloud and to teach the children about the language.
- Failing that, the children can look for clues in the spelling, syntax and punctuation of the poem for ways into the pronunciation. Tapes of speakers talking or reading in the appropriate dialect can also be a great help.
- Dialect phrases can be glossed in standard English terms.
- You could try 'translating' the whole poem into standard English. What has been lost in the translation in terms of sound, rhythm and meaning?
- One poem – Robert Burns's 'Up in the Morning Early' – can be found on **activity sheet 3** for photocopying and annotating (see *Activity 5* below).

# Activity 4

***Using some of the poems as models for the children's own poems***

### Learning objectives

- to write creatively, using a model
- to recognise and understand the elements of several poetic forms

- At this stage in their writing career the children will have had a good introduction to the writing of

poetry in different forms. Given that the 'green' theme is one which interests them, the opportunities for writing poems on the subject, using the forms they have been introduced to, are obvious. However, you might want to use some of the poems in the book as models to extend children's poetry-writing skills. The following list offers models which the children can 'borrow' to write their own poems:
- **question and answer form:** 'Landscape' (p. 12);
- **haiku:** 'Haiku Moment' (p. 18);
- **prayer:** 'The Prayer of the Little Bird' (p. 19);

- **'Be like the...':** 'Be Like the Bird' (p. 20). The children begin their poem with this phrase but substitute another animal.
- **'Trees are great, they...':** 'Trees Are Great' (p. 23). The children substitute another subject from nature.
- **an atmospheric description:** 'Pine Forest' (p. 25). The children write an atmospheric description of a place, concentrating on its unique elements: How does this place make them feel? What do they remember most clearly about it? How is it different from any other place?

- **rewriting a well-known song or hymn:** 'Harvest Hymn' (p. 10) or 'A Bright Future?' (p. 38);
- **rap:** 'Baby-K Rap Rhyme' (pp. 40–41) paying attention to the repetitive and rhythmic style of rap;
- **song:** 'Blowin' in the Wind' (p. 68) using a strict verse form and an appropriate chorus or refrain;
- **chant:** 'I Sing for the Animals' (p. 52) trying to capture the solemn, ceremonial style of the chant, perhaps using repeated lines to emphasise important issues;
- **reincarnation:** 'Elephant' (p. 66). Which animal would the children like to be reincarnated as?

# Activity 5

## *Annotating more challenging poems*

### Learning objectives
- to practise the skill of annotation
- to develop understanding of difficult concepts and language

- This activity will have most impact when used with more complex and challenging poems, although differentiation can easily be achieved by varying the choice of poem.
- If the children have not yet used annotation as a technique for recording responses to a poem in group discussion, then you will need to explain the process. Explain that parts of poems can be difficult, or use unusual words or phrases; they are often ambiguous in meaning, open to different interpretations, and only yield up meaning after a lot of discussion. Some responses remain in the form of questions waiting to be resolved.

- The technique is simple. Having written or typed onto the word-processor the poem they are going to annotate, the children circle words or underline lines and phrases which merit discussion. In the margins around the poem they record:
  - ideas about meaning ('Perhaps this means..., or it could mean...');
  - personal reactions ('This is brilliant!' or 'This makes me shiver.');
  - questions ('Does this mean...?');
  - definitions of words ('This word means...');
  - notes on how it should be read aloud ('Quiet, slow bit.' or 'Emphasise this.').

  Write these options on the board or on a sheet of paper for the group to use as a guide.
- Use **activity sheet 3** to demonstrate the approach.
- The advantage of using the word-processor to annotate a poem is that children can interpolate their own notes into the body of the poem, perhaps using capitals or a different font.

# Twinkle, Twinkle, Planet Blue    Activity sheet 1

Name _____    Date _____

When you have read a section of poems, use questions 1 and 2
below to help you discuss your responses. Try to give reasons
for all your answers.

1.  Which poem in the section did you:
    - like best?
    - find the most thought-provoking?
    - think had the most interesting form?
    - like least?
    - wonder about?
    - think said the most about conservation?

2.  What images and lines did you particularly
    admire?

# Twinkle, Twinkle, Planet Blue     Activity sheet 2

Name _____     Date _____

Once you have read the poems in a section, use this sheet to help you
decide what sort of poem each one is. Some poems are best described
by one box, other poems by more than one box.

| | | |
|---|---|---|
| a lament for things lost or passing | a complaint; an expression of anger | a private world; thoughts confided |
| a thoughtful question | defiance | enjoyment; fun; delight in nature |
| a telling observation or description | advice | a celebration |
| an atmospheric description, (usually of a place) | contains a powerful image | contains a powerful idea |
| a prayer, hymn, song, chant or rap | amazing metaphors | a story |
| Write here any types you have discovered for yourself. | | a plea to preserve |

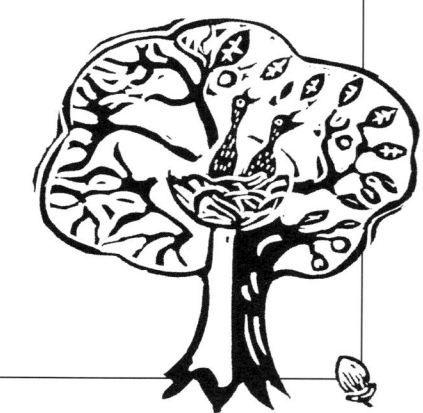

© Cambridge University Press 1999     Original artwork by Mario Minichiello

# Twinkle, Twinkle, Planet Blue   Activity sheet 3

Name _____   Date _____

Underline words and phrases in dialect and write in the
margin what you think they mean.

### Up in the Morning Early

Cauld blaws the wind frae east to west,

The drift is driving sairly;

Sae loud and shrill's I hear the blast,

I'm sure it's winter fairly.


Up in the morning's no for me,

Up in the morning early;

When a' the hills are cover'd wi' snaw,

I'm sure it's winter fairly.


The birds sit chittering in the thorn,

A' day they fare but sparely;

And lang's the night frae e'en to morn,

I'm sure it's winter fairly.


Up in the morning's no for me,

Up in the morning early;

When a' the hills are cover'd wi' snaw,

I'm sure it's winter fairly.


*Robert Burns*

141

# Whisked Away

**Author**   *Richard Brown*

**Illustrators**   *Robina Green, Jackie Morris, Shevanthi de Silva, Polly Noakes*

**Poetry**   *A collection of poems for more than one voice, originally published as part of Talk Poetry*

## Description

This book of poems covers many subjects and uses a variety of different forms. It has proved popular in schools (including at Key Stage 3), particularly in the context of group reading and poetry performances. Most of the poems have been written especially for more than one voice; the rest have different voices suggested for different parts of the poem.

The introduction to the book (pp. 4–5) suggests three ways to enjoy the poems with others. The first is exploring and practising ways to read a poem aloud in a group. The second gives six key questions to prompt discussion. The third suggests that the poems are rather like mini-plays which can be performed. Detailed suggestions on performing each poem are given at the back of the book.

There is a companion volume, *The Midnight Party*, at the Independent Reading phase of **Cambridge Reading.**

## Using the poems

The poems can be enjoyed in a number of ways, for example:

- for reading to the class, treating them as poems for one voice;
- for use in a shared reading to the class, you and some of the children combining to present the poem;
- for individual reading;
- for pairs to read aloud and discuss informally;
- for groups to read aloud and discuss more formally (read the introduction with the group at the outset, and use the key questions on p. 5);
- for rehearsed performances, using the notes at the back of the book.

### Performing the poems

Pages 49–50 of the book contain general questions and detailed advice on performing the poems. If the performance of the poems is going to be a major literacy activity for the class, it is worth spending some time talking through these pages with the whole class. (Brief performance notes on the individual poems follow on pp. 51–56.)

### Writing ideas

In addition to the performance element, the poems can act as models or prompts for the children's own writing. Here are some suggestions for writing activities on specific poems.

### 'The Elements Reminisce' (pp. 6–7)
### Writing a poem based on the original

- Ask the children to write their own version of the Creation, using the four elements to organise their poems. For example, you could ask, 'How was Earth created?' (or Air, or Fire, or Water). The children should then make up their own scenario for each one. Alternatively, pairs could work on different elements and then put their poems together to make a group poem.

### 'A Creature to Sum Up Creation' (pp. 8–10)
### Writing a poem based on the original

- Ask the children to write their own variation of this poem. It needs to be done in three parts.

**Part 1:** from the beginning down to 'salmon leapt'. The children should change the verbs in each verse. So, for example, instead of 'flowers teemed', you might have 'flowers flourished'; instead of 'trees stretched', you might have 'trees soared'.

**Part 2:** from 'Unmade' down to 'But what should they be like/inside themselves?' Brainstorm a different set of animals. For each animal, the two-line verse can follow the pattern used in the poem (i.e. 'They should have...').

**Part 3:** from 'They should have shyness...' to the end. Brainstorm another set of animals and ask the children what special quality each one suggests. Once again, they should follow the pattern of the original to complete the poem.

### 'The Future' (pp. 11–13)
### Responding to written questions

- Part of the poem is reproduced on **activity sheet 1**. Pairs or small groups should discuss their answers before writing them in the spaces provided.

### 'Whisked Away' (pp. 14–16)
### Story writing (science fiction or horror)

- This poem could provide the stimulus for a science-fiction or horror story which explains what happened prior to the events described. Ask the children what they think came to the village and why, and what happened to make it deserted.

### 'Pink Flamingos' (pp. 17–19)
### Deducing the moral of the poem

- Ask the children to write what they think is the message or moral of this fable. You could suggest a two-part framework:
  - 'I think this story tells us that...'
  - 'This is because...'

### 'Aunt and Uncle's Travels' (pp. 20–21)
### Writing a free verse poem

- Ask the children to imagine something unusual, exciting and wish-fulfilling at 'the rainbow's end', and then try to describe it in a free verse poem.

### 'One Christmas Eve' (pp. 22–25)
### Comparing versions of the Christmas story

- The children could match individual verses to their corresponding parts in other versions of the Christmas story, from the Authorised Version of the Bible to modern picture book retellings. Then, they can compare and discuss the similarities and differences between the approaches, considering why the various authors chose to write as they did. What audience did each one have in mind?

- They could also discuss the child's question, 'Why do you come now,/why to me...' and the meaning of the reply (p. 25).

### 'Hey, Little Pond Skater' (pp. 27–29)
### Writing a poem based on a model

- The children could write a poem on one of the themes of the poem – the contrast between being in the pond and being above it. They could use an alternating verse framework, for example:

Down below
all is dark, murky with seaweed...

Up above
all is light, sunlight glancing...

### 'What the Trees Say' (pp. 30–31)
### Poetry writing in the form of a monologue

- Ask the children to write a 'tree monologue' (i.e. the thoughts of a tree) reflecting the theme of the poem. Brainstorm with the children a list of different tree locations, from the paradise of the wild wood where there is no apparent threat, to the lone tree beside a busy road or a dying tree in a parched garden. The children can then choose a tree from this list to write about.

### 'Headlines of a Very Ordinary Day' (pp. 32–34)
### Writing a poem based on a model

- Ask the children to use this poem as a model for a similar poem of their own. The first task is to describe an ordinary day in undramatic language, leaving space between each sentence for the headline version. (You might prefer to do this stage as a whole-class activity.) The second is to 'hype' each part of the day using newspaper-style headlines.

- Discuss the language of headlines: the use of adjectives like 'miraculous' and 'brilliant'; the use of strong verbs like 'stuns' and 'fights'; the use of categories of people such as 'explorer', 'linguist', 'top selectors' and 'vegetarians'; and the use of clichés such as 'a cert', 'meat lobby', 'throw in the towel' and 'brainwashes'.

### 'The Dinner Report' (p. 35)
### Writing a poem based on a model

- The preamble to the poem asks whether the children can describe their own family in the language of a weather report. See if they can take up the challenge. To get the children going, brainstorm a list of phrases commonly used in weather forecasting.

### 'What Shall we Do with Jason?' (pp. 36–37)
### Options for personal writing, letter writing or scripting a dialogue

- You could give the children a number of writing ideas sparked off by this poem and let them choose one.

  1. Write about a sadness in your own life. Say what happened, how you felt, how your feelings changed over time and how you view the cause of the sadness now.
  2. Jason has written to the letters page of a magazine asking for advice on how to cope with his grandad's death. What would you write in reply?
  3. Write a dialogue between Jason's mum and his step-father. She is sympathetic and protective of her son; he is unsympathetic and thinks that Jason is over-reacting.

### 'Give Us a Job' (pp. 38–39)
### Writing verses of a group poem based on the original

- Ask the children to write further outlandish 'wanted' adverts in the four-line rhyming form used in the poem. Put the best ones together to make a group or class poem to be chanted using the poem's existing refrain.

### 'Traveller's Child' (pp. 39–42)
### Writing verses of a group poem based on the original

- The children could use this poem as a model for a group poem, using the idea of multiple viewpoints. Work with a group or the whole class to create a child character, paying particular attention to their home circumstances, their clothes, their personality and the way they relate to other children. Alternatively, you could use a character from a novel currently being enjoyed by all the children.
- List words on the board which sum up a basic attitude to the child or a viewpoint (e.g. love, hate, envy, jealousy, desire for friendship, admiration, puzzlement, fear, shyness). Each child should then choose one of these words as the theme for their verse, to be written in free verse and in the first person, as in the original. The best of the verses can be put together to make a group poem.

### 'Jack-a-Penny' (pp. 43–45)
### Reflecting on the experience of writing a poem

- Discuss the poem with the children; talk in particular about why Jack buried the coin when he was a boy and why he is now obsessive about it. Now return to the introductory note. It gives a glimpse into the creative process.
- To stimulate a discussion, ask: 'Where do poems come from?' Then ask the children to write a short piece explaining how they approach poetry writing, for example:

  – Where do ideas come from?
  – Is poetry writing a struggle?
  – Do the children have a favourite form (free verse, rhyme)?
  – What does it feel like to write a poem that other people enjoy?

  You could brainstorm a list of more questions like this to help the children get started.

### 'Granny and Child' (pp. 46–47)
### Options for writing persuasively or imaginatively, exploring points of view

- The introductory note asks if there is something a little strange about Granny. Make this the theme of a piece of writing in two parts. The first part begins, 'I think Granny is...' and sets out what the reader thinks about Granny, based on the evidence in the poem. The second part begins, 'I think the girl is...' and sets out the reader's view of her. Alternatively, the two parts could be written in the first person, reflecting the thoughts of the two characters after the light has been turned out.

### 'Nightmare' (p. 48)
### Discussion of what the poem might be about

- This is a potentially disturbing poem. You might want to ask the children to say what they think is happening – for example, why the girl is frightened and who is coming up the stairs. If you do, be prepared for possible revelations: the poem could be about child abuse.

# Whisked Away    Activity sheet 1

Name _____    Date _____

Read this extract from 'The Future' by Richard Brown.
Discuss the questions and then write down your answers.

**First son**
I'll build a castle
of crystal glass,
our secrets open
to all who pass.

**Second son**
I'll ride horses
through the foam of the sea,
in the moonlight a-riding,
just phantoms and me.

**Third son**
I'll grow a garden
so secret and tall
tongues will whisper
beyond its great wall.

**Fourth son**
I'll draw a map
of an island unknown
where thoughts are reflected
in each polished stone.

**Fifth son**
And I shall plant
on the tallest peak
our family's motto:
"Horizons we seek."

**Father**
And you, my youngest,
where will you go?
Nothing you say, yet
your wits are not slow.

**Sixth son**
I'll keep this house
where our memories are.
Who'll tend your grave
with the family so far?
I'll take my journeys
through the lands of the mind,
no shortage of wonders or
treasures I'll find.
So father, be sure,
we'll discover ourselves,
with angels and monsters
and mischievous elves.

1.  Who gave the most interesting answer?

    _____

2.  Who gave the most mysterious answer?

    _____

3.  Which son is the most

    romantic?_____

    secretive? _____

    thoughtful? _____

    honest?_____

    shy?_____

    imaginative? _____

    family-orientated? _____

4.  Which son's answer best matches what you
    would have said in the same situation? Why?

    _____

    _____

5.  What does 'discover ourselves' mean?

    _____

    _____

# Author profiles

## Judy Cumberbatch

Author of *Sandstorm*

Judy was born in England but spent her childhood in Ghana. After going to university, she taught English in several countries in the Arab world. She now lives in London and works as a journalist and television researcher, as well as writing children's books.

### What was it like growing up in Ghana?

Ghana was a great place to grow up. We had lots of pets, everything from an iguana lizard to a pair of owls and a hedgehog which lived under the bath. There were also nasty things like snakes and scorpions. One day a whacking great python got into the hen house and ate my pet hen!

### Did you like reading? What was your favourite book?

I've always loved reading. We had a travelling library, which called every three months. I was allowed fourteen books. I would read the lot in the first couple of weeks and then have to read them over and over until the library called again. I used to love *Swallows and Amazons* and their adventures on boats. We lived in a very dry part of Ghana which didn't have any rivers and certainly no boats, and I've wanted to have a little boat ever since. That's what I like about books. You can travel with them and meet lots of different people and do things you wouldn't normally do.

### When did you decide you wanted to be a writer?

When I was about ten I decided I wanted to be a journalist. Being a journalist is very different from writing fiction, because you have to write about what has actually happened. So when I started writing fiction, I felt very free. I could just write what I wanted without someone standing over my shoulder saying, 'That didn't happen. That's not true.'

### Do you like being a writer?

Sometimes writing comes very easily and then it's the nicest job in the world. Other times, it's like having a headache all day long. The worst thing about being a writer is getting your manuscript back from the publishers with a polite letter saying they don't want to publish it. All the writers I know have very acute hearing and recognise the particular thud of a manuscript dropping on the doormat first thing in the morning.

### Where did you get the idea for *Sandstorm*?

I don't know how I came to think of *Sandstorm*. I wish I could tell you that I was standing in the middle of the British Museum looking at an Egyptian mirror and suddenly became inspired. But it didn't work like that. I've always been fascinated by mirrors and I've always wanted to travel in time, so I suppose the two things came together, and the idea gradually evolved.

When I started writing the book, I did actually go to the British Museum and I read quite a lot about Ancient Egypt. I even found the mummy of a girl called Tet, which sent shivers up and down my back, as this was *after* I had decided on my character's name, Teti! I also got to hold an Ancient Egyptian mirror, which was very exciting, but I didn't see any strange faces in it!

# Rosalind Kerven

Author of *Sorcery and Gold, In the Court of the Jade Emperor* and *Earth Magic, Sky Magic*

Rosalind lives in a stone cottage in the wild hill country of Northumberland with her husband, two school-age daughters and a beautiful rough collie dog. She has been writing children's books professionally since 1980.

## How do you write?

I work regular hours each day in my study, but the most important and time-consuming part of any project is done away from there, in my head. That can happen any time, any place, but most often when I'm out walking, relaxing in a hot bath, or dropping off to sleep. By the time I sit down at my desk, I know almost exactly what I'm going to write: the words come tumbling out.

I always write a first draft in longhand, scribble corrections and revisions all over it, then type it on my word-processor, print it out and revise it another four or five times. Finally I read it aloud and make further changes to make it sound more natural.

## Where did you get the ideas for *Sorcery and Gold*?

For a long time, I've been fascinated by the independently minded women and men of the Viking Age, and also by the stunning Icelandic landscape. I started to research the Norse settlers' archaeology, history and literature. I grew increasingly intrigued by all these facts and ideas, until they crystallised into my own dreaming of the long-lost world that you'll find in *Sorcery and Gold*.

## Why do you write historical novels?

I believe we need stories that lift us right out of the confines of our everyday world, stories that really exercise and stretch our imaginations. Someone who's never learnt to use their imagination is severely handicapped when they're confronted by new situations or people as they move through life. Going back to a distant period of history frees a writer from all the constraints of a contemporary setting. You can send your child characters on blood-curdling adventures that really test their inner resources without having to worry about whether it's 'suitable' or realistic. You can introduce the most sinister adult characters and the scariest situations, but because they're so remote, the reader doesn't feel seriously threatened by them. And you can explore a strange world where every detail is exotic and fascinating.

## Does retelling myths and legends require different skills from writing a historical novel?

In many ways, the skills are the same. Firstly, you need an imagination vivid enough to immerse yourself easily into any totally different culture. The other vital skill is the ability to make words work in whatever way you need – to adapt your style to the particular culture and story.

But retelling myths, legends and folk tales also requires a very special approach. You have to remember that they are like priceless antiques: some of these stories are hundreds or even thousands of years old. You can't escape your responsibilities to the original tellers. You have to be true to the plot, respect the characters and be faithful to the culture from which the story comes. Most importantly, you have to care about the story and spare no effort in making today's audience enthralled by it, so that, in turn, they will remember it and want to pass it on for the next generation.

# Nell Marshall

Author of *Letters to Henrietta*

Nell was born in 1936 in India, where her parents were missionaries. In 1946 she went to boarding school in England and for the next three years she didn't see her parents or her two younger sisters. When she left school she returned to India, where she met her husband Geoffrey. They got married in 1957 and lived in Madras and Bangalore for the next twelve years. Since 1970 they have lived in England, in a 300-year-old house. Once Nell's children had all started school she did a history degree and became a secondary school teacher, which she loved. Since she retired she has helped to set up a museum in her home town of St Neots in Cambridgeshire.

### Did you like reading when you were younger?

Yes, I loved it. I was very upset when my favourite copy *of Snow White and the Seven Dwarfs* got eaten by white ants in India, but I still have my copies of *Black Beauty* and *Little Women*.

### Why did you decide to write *Letters to Henrietta*?

My father-in-law Henry lived with us until his death in 1981, and it was his stories about his childhood in the vicarage at Sutton, and then his time in the First World War, that led to *Letters to Henrietta*. I was very keen that his experiences and memories, and also those of my own parents, should be passed on to my children.

### Do you tell a lot of family stories?

Well, I have eight grandchildren who all love to hear stories about when their parents were little! My mother is 88 and she is currently writing about her life in India so that all her memories and experiences will not die with her.

### Will you write another book about your family?

Maybe! I have a vast hoard of family letters, including some from the Second World War and some from the eighteenth century. There are lots more family stories waiting to be told...

# Judith O'Neill

Author of *Spindle River*

Judith was born in Australia. Her eight great-grandparents sailed to Australia from England, Ireland or Scotland between 1840 and 1860. She grew up in Mildura, a town on the Murray River. As a result, she loves rivers and often writes about them in her stories. In 1964, she and her husband, John, and their three young daughters came to live in Cambridge in England. There Judith wrote two history books for schools (one about her convict ancestors) and later taught English in a Cambridge secondary school. At last, when she was 49, she began to do what she most wanted – to write novels for children. She and John now live in Edinburgh in Scotland, where they hope to stay.

## Did you read and write a lot when you were younger?

Yes, I devoured books and wrote a lot of stories and poems. We had plenty of books at home and there was a very good children's library in Mildura. I read with a torch under the bedclothes too.

## What sort of things do you like reading?

I love reading novels – the great stories from the past and new stories written today. I love reading Shakespeare (out loud) and lots of poetry. I like reading history books, and the lives of interesting people, newspapers, cookery books and the Bible.

## How did you get the idea for *Spindle River*?

The seed of the idea came from a very good history teacher I had in Australia when I was 13. Her name was Miss Anne Hooper. She gave some brilliant lessons on Robert Owen and New Lanark. Those lessons stayed in my mind for more than 40 years. When I came to live in Scotland, I went straight to see New Lanark and the Falls of Clyde. I loved the place and I knew that I wanted to set a story there in the lifetime of Robert Owen.

## What kind of research did you have to do before you wrote your story?

I went to New Lanark many times and explored the magnificent mills. I walked up to the Falls on the Clyde again and again. I watched badgers there. I read every book I could find on the early history of New Lanark. I asked for advice from historians, from industrial archaeologists, from the Education Officer at New Lanark, from wildlife experts, from people in museums who could show me how spinning machines work and from Scots speakers who could help me with the language. The research took me a year and the writing took me another year. They were two happy years.

# 3

# PART THREE: Resources for further work

# Text-based activities to develop literacy: a planning tool

When planning activities and schemes of work around the books in *Cambridge Reading*, the authors and contributors found the following list of teaching ideas and approaches useful for reference. It is likely that you will want to devise your own work around texts which are not in the scheme and would find this list equally helpful.

When deciding which activities are going to be the most appropriate, you will need to take several factors into account, for example:

- the degree to which the activity enhances children's understanding of and engagement with the text;
- the extent to which the activity develops children's literacy skills;
- the children's likely response to the activity;
- the levels of skill, prior knowledge and maturity needed by the children to make the activity successful;
- the opportunities for differentiation of outcome;
- how often the activity has been done before;
- whether the activity is best suited to class, group, pair or individual response;
- classroom organisation and the amount of teacher input required;
- the time you have available.

## Agony aunts

Children examine and discuss examples of problem page letters in magazines (vet them first for suitability!). They then use the form as a model to write a similar letter from the point of view of a character in a story who has a personal problem. Another child could play the role of agony aunt and attempt to answer the letter.

## Alternative plot-lines

Authors constantly make choices about how the story should proceed. This implies that it could have developed differently. Children can be asked: 'What if so and so had done this instead of that?' or 'What else might have happened at this point?'

## Annotation

Children are given a short text (e.g. extract or poem) copied in the centre of a large sheet of paper. They discuss it in small groups, writing annotations in the space around the text – notes, queries, suggestions –

to help them record their exploratory responses to it. In the process, **underlining** and **highlighting** may be used. The annotations then provide the basis for a follow-up discussion with the teacher, either directly with the group or as part of reporting back in a class review of the text.

## Art briefs

This activity is based on the approach which most artists take when illustrating a text. Children write a description of how they would like a passage in the text to be illustrated. Another child then uses this brief to draw an 'art rough' or outline which is then evaluated by the first child. The second child then acts on these comments to create the finished illustration.

## Audio cassettes

The story can be recorded by the children in various ways, from a straight reading to a dramatised retelling with character parts.

Group discussion of a text can also be recorded for assessment opportunities.

## Before that...

The children could try retelling a story backwards, starting from the end or from a particular episode, and 'rewinding the narrative'. Each bit of the retelling begins with the words 'Before that...'. This is particularly good for circle retellings.

## Beginnings

Children examine critically the opening passages of a story and determine the criteria by which it should be judged.

- Does it make you want to read the rest of the story and, if so, how?
- Does it give essential information in an interesting and natural way?
- What expectations does it set up about the rest of the story?

Chapter beginnings could also be examined.

- Why did the author choose to start a new chapter here?
- Has time passed? How can you tell?
- How does what's happening in this new chapter fit in with the rest of the story? (Look for clues like 'Meanwhile...' or 'In another part of the wood...'.)

## Blurbs

With the children, study the art of the blurb.

- How is the blurb written?
- What is it for?
- How much does it tell you about the story?
- Does it make you want to read the book?
- Does it make the story sound better than it really is?
- How else could it have been written?
- How does it compare with other blurbs?

Children could then go on to write a blurb for the next story they read. They could also write blurbs for their own stories.

## Book awards

Over a period of time, children compile a classroom chart which records their 'awards' to books for particular strengths, for example ratings for humour, suspense, originality, style, interest. The criteria can be chosen by the children themselves.

## Book covers

Groups comment critically on the book cover, both before the text is read (e.g. What does it tell us? Looking at the cover, what kind of story do you expect? Does it make you want to read the book?), and after (Was it the best scene to illustrate? What other picture could have been used? Did it give anything away?).

Children could design a new book cover.

## Book reviews

Develop book review formats which reflect different aspects of the book (e.g. theme, plot, genre, characters, mood, settings, language, possibilities for adaptations), allowing for a variety of critical and personal responses. Let the children choose book review formats which best reflect what they want to say about the book, and build in opportunities for sharing the review with others.

## Bubbles

Select a short scene with dialogue. Write out the conversation in speech bubbles. Then, alongside the speech bubbles, write corresponding thought bubbles. This activity can often reveal two simultaneous levels of meaning – the public utterance and the contrasting private thought. For example, 'How nice you look!' is the speech, but the thought might be 'What a ghastly dress!'

## Chapter titles

If the book has chapter titles, discuss them before and after the reading.

- Judging by the chapter title, what do you expect to read about in this chapter?
- Are the titles helpful/misleading?
- What information do they give?

If chapter titles are not given, ask the children to suggest some.

## Character exploration

There are many ways to do this. For example, surround a drawing of the character with the words which best describe them. These words can then be classified in various ways (e.g. good and bad points, aspirations, hidden talents, problems). Compare characters, bringing out differences and similarities. Use relationship diagrams (see 'Sociograms', p. 155) and word-webs. Complete open-ended sentences about the character. Create scenarios and speculate on what the character would do in that situation.

## Close readings

A close reading looks at how individual items of vocabulary, the use of punctuation, spacing and so on affect the meaning of the text. There may be passages of a narrative where a close reading would greatly benefit the children's understanding of the wider text. Provide a photocopy of the passage with wide margins for annotation, or reproduce it on an OHP. Poems in particular often need close readings. Encourage underlining or highlighting, and annotation.

## Clues

We often ask children to find evidence to back up statements, for example about a character or an event. Children find it easier to do this if they understand that they are looking for *clues* to something, for example when they are asked, 'How do we know...?' or, 'What really happened...?' or told 'Let's play detective!'

## Comparisons

Compare two versions of the same story. This is particularly useful when you are working on a traditional story which may exist in a number of different versions.

## Comprehension questions

These are often seen as a dull and ineffective way of responding to a text, but they may have a place if the questions are for discussion, exploring areas where *understanding* is seen as the main objective rather than simply a written response.

## Connections

Children can be encouraged to make connections between the story or poem and the wider world, including their own lives. For example, you can ask, 'Has this ever happened to you or to someone you know?' or, 'Does this remind you of anything?' or, 'What other books have you read by this author?'

## Conversations

Children write the characters' names on slips of paper and mix them up. They then draw out two names (either at random or by conscious choice) and write a conversation which the two characters might have had at a specific point in the story.

## Cue-questions

Choose a key word which is relevant to the story you are exploring. (Key words are descriptive, e.g. 'happy', 'angry', 'worried', 'in authority', 'secretive', 'dishonest'.) Write the key word in the centre of a piece of paper. Than place around it five question cards in sequence: 'Who?' 'Why?' 'When?' 'Which caused what?' 'What was the result?'

## Decisions

Children focus on a character who has just made an important decision. They then discuss the following questions about that decision:

- What decision was made?
- Why did the character make the decision?
- What were the character's intentions?
- Do you think it was the right decision for the character in the circumstances?
- Could the character have made another decision at that point which would have been just as good or better?
- What were the immediate consequences of the decision?
- What long-term consequences can be traced back to this decision? (This is obviously a more sophisticated question for more advanced readers.)

## Diaries (and journals)

These can take several forms, for example:

- the child's own reflections and ideas, written as the story unfolds;
- the diary of a character in a story (before, during and after the narrative);
- a whole-class or group diary where the writing of the text is shared.

## Frieze

Build up a sequence of pictures as the narrative unfolds. Each picture could be done by a different child, with quotes and captions added (or quiz questions attached). Link to a **time-line** if appropriate.

## Genre switch

Take one genre and turn it into another – for example, a story adapted as a playscript, a narrative event represented as a news report, or Walter de la Mare's famously atmospheric poem 'The Listeners' rewritten as a ghost story.

## Hot-seating

A child (or teacher) takes on the role of one of the characters; the rest of the group or class questions them.

## Illustration

Encourage children to compare and contrast different illustrative styles, especially in picture books. Ask key questions, for example:

- How much does the picture add to the story?
- What other picture could the artist have used for this bit of the story?
- What does the picture make you think and feel?
- Why was this particular point in the story chosen for this picture?

(See also 'Art briefs', p. 151 and 'Storyboarding', p. 155.)

## Interviews

These can take several forms, for example:

- an interview with a child in character (e.g. to discover motives and viewpoint);
- an interview with the author or illustrator;
- an interview with the teacher (e.g. 'Why did you choose this book?');
- a child-to-child interview (e.g. 'What do you think of this book/passage/action?').

(See also 'Hot-seating'.)

### Letters

These can take several forms, for example:

- a letter between characters in the story;
- a letter between child and character (see also 'Agony aunts', p. 151);
- a letter between schools;
- a letter to the author or illustrator. (Don't expect every letter to be answered and, as a courtesy, include a stamped, addressed envelope.) If possible, it is best to link this to an author/ illustrator visit.

### Literary fibs

The teacher makes false statements about a text. (Inferential fibs are more challenging than literal ones.) Children discuss them and provide what they consider to be the correct statements, backing them up by reference to relevant passages in the text.

### Map-making

Children can transform textual information (e.g. characters' journeys, story settings) into maps to help them visualise important information and to act as a future reference point (e.g. a map of the island in *The Tempest*). Maps can be annotated as the story unfolds.

### Media celebrity

Characters in stories can be given 'media treatment' in the style of a magazine spread. Give the children plenty of examples of the form as a model for their work.

### Narrative gaps

Authors make skilful use of gaps in narrative to develop pace and, perhaps more importantly, to allow space for the reader's imagination. They are the hidden parts of the story. Children can be asked to speculate on what might have happened in these gaps, perhaps attempting to write sections of the 'missing' narrative themselves in the style of the author.

### News

An episode or narrative can be scripted and presented by children as a TV, radio or newspaper report.

### Personal response

Children can be encouraged to say in discussion and writing how they respond to the story, for example:

- whether it reminds them of something in their own lives;
- their feelings about and insights into the text;
- critical judgements or preferences about characters;
- reflections of a moral or spiritual nature.

### Play scripts

Short stories, picture books and scenes from a novel can be rewritten by the children as play scripts for audio recording or acting. Familiarity with the form helps a great deal in getting this going.

### Points of view

Where a story or episode is told from one character's point of view, it could be retold by the children from another character's point of view. For example, a third-person narrative could be turned into a first-person one, or vice versa.

### Prediction

Children make predictions about the story:

- *Before reading*: on the basis of clues given by the cover, the blurb and reviews of the book.
- *During reading*: what will happen next, based on the clues supplied by the author.
- *After reading*: the children continue the story where the author left off.

### Retellings

Orally, perhaps before a reading (to recap 'the story so far'), or after a reading; occasionally in writing.

### Sequencing

In pairs, children identify the main points of a narrative, write each point on a slip of paper or card, mix them up and then ask another pair who know the story to sequence it correctly. Children will soon discover that to make the task more difficult, the points need to be expressed indirectly. For example, not 'John fell down the ravine and broke his leg', but 'Something terrible happened to John and he was in agony.'

## Sociograms

Children can construct flexible spider-charts showing the relationship between characters. Names of characters are written on counters and positioned on a sheet of paper in relation to other characters. Then lines are drawn between the characters. The children then write along the lines the chief characteristics of the relationship, for example love, hate, greed, indifference.

## Storyboarding

Children translate a text into a sequence of drawings to show how a camera would represent it visually.

More generally, the story can be retold in a series of pictures with captions, perhaps made into a book.

## Structure

Explore how short stories and picture books are structured. Use key words and phrases such as **opening** (how?), **orientation** (where, who, what?), **inciting moment** (what gets the story moving?), **development of the main action**, **sub-plot** (if there is one), **dénouement**, **climax**, **resolution**. The use of such terms will help the children recognise and describe the way the story is structured. Also use words like **theme**, **character**, **suspense**, **pace**, **narrative gaps**, **element of surprise**.

The problem-solving model is often used in stories too. This is easier to explain and recognise than the model outlined above and is therefore more suitable for less experienced readers.

(See also 'Time-lines' below.)

## Thought-tracking

Thought-tracking is especially appropriate for stories where characters' inner experiences are left to the reader's imagination, for example in many traditional stories (myths, legends, folk and fairy tales). Children are asked to consider what a character is thinking and feeling at various points in the story. This can be done informally through discussion, or it can be a written exercise (e.g. the character's key actions are listed on one side of a sheet of paper, with space on the other side for the child to write down what the character is thinking and feeling at this point). In picture books, Post-it notes can be used, with the child writing the character's thoughts in thought bubbles.

Thought-tracking is often used in drama.

## Time-lines

Individual children (or the whole class) draw up a time-line to show how events link in a linear sequence. This may be done either as the narrative unfolds or after reading the story. It acts as a useful *aide-mémoire* for the class and helps to show how the story is structured. Large time-lines can be displayed in class and developed as the story progresses.

## Transported

Children imagine that they have been transported (or 'beamed down' as in *Star Trek*) to a scene in a story. They have to describe what they see, hear, touch, feel and understand. What impresses them most?

Variations of the game:

- You are simply an invisible spectator.
- You are invisible but can change the course of the action.
- You participate in the scene for only a few seconds.
- A scene is picked at random.
- A scene is carefully chosen.

## Tribunals

A challenging whole-class approach, particularly suitable for classes that have had plenty of experience of hot-seating and improvised drama. Characters with questionable actions or motives are role-played and put on trial, with prosecution, defence, witnesses, judge and jury. This activity needs plenty of preparation! Start with something familiar, like the Wolf in *The Three Little Pigs*.

## True/False/We can't tell

Children make statements about a text for others to sort into these three categories. Finding evidence in the text to confirm their classification is an important part of this activity. Alternatively, the teacher makes the statements and the children sort them with reference to the text.

# Cambridge Reading books at Key Stage 2

## Independent Reading A

### Short narrative

| | |
|---|---|
| *The Proper Princess Test* J. Burchett and S. Vogler | 0 521 63946 8 |
| *Rachel's Mysterious Drawings* Richard Brown | 0 521 63947 6 |
| *How to Trick a Tiger* Richard Brown | 0 521 63570 5 |
| *The Best Present Ever* Sally Grindley | 0 521 63945 X |
| *Ollie* Irene Yates | 0 521 63944 1 |

### Picture/Cartoon

| | |
|---|---|
| *Captain Cool and the Ice Queen* Gerald Rose | 0 521 55649 X |
| *A Walk with Granny* Nigel Gray | 0 521 46928 7 |

### Poetry

| | |
|---|---|
| *Bananas in Pyjamas* Morag Styles and Helen Cook | 0 521 63516 0 |
| *Pussy Cat, Pussy Cat* Morag Styles and Helen Cook | 0 521 63517 9 |
| *A Door to Secrets* Tony Mitton | 0 521 49841 4 |

### Extended narrative

| | |
|---|---|
| *Garlunk* Helen Cresswell | 0 521 46890 6 |
| *Carnival* Grace Hallworth | 0 521 47703 4 |

### Teacher's resources

| | |
|---|---|
| *Passports to Literacy: Texts 1* | 0 521 64817 3 |
| *Passports to Literacy: Sentences 1* | 0 521 64813 0 |
| *Passports to Literacy: Words 1* | 0 521 64809 2 |
| *Text Extracts 1* | 0 521 64805 X |
| *Exploring Texts IRA* | 0 521 63410 5 |

## Independent Reading B

### Short narrative

| | |
|---|---|
| *Great-grandma's Dancing Dress* Helen Dunmore | 0 521 63744 9 |
| *Clyde's Leopard* Helen Dunmore | 0 521 63743 0 |
| *Leaving the Island* Judith O'Neill | 0 521 63745 7 |
| *Tower Block Blowdown* J. Burchett and S. Vogler | 0 521 63746 5 |
| *Harry and the Megabyte Brain* Jan Dean | 0 521 63742 2 |

### Picture/Cartoon

| | |
|---|---|
| *Captain Cool and the Robogang* Gerald Rose | 0 521 55648 1 |
| *Never Meddle with Magic Mirrors!* Kate Umansky | 0 521 47627 5 |

### Poetry

| | |
|---|---|
| *Half of Nowhere* Richard Burns | 0 521 47626 7 |
| *Don't Do That!* Morag Styles and Helen Cook | 0 521 63521 7 |
| *The Midnight Party* Richard Brown | 0 521 63518 7 |

### Extended narrative

| | |
|---|---|
| *Leopard on the Mountain* Ruskin Bond | 0 521 47704 2 |
| *A True Spell and a Dangerous* Susan Price | 0 521 49764 7 |

### Teacher's resources

| | |
|---|---|
| *Passports to Literacy: Texts 2* | 0 521 64816 5 |
| *Passports to Literacy: Sentences 2* | 0 521 64812 2 |
| *Passports to Literacy: Words 2* | 0 521 64808 4 |
| *Text Extracts 2* | 0 521 64804 1 |
| *Exploring Texts IRB* | 0 521 63411 3 |

## Extended Reading A

### Short narrative

| | |
|---|---|
| *Earth Magic, Sky Magic* Rosalind Kerven | 0 521 63525 X |
| *Truth or Dare* Tony Bradman | 0 521 57552 4 |

### Picture/Cartoon

| | |
|---|---|
| *Psyche and Eros* Marcia Williams | 0 521 47786 7 |

### Poetry

| | |
|---|---|
| *Dream Time* Morag Styles and Helen Cook | 0 521 63519 5 |
| *My Brother's a Beast* Morag Styles and Helen Cook | 0 521 63522 5 |
| *Words Alive: Poems to Perform* Barry Wilsher and Jill Wilsher | 0 521 48577 0 |
| *Words Alive: Poems to Perform (cassette)* Barry Wilsher and Jill Wilsher | 0 521 64867 X |

### Extended narrative

| | |
|---|---|
| *Tom Tiddler's Ground* John Rowe Townsend | 0 521 46889 2 |
| *Star Child on Clark Street* Jamila Gavin | 0 521 47624 0 |
| *That Rebellious Towne* Frances Usher | 0 521 47705 0 |
| *Once upon Olympus* Jenny Koralek | 0 521 47630 5 |

### Teacher's resources

| | |
|---|---|
| *Passports to Literacy: Texts 3* | 0 521 64815 7 |
| *Passports to Literacy: Sentences 3* | 0 521 64811 4 |
| *Passports to Literacy: Words 3* | 0 521 64807 6 |
| *Text Extracts 3* | 0 521 64803 3 |
| *Exploring Texts ERA* | 0 521 63412 1 |

## Extended Reading B

### Short narrative

| | |
|---|---|
| *Heroes and Villains* Tony Bradman | 0 521 57551 6 |
| *In the Court of the Jade Emperor* Rosalind Kerven | 0 521 63524 1 |

### Picture/Cartoon

| | |
|---|---|
| *Letters to Henrietta* Nell Marshall | 0 521 47625 9 |

### Poetry

| | |
|---|---|
| *By the Pricking of My Thumbs* Morag Styles and Helen Cook | 0 521 63520 9 |
| *Whisked Away* Richard Brown | 0 521 63523 3 |
| *Twinkle, Twinkle, Planet Blue* Morag Styles | 0 521 55558 2 |

### Extended narrative

| | |
|---|---|
| *Sorcery and Gold* Rosalind Kerven | 0 521 46878 7 |
| *Spindle River* Judith O'Neill | 0 521 47629 1 |
| *The Hermit Shell* Frances Usher | 0 521 55666 X |
| *Sandstorm* Judy Cumberbatch | 0 521 62927 6 |

### Teacher's resources

| | |
|---|---|
| *Passports to Literacy: Texts 4* | 0 521 64814 9 |
| *Passports to Literacy: Sentences 4* | 0 521 64810 6 |
| *Passports to Literacy: Words 4* | 0 521 64806 8 |
| *Text Extracts 4* | 0 521 64802 5 |
| *Exploring Texts ERB* | 0 521 63413 X |